MURDER AT VASSAR

Also by Elizabeth Atwood Taylor
In Thorndike Large Print

The Cable Car Murder

MURDER AT VASSAR

Elizabeth Atwood Taylor

THORNDIKE PRESS • THORNDIKE, MAINE

Library of Congress Cataloging in Publication Data:

Taylor, Elizabeth Atwood.
  Murder at Vassar.

  1. Large type books. I. Title.
  [PS3570.A9286M8 1987b]   813'.54   87-7063
  ISBN 0-89621-832-5 (lg. print : alk. paper)

Excerpt from *Three Guineas* by Virginia Woolf. © Copyright 1938 by
Harcourt Brace Jovanovich Inc; renewed 1966 by Leonard Woolf.
Reprinted by permission of the publisher. "Souvenir" by Edna St.
Vincent Millay. From *Collected Poems*, Harper & Row. © Copyright
1923, 1951 by Edna St. Vincent Millay and Norma Millay Ellis. Used
by Permission. "Hobo's Lullaby" by Goebel Reeves. © Copyright 1961,
1962 by Fall River Music Inc. All Rights Reserved. Used by Permission.
"This Land Is Your Land." Words and Music by Woody Guthrie.
TRO— © Copyright 1956 (renewed 1984), 1958 (renewed 1986) and
1970 by Ludlow Music Inc. New York, NY. Used by Permission. "If
I Had a Hammer" (The Hammer Song). Words and Music by Lee
Hays and Pete Seeger. TRO—© Copyright 1958 (renewed 1986) and
1962 by Ludlow Music Inc. New York, NY. Used by Permission.
"Where Have All the Flowers Gone?" by Pete Seeger. © Copyright
1961 by Fall River Music Inc. All Rights Reserved. Used by Permission.
"We Shall Overcome" by Zilphia Horton, Frank Hamilton, Guy
Carawan and Pete Seeger. TRO—© Copyright 1960 and 1963 by
Ludlow Music Inc. New York, NY. Used by Permission. Royalties
from this song are being contributed to the Freedom Movement under
the trusteeship of the writers.

Large Print edition available in North America by arrangement with
St. Martin's Press, Inc., New York.

Cover design by James B. Murray.

To Esther Wanning

I had a little help from my friends on this one: feedback, suggestions, and ideas for the places that wouldn't come quite right. I want to thank here, in order of appearance, Peter Cosgrove and Esther Wanning; Virginia Mathias and Jennifer Chinlund; Sandra Larsen and Margaret Anstin; John and Susie Glazer; and Bill and Tekla Deverell. And to Hope Dellon, I am especially indebted for the kind of criticism that the book required to find its final form.

. . . what is this "civilization" in which we find ourselves? What are these ceremonies and why should we take part in them? What are these professions and why should we make money out of them? Where in short is it leading us, the procession of the sons of educated men?
—Virginia Woolf

Prologue

It occurred to me, that woman, having received from her Creator the same intellectual constitution as man, has the same right as man to intellectual culture and development.
—Matthew Vassar (1860)

Green leaves, millions of them, rustle uneasily above the thousand acres that are Vassar College, in the thousand shades of green that are early summer in the state of New York. Leaves of huge ancient trees, of orderly clipped bushes, of new-mowed grass; large and small, pale and dark, all are luminous against the gray afternoon June sky. No sun can be seen behind that uniform gray, but the landscape is saturated with the lovely light of summer, and the air is warm and filled with a feeling of anticipation. Graduation is some days past,

9

and the thousand acres are mostly empty of people.

A blue-uniformed man stands, bored and sleepy, by Taylor Gate. A man and a woman sit talking quietly on the steps of Thompson Library. In front of Main, the original and still central building of the college, a gardener is on his hands and knees in the grassy circle, doing something at the roots of one of the peony bushes whose large bright flowers, white and many shades of pink, contribute their part to the air of abundance, plenty, happiness, and ease that spreads over the campus like a benediction. Behind him the white stone slab over the doorway glistens in the strangely shining light of the cloudy summer day:

ERECTED 1861—MATTHEW VASSAR FOUNDER

The man who convinced the childless, prosperous, seventy-year-old brewer to found the world's first endowed college for women promised that the institution would be a monument to him "more lasting than the pyramids." Some hundred and twenty-five years later, however, the original building of dark red brick, with a round central roof, white cake-icing oval windows, and gay towers at either end looks rather more like a giant elderly steamboat than like a pyramid.

Inside, the administrative work, which does not stop for summer, has nevertheless hit a lull, and those who haven't taken vacation work slowly this Monday morning, getting up and going to the snack bar or to the post office, or taking walks outside before it rains. It is hot and muggy, the beginning of summer, the rain a certainty, and it is hard to concentrate.

Upstairs in the old building on the second, third, and fourth floors, maids are getting the rooms ready for the two hundred alumnae who will arrive at the end of the week for their twenty-fifth and fifteenth reunion weekends. Other maids in the four quadrangle dormitories, and in Noyes and Josselyn and Jewett, mop the long hall floors, vacuum the parlors, and put out linens in rooms that will house the graduates of ten, thirty, fifty, and sixty years ago.

Over in the Shakespeare Gardens, a girl is propped against a tree with a large heavy book in her lap, staring abstractly at the gray sky and frowning. Next to the Shakespeare Gardens is the Outdoor Theater, a long grassy hill sloping down to a flat place, and beyond that is Sunset Lake. Trees and bushes of several hundred varieties form a barricade at the back of the lake, an impenetrable area of green

11

leaves and thorny blackberry vines broken only by the one thin path that cuts through some distance beyond to a little-used back gate that puts you out onto Route 376.

About halfway down the path, still well back in the woods and not seen from the lake, two women come walking along slowly from the direction of the highway. One of them, very old, supports herself with a cane on one side and the arm of her companion on the other. She is breathing heavily, and the younger one says, "Don't go so fast, Aunt Chloe, the path's too narrow. We're not going to a fire, you know."

"Don't want," the older woman puffs, "to hold you up, my dear Pudgie. I know you wanted to take the car today, and I know you have things to do at the college, and I know—" Her autocratic old voice stops abruptly as she looks up and sees a man in a mask blocking the path and holding a large gun pointed directly at them. The mask is a bright pink rubber, with small holes for the eyes through which only mirrored sunglasses can be seen. Bushy brown hair sticks out all around the mask, and the old woman notes confusedly that the long black robe looks a bit like a graduation gown. She grasps at the idea that it's all some unpleasant student prank, and begins to feel highly irritated. Really, such behavior is insufferable and must not be permitted—

"Don't move," a thin, whispery voice says from behind the garish rubber mask. "Stop right there . . . good. I want your jewelry and your purses. Hand them over quietly and you won't get hurt. Take off your rings, old lady — *don't* just *stand* there, I don't have all day. That big diamond first, come on now, hand it over—"

"Young man!" the old woman raps out — though the mask's whispery voice could as easily belong to a woman as a man. She raises her silver-tipped cane and shakes it with such authority that the mask stands silently for a moment, listening. "This ring has not been off my finger in sixty-five years—" She shakes her cane again — "and it's not coming off now! My dear husband gave me this ring—"

The younger woman's voice interrupts the older woman's as the masked figure raises the gun and points it carefully at the old woman's chest. "Aunt Chloe, maybe you'd better give—"

But there is a very loud noise that knocks the old woman backward and leaves a large black hole that quickly turns red in the center of her white linen jacket.

"Okay, you — get over there to the tree," the voice hisses quickly. "I said *move,* unless you want me to shoot you, too? No, wait — first take off the old lady's rings; take yours off, too."

The gun is pointed quite steadily at the woman called Pudgie, and she does what she is told. Her aunt's rings come easily off the thin old fingers. She tugs off her own and holds them out. Her hands are shaking and so is her voice as she says, "Here. Here they are."

"No. Put them there on the ground. That's right. Now walk over to the tree and put your arms around it — *move!* I'd just as soon shoot you, too, at this point."

Pudgie moves off the path like a sleep-walker, staring blankly, and goes to the big maple tree and rather tentatively raises her arms and wraps them around it. The man — or perhaps woman — muttering, holding the gun in his gloved left hand now, from under his robe produces a rope and goes behind the tree. Pudgie's arms are pulled tight, the wrists tied. Next he walks back around the tree, puts down the gun and ties her feet. "Stupid old woman, stupid . . . stupid . . . stupid . . ."

He picks up the gun by the barrel and gives Pudgie a hard clip on the side of the head, and she slumps against the tree. Then he walks behind the tree again and presently comes out and stands still, looking around, listening, but hears nothing to worry about. He goes over to the body of the old woman, drags it off the path, picks up the women's handbags and rings, gives a last look around, and takes off in the direction of the college. The black cape and bushy brown head disappear almost immediately in a tangle of bushes, and it begins to rain, a sudden hard, steady downpour.

The body of the old woman, in its white suit and blue-and-white spectator shoes, lies jackknifed on the ground with stocking-covered legs sticking out at peculiar angles, looking like an old doll that has been dropped by some careless giant-child. The sparse blue-gray hair is spattered with red splashes of blood, as is the face. The round black eyes, so recently glittering with outrage, stare dully at the somber sky. The only sounds are the steady beat of the rain on the leaves, the faint hiss of traffic from the highway, the scattered notes of the summer songs of birds, and the splashing of a little creek over the rocks. It's called Fonteyn Kill, and it runs from Sunset Lake down to Vassar Lake some distance away.

After quite some time has passed, Pudgie makes a low moaning sound, then hiccups and gasps for air. She moves her head and shakes it, looks around groggily, then starts pulling and tugging on her arms. Scraping the skin, but still rather easily she gets her left hand free, stretches it farther around the tree, and after a while loosens the other hand. She brings her hands forward and stands rubbing her wrists, sees the body of her aunt, hiccups again, and hurriedly bends over and unties the ropes around her ankles. Then she hobbles over to the old woman and kneels and touches her face. The head lolls loosely to one side in a horrible way, and Pudgie pulls her hand back abruptly and gets up. She looks around, confused, then sets off down the path toward the college, lurching rather than running, falling down so that she puts out bleeding hands to break her fall, scrambling up and starting off again. She runs up the long grassy hill, out of breath and hiccupping, across the Shakespeare Gardens and past the science building, past the old New England Building, past the President's House, past the gardener working in the peony circle, who looks at her with astonishment, and finally up the steps and in through the big front doors of Main. At the window of the Message Center she raps

16

weakly on the glass to get the receptionist's attention, breathes heavily several times, and finally gasps out, "My aunt — she's dead. Get the police — it was a masked man . . ." The elderly woman sitting at the desk on the other side of the glass doesn't do a thing, just stares, so Pudgie, with better control of her voice now, again says, "The police, *call them!* My aunt's been *shot* and she's *dead!*"

The receptionist, still staring, still silent, her mouth open now, reaches for the receiver and looks down and punches the button for operator. She speaks in a clear, dry voice that could just as well be ordering office supplies: "Connect me with the police, please, this is an emergency . . . er . . . the homicide department."

ONE

Driving in through Taylor Gate that Friday gave me the strangest feeling, but I'd expected that. Driving into that safe, rich green world where I'd lived for four years — suddenly I didn't know whether it had ended yesterday or a hundred years before. Fifteen years was the counted calendar number and for the moment as meaningless to me as the scratchings made on a log by an insect. For I saw myself suddenly as I'd been, clear as clear, walking in summer clothes down the path toward Taylor Hall with an expression on my face — her face — that I couldn't read but that seemed to look at me questioningly.

And then other pieces of the past came down the drive from Main to greet me in a rush of images so strong and unexpected they took my breath away. I must have stopped the car then, for I was startled out of my reverie by an impatient honking sound; I hurriedly shifted into first and drove on. There was a

18

smallish new parking area — new to me — to the left of the big circle of pink and white flowers — peonies, were they? — that glittered and waved in front of Main. I hadn't seen peonies in years and years. And the air was so muggy and warm, and moist, the trees so huge and spreading and old, the vegetation so lush and green and thick — I'd forgotten how much summer in the country in the East is like a well-tended, orderly tropical jungle. Funny, the things one forgets.

A number of cars were parked in the new lot and I slid my small rental in alongside a glistening green station wagon. There were a lot of people about, almost all women and most of them wearing the kind of pale beige poplin raincoats you buy at Brooks Brothers or Saks Fifth Avenue. They were all different ages, these women, strolling about in small groups and talking, talking, but I didn't recognize any of them. I felt a small chill then, suddenly worried I wouldn't recognize anyone the whole weekend — or they me. Fifteen years, some of them hellish . . . but this was nonsense, and a voice put it to rest.

"Maggie! Maggie Linden! *Maggie!*"

I turned, and there was Nancy Porter, looking, I swear, exactly the same as she had that sunny June day we'd graduated. Her round freckled face was a little girl's face still, and it was all smiles, and, I realized, so was mine.

"Why, you haven't changed at all," she said, "not at all, you look *exactly* the same. I'd have known you anywhere, isn't it amazing? Isn't it wonderful to be back? Mary's here, and Georgia and Muffy, Tully's coming up tonight, and Caroline too — oh, Maggie! It's so great to see you. And you've come all the way from *California?*" An Easterner of the Mayflower type, Nancy said "California" as I would say "outer space." "Can I help you carry anything? Oh, how long has it *been?*"

"Fifteen years, I guess. Hullo, Nancy." We exchanged hugs and I pulled a small case out of the back seat. "No, I've got it. *You* look just the same, anyway, you look *great*. It's hard to believe that I do, though — after the little ghost I saw a minute ago walking down the drive . . . brr." I shivered as the first fat drops of rain came down and the June afternoon turned suddenly cool. "Where is everyone? We're in Main?"

"Come sign in. Muffy's registering and we've all got rooms together; the doors have locks now and they're hard as hell to get open. . . ."

The inside of Main was as drab and dingy as ever, and the wide stairs, lit by what surely

20

couldn't have been more than a forty-watt bulb, were just as gloomy. Nancy kept talking as we walked up to the second floor, where a long table had been set up, and most of the faces around it looked as familar as if we'd shared a class, or a late-night cup of coffee and anguish over a paper due the next morning, only the day before. There were about sixty women standing around the table, and it sounded as if all sixty of them were talking at once — and at the top of their voices. An even louder roar came from a larger group gathered in the living room across the hall — the twenty-fifth reunion, according to Nancy. A few men, husbands or boyfriends, and a sprinkling of children stood awkwardly in the hall between the two rooms like a thin line of foam edging a vast and restless sea. Three of the eight roommates I'd had senior year saw us then and came swooping toward us with cries of delight and beaming faces. I'd looked forward to seeing those faces and had dreaded it a little, too. How would I measure up — in their eyes, and, maybe worse, in my own?

As that group of familiar faces headed toward me, though, with others all around them, talking, laughing, and beaming good will, I felt a simple affection, a rush of belonging and connectedness with those women who, like

21

me, had managed to survive the fifteen years that had passed since we'd shared — what? An education, whatever that is. The end of youth, maybe? Whatever it was, I felt as immediately comfortable with Nancy and the others as if our lives had never taken different paths; the links of affection between us, it seemed, were ones that time and distance hadn't affected much, and I found myself smiling, unable to stop, and talking at the top of my voice nonstop just like the rest of them, trying to catch up on fifteen years in ten minutes. Finally, I moved over to the table to register and find out about my room. Muffy Tucker, one of the few women I'd seen in the years since college, was in charge and gave me a piece of paper with Room No. 349 at the top and a list of steps to take to open the door.

"Turn knob to right," I read, "depress proper buttons in correct order, press simultaneously—"

"Vassar College, though remote, is not entirely unaffected by world conditions, the rising crime rate, et cetera," said Muffy, who worked for *Time*. "All the rooms have locks now, but that should present no problem to a private detective. Hello, Maggie, how are you?"

"A little blitzed out by all this" — I waved my hand vaguely toward the crowded room — "I'd no idea I would feel this enormous pleasure at the sight of this particular collection of people." I looked down at the paper she'd handed me and asked, "Who's my roommate? You have a list? Three-forty-nine?"

"Caroline," Muffy answered without looking. "She's coming in tonight; she lives in Rome now, did you know?"

"Only because I looked everyone up in the reunion book on the plane — but I'm holding up the line, I'll see you later."

I picked up my bag and headed for the stairs. The third floor was almost as dark as the stairwell; it was gray and raining outside, and the overhead lights hadn't been turned on yet. I could barely make out the directions but finally got the door open, went in, and put my bag down on the bed nearest the window. I'd had a bad cold that I was just beginning to shake off, or hoped I was, and I was feeling both tired and jangly. I lay down, which felt absolutely wonderful, and stared out at the rain and the green that covered the campus like the smooth, silky flow of a debutant's coming out dress, listening to the rain and the rustling leaves. The soft, steady plopping of raindrops was soothing and restful. It had been a long day, and pieces of it knocked about in my mind: the Oakland airport at midnight; early morning New York and breakfast at a place called Eat and Run, followed by some research for my partner at a title company; then driving up along the Hudson River and not quite remembering the way, after all those years I'd known it so well. . . . Then Taylor Gate and Vassar College and that unexpected glimpse of myself as I'd been . . . as I'd been . . . that little young ghost . . . and how differently it had all turned out. Would she be pleased with what I'd made of her life, or managed to salvage of it, that little ghost? Or disappointed? I wondered.

Oh, yes, Vietnam was long over, that horror she'd worked against so long and hard, and civil rights before that . . . but then there'd been David's death and the years zonked on alcohol, valium, and self-pity. After finally emerging from that, my sister had been killed when she supposedly fell in front of a cable car — then her husband's remarriage and my suspicions in the end getting me and O'Reagan together to find her murderer, and a new career as well. The detective agency, rather unexpectedly, was thriving; I'd just gotten my own license after

24

a year of working under O'Reagan's. What would she have thought of all this, that young thin ghost? And of the world around us, with all its confusion about where and how to make a stand? No doubt she'd have preferred to see me down in Nicaragua helping with the coffee harvest, doing what little I could to help redress the balance of misery and suffering my government was causing down there, instead of attending to my own life, or trying to; my own life that was so unsettled at the moment that worrying about the state of the world was pretty ludicrous. But it was an old habit of mine, worrying about the world, and hard to break.

My thoughts rattled around like flies, never quite settling; distracting, irritating. At the moment I was virtually homeless, most of my belongings in storage, and the rest, but for the few clothes I'd brought East, residing dejectedly in boxes in a friend's basement in San Francisco. Richard was now pleading for me to come back "home," but I wasn't even sure where home *was* these days. When my thoughts reached this point, I knew it was time to put my mind on something else.

I got up and took the white towel and washcloth off the plain brown chest of drawers, got a slip and a red silk party dress out of my suitcase, and wandered down the vast hall looking for a shower. How could I ever have forgotten those halls, those endless miles of brown linoleum?

TWO

It was at the cocktail party about an hour later that I first heard about the murder.

I'd taken the time to telephone my partner O'Reagan with the information I'd found for him in New York, and everyone else had already left by the time I was finished. So I walked over to Taylor Hall by myself, through a thin, steady rain and up flagged stone steps into a noisy, bright, large room filled almost to overflowing with my old classmates and their husbands and boyfriends.

I stood there just looking for a minute, getting used to the brightness and the noise and the intensity after the quiet gloom outside. As I stood there in the anonymous wash of a roomful of people talking at the tops of their voices, laughing and squealing, I clearly heard the words, "The murder, oh, the murder!" I pricked up my ears and focused my attention in the direction the words had come from — simply professional habit, though not one of

27

long duration. But I couldn't tell who it was that was speaking, as the voice continued, ". . . Shakespeare Gardens or Vassar Lake, I think, here for her sixty-fifth reunion she would've been, can you *imagine?* How old would that make her, ninety something, a hundred?" Whoever was speaking was not a mathematics major, apparently.

Then cries of "Maggie, Maggie!" captured my attention. A small group over by the bar was waving and calling, and I headed toward them, but it was slow going because of all the pauses and hellos to almost every face.

The next thing I knew, a tall man in a beautiful suit and an intent expression was heading straight for me, holding out a drink. I looked over my shoulder to see who it could be for, but the people behind me were busy with their own conversation, and when I turned the man was saying, "I've brought you a drink, here you are."

He handed it over with such a pleased smile and boyish air, though he was somewhere over thirty, that I said "Thanks" and took the drink. "Have I somehow misplaced those of my brain cells that know you?"

"Well, no, I saw you earlier, signing in this afternoon. Cici said you're a private detective, and I thought I'd like to meet you, but you'd gone before I had the chance. Then I saw you

28

come in tonight, standing there at the door, so I grabbed you a drink and hurried over." His smile said he expected me to be as pleased about all this as he was, an engaging grin that I couldn't help but return as he raised his glass and said, "Cheers."

Because I'm an alcoholic, I don't drink (anymore, that is), so I merely looked him over as he knocked back a good portion of his drink. He was quite good-looking, tall, a bit on the thin side, with light gray eyes that were almost startling in his suntanned face. Soft mousy brown hair with a cowlick cut fairly short, wearing a lovely mud-colored linen suit and a casual air that I thought might be masking something else. Worry, maybe? I asked, "Who's Cici? Cici Warren? And why did you want to meet a private detective?"

"Cici Warren, yes. My name's Peter, by the way. Come over and join us, why don't you? I know Cici would like to see you."

"There're some people over by the bar I want to see first — maybe I'll see you later, if you're here for the weekend."

"I won't be here, I'm afraid. I have to be in Boston tomorrow. Came here today for a funeral, actually, and then just stayed on for the party."

"A funeral?"

"A very elderly great-aunt by marriage whom I hadn't seen in several years." He paused, as if undecided whether to go on, then continued. "But it was . . . pretty horrible, all the same. She was murdered, poor old thing."

"Murdered?"

"Some thug in a Halloween mask held them up, then shot the old lady in cold blood when she wouldn't give him her rings. My cousin was with her; he knocked her out and took the loot and ran."

"How . . ." I tried to think of a word that fit the situation, and couldn't.

"Yes," he agreed with the word I'd not found. "Very."

"Who did you say was with her? And when did it happen? And where?"

"It was Monday — right here on campus, oddly enough. Behind that lake over there by the golf course."

"Ah. That's what someone was talking about when I came in, what's it called . . . Sunset Lake. What in the world was she doing there? Who did you say was with her?"

"My cousin — Pudgie Warren. They'd been to see someone in a convalescent hospital on the highway back there; they always walked back that way to the campus afterward, apparently."

"Pudgie Warren," I said slowly. "Why, I know her — I was a friend of her sister, Lee. Lee must have been your cousin also."

"That's right." He nodded, and a fleeting look of sadness that I felt too crossed his face as I remembered my classmate Lee Warren, who'd become a top photographer right out of college and had been killed in Vietnam while working on a film. "Cici said you and Lee were good friends."

"Yes. I used to visit her out at her aunt's — is it the same aunt who's been killed? With a great big railroad tycoon sort of place out on the Hudson? Old Mrs. Warren?" He nodded, and I continued slowly, remembering. "Pudgie was there sometimes. We thought her very straight at the time, but she was very patient and courteous with our sixties' tendency to know-it-all, now that I think about it. . . . When did all this happen? You said Monday?"

"Monday, yes. The funeral was delayed because of the police having the body."

"And have they found the person who did it, this masked man? It all sounds . . . rather dramatic. Like a play or something."

"Yes, well, no, they haven't caught him. In fact, I'm not sure if they entirely believe in him."

31

"What do you mean, they don't believe in him?"

"I mean they seem to spend most of their time questioning poor Pudgie. Maybe that means something, maybe not."

"Hard to tell at this stage," I agreed. "Are you close to her, to Pudgie?"

"Yes — after Lee's death, we all sort of . . . pulled together. Closed ranks. I was wondering, as you were a friend of Lee's and you're a private detective, perhaps you could work on this a bit, maybe help take the pressure off Pudgie. In your spare time this weekend?" He smiled the appealing crooked smile to show he wasn't entirely serious. Not entirely.

"If I find any spare time you'll be the first to know about it," I replied evasively, thinking of all the old friends I wanted to spend the weekend talking to. "And meanwhile there're those people over by the bar I want to see. I'm very sorry about Mrs. Warren."

"Thank you." He hesitated, his eyes looking directly into mine, no longer smiling. "To be serious for a moment, I am really worried about Pudgie. Maybe we could get together next week, if the police are still bothering her, and talk the situation over? I've been trying to get her to get herself a lawyer all week, but she refuses, says she doesn't need one, the police couldn't possibly suspect *her*. But I'm not so sure about that. Not so sure at all. Cici said you live in San Francisco — were you planning to go right back? Or could we have dinner and talk about what we can do to help her, some night this week? Of course I'd pay whatever's the usual fee for your time."

"I'll be in New York for a couple of weeks, as a matter of fact. And if Pudgie is in trouble I'd certainly want to help, if I could. But a lawyer sounds like the best idea, and I will be fairly busy. . . ."

"Working on a case?"

"No."

"Then I'll call you, if I may."

"All right. What are you to Cici, anyway? Another cousin, a husband?"

"No, no, merely a brother."

I gave him my New York phone number and went to join my friends.

THREE

". . . tied to a tree," Nancy Porter was saying as I joined the group at the bar. "She's here this weekend for her twenty-fifth I understand, Lee Warren's sister — ah, Maggie! Do you know Jake? I don't think you've met, he's my whatta-ya-callit — this is Maggie, my ex-roommate from California."

I exchanged appropriate formulae with a young-looking gray-haired man who wore silver wire-rim glasses and had a beaky nose in a thin face. Others joined the group and the talk went on to the sorts of lives we variously were living now.

We kept talking steadily through a long walk in the rain over to Student's Building and dinner, then back again to one of the small parlors in Main. From time to time one of us would go and get a fresh batch of drinks from the dining room. We were a fairly large group now, ex-roommates and friends, husbands and boyfriends — ours was the last class of women-only to graduate from Vassar — and we were talking in rather loud voices because the twenty-fifth reunion in the main parlor, just down the hall, was still going strong and loud though it was well after midnight.

"I wonder if there's much difference" — I nodded my head in the direction of the noisy twenty-fifth, thinking especially of Pudgie Warren — "between them and us. Women who went out into the world twenty-five years ago as opposed to fifteen. . . ."

"Lifestyle, values, work? Married or single? Mmmm," said Caroline. "All the books would say so, wouldn't they? Separated by the sixties . . ."

"Oh God, the sixties!"

"Civil rights and SNCC—"

"The Beatles and Bob Dylan—"

"Let's not forget birth control pills—"

"The end of the war," put in Jake, who was a journalist, "the White House tapes, the resignation of the poison toad—"

"But that was the *seventies*—"

"And did any of it," Caroline interrupted, "make any difference, do you think?"

"Those women down the hall," a short bullet-headed boyfriend said in response to my original question, "those women having their twenty-fifth, *have* your lives been significantly

35

different from theirs, do you think?"

There was a pause while we all thought about it.

"Well, but do we know what their lives have been?" asked Caroline, who had been a science major.

"Most of them are housewives, don't you think?" I said. "Primarily wives and mothers, and if they have jobs they're secondary. And often unpaid."

"Riley Sloan's done a survey of our class from the reunion book," Nancy put in. "She says we've hardly *any* children compared to those earlier classes, more careers, and fewer marriages, too."

"But inner things," I said. "I wonder."

"I doubt it," Caroline said. "I hope I'm wrong, but I doubt it. Ten years isn't very long, really. Even those ten years."

"Well, but have you read *Why Do I Think I Am Nothing Without a Man?*—"

"Excuse me," a voice said loudly from the door. "Excuse me, but someone said I could find Maggie Elliott in here."

I turned around and saw a rather heavyset woman in a shiny green cocktail dress a little too tight for her standing in the doorway. She had a sharp, pointed nose, wispy, untidy brown hair, and beady brown eyes.

"I'm Maggie," I said.

"Oh, *good*. I am Alice Langley Worthington, from the twenty-fifth reunion. Would you mind coming out — I'd like very much to talk with you a moment."

I didn't particularly want to leave my friends but I did, following the woman in the green cocktail dress down the hall until we were far enough away from the noise of her reunion party to hear each other without shouting.

"I am Alice Langley Worthington," she repeated, "and I am a lifelong friend of Pudgie Warren Brown. We were roommates here at Vassar, in fact. And when I ran into Cici and Peter Warren — I know the whole family, known them all my life — anyway Peter mentioned you, and I thought you might be just the person we want. You know there's been this horrible murder of old Mrs. Warren? I feel it needs looking into. By someone other than the police, I mean. And Cici said you're a private detective — or was it Peter? Anyway, you're *here*, that's the main thing. So, I thought I'd just track you down and ask you to look into the matter." She paused for the first time in her long speech and nodded her head with an abrupt downward motion that shook loose several more wisps of hair, and

37

smiled rather mechanically, her beady eyes remaining intent and worried.

"Why do you want a private detective?" I asked. "What's wrong with the police?"

"Well. For investigating this sort of . . . I mean the sort of people involved . . . the police just aren't — how can I put it? I mean I'm the last person in the world to be a *snob*. Anyone will tell you that. But really! They've been just dreadful to poor Pudgie all week, simply *hounded* her. Imagine, after that horrible ordeal, the old lady shot right in front of her, and the police keep questioning *Pudgie!* I can't imagine why, when they ought to be spending their time looking for that townie who did it. Blockheads. Obviously we can't count on much from *them*. So I thought when I heard about you, someone of our own sort, of our own class, you know, and then, your being here, it's obviously *meant*."

"Have you suggested to Pudgie that she get a lawyer?"

"I have actually — but — she says she hasn't been *accused* of anything. Yet. But do you think — her husband is with her, though."

"It sounds to me like it would be a good idea for her to get a lawyer. And then if the question of a private detective arises, it should really come from her. Or at least with her blessing."

"Oh, but I thought, you being here, you could get right to work on it. No? All right, I'll speak to Pudgie. She's not here tonight, but I can do it before the AAVC meeting tomorrow. She's in charge of our Class Gift, so she'll be up there on the platform. And she's probably going to be elected a trustee of the college also, so I'm sure she'll be there. Unless those dreadful police — well. Sufficient unto the day. And I'll get the other roommates — we all want to help. I'll talk to Pudgie tomorrow, and then you can meet with us."

"I'd work on getting a lawyer first," I repeated. "Time enough to think about hiring some investigation after that."

"Where is your room? Here in Main, aren't you?"

I gave her my room number and then went back to the small parlor, but the group was breaking up. It was almost three A.M., my throat was aching again and it hurt to breathe, and I was more than ready for the narrow bed awaiting me in Room 349. Caroline and I walked back together, and as I dragged my weary body up the stairs I thought over what I knew about the murder, and about how I really didn't want to have anything to do with it — at least not until the weekend was over and I'd had my full share of visiting with old friends and classmates.

When we got upstairs neither Caroline nor I could find our instructions for opening the wretched lock, so I picked it. Then I crawled into the skimpy bed, and very soon the images of Nancy and Muffy, of Pudgie Warren and Peter Warren and Alice Langley whatsit, of the thin little ghost and the giant trees and wide soothing lawns, turned into dreams, and I slept.

During the night the wide lawns and spreading trees turned into the beach at Los Angeles. There were a lot of people around, all walking hurriedly in one direction or the other as if the beach were merely something they had to walk over on their way to someplace more important. I stood on the sand and watched a man in bathing trunks trying to swim toward the horizon in a sort of breast stroke. He was having difficulty because the surface of the water was hard and black and metallic, and it tilted sharply toward the horizon. Silhouetted there, where sea met sky, was an endless barricade of barbed wire and old dented metal garbage cans and oil rigs and other rubbish. I started pointing to the horrible sight and saying to the passing people, louder and louder until finally I was yelling, "See that! *Look*, can't you *see* it? Is that what you want the whole *coast* to look like? *Look* at it!" But no one paid any attention.

A blue-uniformed policeman, rather portly, wandered up, and I yelled at him, too, though I was afraid he'd retaliate by beating me up. He approached menacingly but then started mouthing some Chamber of Commerce bullshit at me about how it was perfectly pleasant to have a barricade of oil rigs and barbed wire and other garbage between you and the sea and the sky. Then he walked on, telling me sneeringly over his shoulder not to be so "sensitive." My mother and father, standing farther back on the beach, looked on passively.

FOUR

Waking up with a feeling of frustration after my encounter with the heedless people and the cop on the beach in L.A. during the night, I decided to go for a walk before breakfast. The cold was still hanging on; I didn't feel up to a run, but I thought a good fast walk might at least clear my head. After I wrote the dream down, with Caroline still asleep and snoring softly, I put on a pair of shorts and some Adidas, then headed out behind Main toward Sunset Lake. The rain had stopped during the night and the sky was a clear, fresh blue, with puffy white clouds to the south.

I was just starting to wake up as I approached the lake when I saw a lot of people standing around. As I came closer I saw that the lake was very low, with a wide swath of mud edging the water. There was a dank, moldy smell in the air. Men in high rubber boots walked back and forth through the mud and the others standing around were all men, too. I'd seen enough policemen to know when a whole group of them was actively at work, so I went a bit closer and watched. A tall heavyset man in a black raincoat seemed to be in charge; he would say something to one of the others, who would listen and nod and then take off to search some new part of the lake. There was a growing pile of debris near the man in the raincoat: old tires, beer cans, and so forth. Obviously, they were searching there because of the murder of old Mrs. Warren nearby, but if they were looking for the gun, they didn't have the air of people who'd found what they were looking for. I watched them for a few more minutes but nothing new happened, so I went on my way. When I came back a bit later the lake was lower but nothing else had changed, so I just kept going.

After breakfast — more nonstop talking over fresh-baked sweet rolls and cups and cups of coffee — we all walked over to the chapel for the AAVC meeting, the gathering of all the reunion classes. The chapel was dark inside, being Gothic in style and paneled in wood, and featured carved female heads with winged torsos jutting out from just beneath the ceiling like the prows of ships. As I sat down I heard singing from behind me as the fiftieth reunion class straggled down the central aisle and filled the three empty rows in front:

> vivi vivo vim
> *oh seniors hail all hail our cry*
> *we're out for play today*
> *marching forward in a mass*
> o salve . . .

Salve night — that night at the end of spring when kegs of beer (in memory of Matthew Vassar's source of income) dotted the campus and the juniors drank as much as they could and ran around being wild and crazy and then officially became seniors . . . or was it the seniors getting drunk? Or both? Funny, I couldn't remember. . . .

The president of the college began to speak about the college's decision to admit men. Vassar had been invited, I remembered, to move to New Haven and join up with Yale, selling off the grounds and buildings and taking the proceeds with them as a sort of dowry — in which case Matthew's monument would have lasted about five thousand years less than the pyramids, depending on which pyramids you were talking about.

My attention wandered back to the president, who was talking about Vassar's determination to provide a highest quality liberal arts education that exemplified and nurtured true equality between the sexes, which was more possible at an institution originally established for women. She mentioned her own universities, supposedly coeducational, where there'd been only one female professor, in both cases having something to do with the school library. The president continued talking and soon came to the subject of money. She then introduced the various class chairmen, who in turn announced the amounts of their class gifts. I was feeling restless and bored and wishing I'd had the sense to skip the meeting, when the chairman of the twenty-fifth was called: Pudgie Warren Brown.

I looked at her with a good deal of curiosity, remembering her only vaguely from the visits to Lee all those years before, and found her not much changed from what I remembered. She was, in fact, a bit pudgy, with a baby-fat look that had presumably been with her all her life and inspired her nickname. She had shiny black hair lightly dusted with gray, straight and thick and cut close to her rather round head, large hazel eyes, and she wasn't very tall. Even from a distance her skin was strikingly pale and clear, with a kind of translucence to it that was amazing considering she must be well into her forties. She wore a neat but unexciting pale blue suit, plain white shoes, and clasped a white purse. She had an air that I remembered immediately of calm competence and something else — efficiency? It was a kind of attitude that suggested that whatever was put into her hands would be taken care of perfectly, if not, perhaps, very imaginatively. She'd seemed, the little I'd seen of her in the past, an unlikely sister for Lee, who'd been so gifted in so many areas; she seemed, now, even more unlikely as a murder suspect. After a brief colorless speech about the pleasure of her class in giving the gift, she announced the amount, which came to slightly under one million dollars. There was a swell of applause and the president came back to say that that was a great deal more than had ever been given before by a twenty-fifth reunion. So she was very efficient, anyway. Efficient enough to plan a murder and not immediately find herself the number-one suspect, you'd think.

Pudgie smiled graciously at the applause and returned to sit quietly in her seat with her hands clasped together in her lap, seeming to give her full attention to the continuing announcements. She showed no sign that earlier in the week her aged aunt had been murdered before her eyes, or that she'd spent a good part of the week being questioned by the police. Whatever her feelings, they would remain quite private.

Finally, the last gift was announced; I totaled the lot in my head and came out with about four million dollars. Not bad for the place old Mr. Vassar had launched with four hundred and eight thousand dollars brought to the endowment ceremony in a tin box. . . .

As the fiftieth reunion filed out again, I thought of something Virginia Woolf wrote somewhere about the procession of the sons of educated men. Where was it leading us? I wondered gloomily, finding myself suddenly back to world-worrying. Perhaps from the thought of all the money, and all no doubt for a good cause, and yet. . . . The path of the mind obviously wasn't making it; if only there were colleges for the path of the heart. . . .

I sighed so deeply that Caroline, sitting next to me, whispered, "Are you all right?"

"Fine," I whispered back, and then shook my head to try and dislodge the dreary judgments on this place that I did, after all, feel a lot of love for, where I'd had an awfully good time, and where I'd learned a fair amount that *had* been useful . . . and who was I to judge? Loud clapping brought my attention back to the meeting and the people getting up and leaving. Good!

Outside, it was raining again — softly, lightly, steadily. I walked with Caroline over to Main and downstairs to the bookstore, where she went to the art books section to get something by an ex-professor while I looked through the postcards. I chose several but had to wait in line to pay for them.

"I'm so sorry," an elderly woman with hennaed hair said as my turn came. "We're short today, one of our dratted girls simply didn't show up this morning, and not a word! And of course the whole point of her being here was to help with this reunion crush. Will these be all?"

I paid for the cards and waited outside for Caroline, who had never been very speedy. I thought about Lee's sister, the woman who was so good at raising money, was a newly elected trustee of the college, and who was being "badgered" by the Poughkeepsie police. Did I want to work for her, if I was asked? I was planning to go on to New York after the reunion for a couple of weeks of much needed time away from work, and away from my own life, specifically from that disaster of a relationship back in San Francisco. Away from the man I'd been living with for the past year, whom I'd bought a house with and who'd had, it turned out, another girlfriend on the side he hadn't mentioned, who'd lied and lied but now claimed he wanted me back. When I'd found out, two weeks before, that Richard had been sleeping with Ilsa off and on the whole time we'd been together, I'd walked out and gone for a long, long walk on the beach, thinking hard, or trying to. Did I really mind the lies the most, or was it his sleeping with Ilsa, period? Thinking about the relationship, thinking about Richard who was so smart and witty, who made me laugh as no one else did, who could be so charming and sexy and loving, but who also rather frequently retreated into implacable rages, followed by violent verbal outbursts, followed inevitably by remorse and apologies. The last one before the Ilsa blow-up had been over a chicken not cooked (by me) for dinner. How ridiculous! We'd been involved with each other off and on for about three years — since I'd stopped drinking — but the temper tantrums had started only after we bought the house together almost a year ago. Struggling along trying to work out the problems of an always difficult relationship, only to find out he was sleeping with Ilsa — God, that had been painful. It was still painful. And now he

49

swore that was all over, all a big mistake, but could I trust him? Did I even want to, anymore? Did I want to continue living the way we had been, even without the Ilsa thing? Had there been anywhere near enough good times between us to balance the bad?

On the way back from the beach I'd stopped off at three grocery stores, collecting cardboard boxes. Most of my things had been in storage anyway, the house being small, with only one room and the kitchen really liveable because we were still doing major restoration work on the rest. It hadn't taken very long to pack up most of what I had kept there, to leave a note saying I'd be in touch, call the dogs, and shut that self-locking door on the tantalizing — and outdated! — dream of living happily every after, white picket fence and et cetera. Of course, it was always possible I'd come to feel differently; Richard remained convinced we could work things out if only I'd give it time, more time. But did I want to spend any more time on the relationship? I wasn't sure. At the moment the break felt pretty final, and along with the sadness there was a certain sense of relief, as well. . . .

"Maggie? *Maggie!*" Caroline was shaking my arm.

I returned abruptly from the West Coast

and said, "Sorry — you ready to go? Listen — *some* people do seem to find the right mate, don't they? And have children *and* work they care about, and *homes*. Why don't I, I wonder? Why haven't you, for that matter?"

"Ah," replied Caroline, looking quite unperturbed, "now *that's* a very long story. . . ."

FIVE

Later that afternoon several of us went to Avery Hall to see the Vietnam film Lee Warren had been working on when she'd been killed. If Main was a huge antique steamboat, Avery is the little tug that goes with it, built of matching dark red brick but short and squat, with a whimsically curved roof and thin oval windows.

There were two police cars and an ambulance outside when we got there. The tall man I'd seen at the lake that morning was standing outside the door talking to a uniformed policeman and a man in plainclothes, and they were blocking the door.

We walked up, and Muffy said, "We're supposed to see a film in here. What's happened?"

"Student — we think — found dead," the tall man answered.

"Murdered?" asked Muffy.

"Why?"

"Well, you look like Homicide to me. And

since there was a murder here earlier in the week I'm wondering if there's a connection." When he said nothing, she went on, "*Is* there a connection?"

"Free country for speculation, Nancy Drew, but it's early days yet." He hesitated, then seemed to make up his mind and added, "But come in, if you wouldn't mind looking at the body, maybe you've seen her before, know who she is."

"Sure," Muffy agreed. "Who found her? And when?"

We followed him into the building. "Cleaning woman," he said over his shoulder. "Few hours ago."

He led us down a shadowy hallway with closed doors on both sides to the far end, where a door was open.

"Oh, the costume room," Muffy said. "It looks just the same, doesn't it? *Phew!*" There was a terrible smell in the air despite the white powder sprinkled all over everything — the substance the police use for neutralizing a smell when they come across a body that's been dead a long time. The policeman led us to a floodlit corner in back and said, "Don't go any further. If you'd just step over here one at a time."

Muffy went first and looked long and hard,

probably gathering details for a piece for her magazine. Then she shook her head. "No, never saw her before, I'm afraid. Sorry."

She stepped back, and I walked up, looked down, and saw the sprawling, bloated body of a tall, thin girl with a purple-and-blue face and horrible bulging eyes. A long navy-blue cord was embedded in her throat. She had on short white shorts and a brief white halter, and she was lying on a pile of clothes, probably costumes from the rack behind her. Her dark brown hair would have reached halfway down her back had she been standing, which she'd obviously never do again, and she had long, graceful legs that put me in mind of a colt who'd by some horrible chance ended up at the slaughterhouse.

"No," I echoed Muffy. "Sorry, no." I felt like throwing up; the smell was horrible. "When did it happen?"

"Several days ago. Why?"

"Probably nothing, but in the bookstore this morning a woman was complaining they were short because a girl hadn't shown up for work and hadn't let them know."

"She missed all week?"

"I don't know."

"All right. Thanks. Next?"

Caroline looked very briefly, then backed

away shaking her head.

"Thank you, ladies, now if you'll just follow me." Caroline, however, was already out of the room and halfway down the hall.

Muffy mumbled something and hurried off toward Main and, no doubt, the bookstore. The cop stopped at the front door to say something to the uniformed guy there, then headed in the same direction as Muffy. I went on into the auditorium, which eventually darkened, thin flute music came up, and the film began. But I wasn't paying attention. Pity and terror . . . the Greeks had known all about such things, and I'd studied them in this very building. What a gruesome piece of lifeless stuff that young girl had become. Who was she? And *had* her death been connected? How could it not be? The Vietnam film continued on, pretty good, but those particular horrors were not as gripping for the moment as the memory of the strangled young girl lying on the heap of costumes.

When the film was over I walked back to Main and poked my head into the Retreat — a modern glass-and-brick space built against one of the old outside brick walls of Main — where coffee and doughnuts and such were sold during the day. Sure enough, Muffy was sitting at a table scribbling furiously in a notebook. I got some coffee and sat down beside her but kept quiet.

After a few minutes she looked up. "There. That'll do, for now."

"Will you get a story out of all this?"

"When I called in they said act as if. From what the woman in the bookstore said, it *is* the same girl. Long dark hair, brown eyes, tall, thin, and so forth. Name is Deborah Marten. Only due to show up there today. Then along came Lieutenant Bradley, who took the bookstore lady away for the identification, so that was that. Great to get there first, though of course I can't benefit, being weekly, so I called a friend at the *Times* and chalked up a favor. Which in fairness should be half yours, should you ever need it."

"Thanks," I said. "I'll remember."

We talked a bit more about the murders and then went upstairs to prepare for yet another night of overeating and drinking and nonstop conversation. The night before, though I'd felt a steady pressure to see and talk to as many people as possible, I'd also felt the weekend as just beginning. Tonight it felt as if it had already started ending, the time slipping away with dizzying speed. I showered and threw on another party dress, a white Mexican cotton with multicolored embroidery around the edges, then went downstairs past the noisy twenty-fifth reunion and joined my classmates for the cocktail party in the glassed-in area outside the Retreat.

Talking, listening, and Perrier water; conversation, dinner, and coffee; then more listening and talking and more Perrier. Finally, Caroline and I, both very tired, headed upstairs. The twenty-fifth's party, to judge by the loud gabble of conversation as we passed by, was still going as strong as ever. Caroline had been telling me about her life in Rome and a man she was involved with there who unfortunately was married, and Italian, and Catholic. Though he was, as she put it, "somewhat separated."

"Like when you're separating eggs to make a cake?" I asked, "and the white doesn't quite make it into the cup without some of the yellow?" The metaphor was, however, lost due to the noise coming from the twenty-fifth reunion.

"What?" Caroline was nearly yelling. "I can't hear you."

And in like manner, I couldn't hear what Pudgie Brown's friend Alice was saying as her head shot out of the door like a snake on its way to a chicken, but I could guess what she wanted to talk about. I didn't have to guess, though; she soon had a firm grip on my arm and was talking with great vigor only inches from my poor, tired face as she led me away from the door.

"They claim they've found her fingerprints on the gun, Maggie! They found the gun this morning and now they claim they've found these fingerprints. Looks like she may be arrested any minute! It's all some stupid mistake, of course, I *know* Pudgie Warren Brown, we grew up together! You can take it from me, she's as incapable of committing a horrible act like this as . . . as . . ." Her face clouded momentarily and then brightened. ". . . as a princess could become a frog! Flatheads! We better get going right away, I've made a list, and — oh, good, here's Bunny. My cousin," she explained. "Bunny! Come over here! This is the detective I was telling you about."

Bunny looked at me timidly, and I held out my hand and said, "I'm Maggie Elliott, how do you do?"

"Bunny Renick," Alice answered for her, "and she feels terrible. We all do, in fact the whole class is upset, naturally. How do you think it's going to look, for a prominent Vassar alumnus to be arrested for the horrible murder of her helpless old aunt *right here on campus?* Will mothers send their darling daughters here? Or even their sons? Look what's happened to Madeira!"

She paused for breath, and I said, "This doesn't seem quite the same—"

"*Not* to mention the papers! They'll never get off our backs, believe me I know the media *all too well* — but that's digressing. This business with Pudgie, that's the important thing." She turned to her cousin. "Bunny, go get Pudgie and we'll talk — no, too noisy. We'll have to all go upstairs somewhere."

"Wait a minute, Alice," I said. "Did you—"

"Actually, that side parlor will be all right, I'll just tell the people there they have to get out. Bunny, you go get Pudgie and then — what? Speak up! Speak up! I can't hear you when you mumble with all that noise back there."

"I don't think Pudgie is here tonight, Alice," her cousin said softly. "At least, I haven't seen her since before dinner."

"She wasn't at dinner?" Alice asked sharply. "I didn't know that. Probably arrested. We'll have to move even faster than I thought. Go get the rest of the roommates, Bunny. Go get them, whoever you can find."

"What's all this about, anyway," Caroline asked. "No, on second thought, I don't want to know, I'm too tired. Maggie, I'm going

59

upstairs, I'll see you later."

"No, wait, Caroline, I'm coming. Alice, did you talk about me to Pudgie?"

"Yes, briefly, we hadn't much time. Ah" — her face lit up — "here's a roommate now, two of them. This is the detective," she said to two women herded over by Bunny, "here for her fifteenth, luckily. I thought it would be a good idea to have her look into this murder business for poor Pudgie, and Bunny says Pudgie isn't here tonight. Arrested, I suppose."

"Not that I know of," murmured the shorter of the women.

"Well, good. *If* she isn't," Alice couldn't help adding. "Anyway, we should tell Maggie everything we know about the murder and then I hope she can get to work on the case right away. No time to lose, you know, now that the police have the fingerprints all mixed up." She turned a satisfied smile first on the roommates, then on me.

"See you later, Maggie." Caroline sighed and slunk off with a wave to the others.

"Alice," I said firmly, "what did Pudgie say when you talked to her about hiring me?"

"Oh, she said it might be a good idea, and of course it *is* a good idea, anybody can see that."

"As a licensed private detective," I continued, "I'd have to have a client who wanted to hire my services — which are pretty expensive, by the way." I then addressed the two roommates. "But if Pudgie does decide she wants some sort of private investigation, I'll be in New York for the next two weeks or so and I'll be glad to talk to her about it."

Both women were fair-haired, with the taller blonde starting to gray and the short one not, or the gray colored over. Both were thin and beautifully dressed, and both wore gold wedding bands and big diamond engagement rings. The short one had rubies keeping the big diamond company, while with the tall one it was emeralds.

The short one, whose name was Molly, said rather hesitantly, "I think, you know, we would like to talk to you about it now, if that would be possible. I mean, it's hardly the kind of situation any of *us* have any expertise with. What I mean is, we'd like to be helpful, but we don't know how."

The tall, thin, glamorous-looking one, whose name was Cinnie, added briskly, "Well, and if they do charge her then something will have to be done about finding out who actually committed the murder, and quickly."

"Why are you so worried they'll charge her?" I asked.

"The way they've been questioning her all week we think—" Molly began, but Alice easily drowned her out, simply raising her voice until Molly gave up.

"There were fingerprints on the gun for some stupid reason, Pudgie's fingerprints. Also, they've been grilling her all week. It's quite obvious what their intentions are by now. So we need someone to find that hoodlum townie who did it."

"Why are you all so sure," I asked, "that, ah, that Pudgie didn't do it?"

"Impossible!" Alice snorted. "I've known Pudgie Warren Brown all my life and she is a *very* fine person. One of the most distinguished members of our class. Just elected to the Board of Trustees, as you know. And what mother will send her daughter—"

"Never mind that, Alice," Cinnie interrupted briskly, then said, "It seems very unlikely to me. After all, Pudgie's not *stupid*. Creative imagination has never been her forte, but I'm sure if she wanted to murder her aunt she'd have thought up a better story than this one. She's a very competent person, and people don't change character just like that, do they? She'd be as organized about a murder as she is about her committee work. Or so I believe."

"Does she have a lawyer?"

"Hayden has — Hayden is her husband — he has someone coming up Monday or Tuesday from New York, I think," Molly answered hesitantly. "To begin with — well, of course, she never dreamed they would think *she* had anything to do with it, she insisted it wasn't necessary—"

"Unfortunately, all the lawyers we know are corporation, property, estate men, taxes, that sort," interrupted Alice. "And of course you can't find them anyway on the weekend."

"What sort is the one her husband got hold of?" I asked.

"Yes, good question, Maggie!" Alice was enthusiastic about my work already. "She'll need a good criminal man, can't afford to fool around on a thing like that! Is there any reason to think this fellow knows anything about this kind of case? About murder?"

"Or a good criminal woman," Cinnie remarked.

"Huh?" Alice said.

"A good criminal woman lawyer. The one Hayden talked to is more a friend of the family, I think."

"Some of our husbands are coming up tomorrow, to help," Molly added.

Cinnie raised a thin, elegant eyebrow and said, "You think they're coming to help? More likely they're coming to shoo you all out of harm's way. You're such an innocent still, Molly, I can hardly believe it sometimes."

Molly bit her lip in irritation, and I said, edging toward the stairs, "Well, my advice is to find some kind of lawyer for her, tonight, if possible."

"Do you know of anyone?" Cinnie asked.

"Not here — I'm from the West Coast. But there're several lawyers in my class, probably some in yours, too."

"Joan Brooks" — Alice began thumbing through her reunion book — "not here, though. And Mimi Hagen, she's corporate I think but she's here. I'll go find her." And she was off.

"Where is Pudgie now?" I asked.

"We don't know," Molly answered. "She was planning to be here. Maybe that seems strange to you, under the circumstances, but she worked *so* hard on the class gift. And then being elected trustee as well, she felt she should — she felt it would be best . . . to just act as if nothing had happened."

"Ostrich syndrome," Cinnie said dryly. She was, I learned later, a well-known child psychiatrist in New York City.

Alice came running back, slightly out of breath. "I have a name! I have a name and a phone number — Louise Sedgeley lives in Poughkeepsie and she knows this fellow — of course as he's local he probably isn't much good, but it's someone for now. And he's married so he'll be home now."

"Could you meet with us tomorrow, Maggie?" Cinnie asked. "After everyone leaves? For a consultation? We'll pay whatever is your usual fee, of course."

"Yes, good idea," Alice said. "We're in the South Tower; we could meet there, say two o'clock. Or maybe first thing in the morning would be better."

"Two o'clock," I said with finality.

As I dragged myself up the stairs — it was nearly three A.M. again, and my sore throat was back along with an interminable all-over ache — I wondered why Pudgie's roommates of twenty-five years ago were taking such an active role. I tried to put myself in their places, those "housewives" who'd headed out Taylor Gate ten years before we had and who were separated from us by so much water under the bridge you could almost call it an ocean — civil rights and the women's movement, Vietnam and flower children, drugs and Earth Day, our government as good guys turned into government as bad guys. I was awfully tired, but nevertheless I felt a kind of gnawing interest in the murder of Lee's poor old aunt right on Vassar campus, with its supposed masked man, and with Lee's straight, good-girl older sister — now a trustee of the college — the number-one suspect. That old question 'who done it' was tugging at my brain. I wouldn't rest easy until I found out. Or thought I did.

SIX

I woke to the same steady rain that had been the last sound I'd heard the night before and peered out the window at such a dark gray world that I snuggled further beneath my sheet. Then the carillon bells from the nearby chapel started ringing. I'd not thought of them since I'd left college but remembered immediately that there was no question of more sleep with the damn things gonging on and on. Caroline woke up then, groaned and twisted her head around at me out of tangled sheets, and said bitterly, "Why'd they put the horrible things on now, for Christ's sake? Wasn't it enough to torture us with them for four years of college? What time is it? There were some notes on the door for you last night. I put them on the bureau or someplace. . . ." She yawned and retreated back beneath the covers, burying her raggedy yellow head under the pillow.

I got up and found three telephone messages, one to call my partner O'Reagan in San Francisco, one to call Peter Warren in Boston — the man in the beautiful suit at the party Friday night who'd been worried about his cousin Pudgie — and one to call Richard. I suppressed a sharp wave of anxiety as best I could as I put on a somewhat wrinkled cotton dress, widely striped in brown and white, then went down to the bathroom to push a toothbrush around my mouth. A dentist's ad taped to the mirror read, "Ignore your teeth — they'll go away." I brushed a little harder.

Down the hall I found an empty phone booth and called O'Reagan at home. He answered on the first ring and sounded hurried.

"Glad you got me. I'm just on the way out and won't be back till God knows when."

"What's going on?"

"The Blackwing thing's exploded and I've got to go up to Reno and see if I can help them find any of the pieces. When'll you be back? Couple days?" He knew perfectly well that I was taking two weeks off in New York after the reunion.

"Two weeks, but listen, Pat, strangely enough there's been a murder here, in fact two murders—"

"Yeah, I know, it was on the news — posh

millionaire college reunion and one of the posh millionaires bumped off along with one of the students. How'd you get involved so fast?"

"Oh, you know, old school ties. Seriously, though, I'm not involved, but I might be later. The millionairess's niece seems to be a suspect and I'm supposed to meet with her and some of her friends this afternoon. They might want to hire me, I don't know. If the woman is charged, that is. But . . . do you need me out there? Should I take this on if it's offered, or what?"

"Take it, take it, and I'll limp along out here without you as best I can—"

"Poor thing."

"We can always use the money, especially if there're millionairesses involved. Sure, take it."

"How long will the Willie Blackwing business take, do you think?"

A loud sigh came drifting across the continent. "Couple weeks at least. There's considerable tracking to be done on some low-down land deals and they'll be very well covered, if my guess is any good."

"I'm sorry to hear it. I'd feel better about taking on this situation here if you could — if I knew you could come East to help if I needed you. I mean I haven't worked on anything by myself yet, you know. *I* don't know how to go about getting this woman off the hook if she's charged, assuming she didn't do it and I'm hired to prove it."

"Yeah, but you'll find out. You're ready for it. Remember Beatrice? Remember Corny Kelly? Anyway, you'll figure out how to handle it as you go along. Christ, Maggie, that's what I have to do. Every time. There isn't any other way."

"Yeah, okay. I suppose I'm glad to know you have such faith in me. You have a phone number in Reno yet?"

"No, and I'll be moving around, but as soon as I get one, Harry'll have it. Best of British luck and all that, old girl."

I hung up the phone feeling a bit forlorn, but cheered at the thought that Pudgie might never be charged, and even if she were, might not want to hire me. New York City, a mere two hours away and her hometown, must be seething with fine, enthusiastic private detectives. With any luck I'd still be able to head down there for two weeks, run around and see people and paintings and enjoy myself, go on the anti-nuclear march. And see lots of films and plays and perhaps meet some new men who didn't fly into jealous rages for no reason at all (while all along secretly seeing other women themselves). Maybe I'd fall a little bit in love with one or two of them, which was always the best cure for heartbreak. Only a little bit, though. The last thing I needed right now was anything complicated or projecting much beyond the present moment. I was going to have my work cut out for me when I got back to San Francisco; there'd be the business of the house to straighten out if I didn't go back there to live with Richard.

I dialed the Boston number.

A female voice answered, and I heard a lot of talking and laughing in the background as she went to get Peter. While I waited I recalled that being in love is apt to involve as much pain as pleasure, and I might better give it a miss . . . though if I were staying in the present and nobody was looking to live happily ever after through the encounter, it could be all right . . .

"Maggie? Glad you could call back, we're about to go over to the Groton graduation." His voice dropped, suddenly becoming intimate. "How are you?"

"Since you ask — no, never mind. I'm fine. Only everything's been such a rush here, there's been another murder, and I seem to have got a little involved with your cousin

71

Pudgie or at least her roommates. . . ." I sighed.

"And no time for it while your reunion's going on. But do you think they seriously suspect Pudgie?"

"Her roommates think so. I don't have any information, one way or the other. Oh, except they say they found her fingerprints on the murder weapon. That needn't mean much, though."

"Doesn't sound so good, either. How about if I stop off in Poughkeepsie on the way back to New York? We can have dinner somewhere and then I'll drive you back to the city."

I hesitated, thought Why not, and said I had a car with me but dinner would be fine. We agreed to meet at Alumnae House at seven.

I sat there and looked at the message to call Richard, then crumpled it up and left the phone booth.

Groups of women passed me in the hallway on the way to Sunday brunch, the last event of the weekend. I joined several who hadn't been special friends at college, and asked about their lives as we walked over to Alumnae House. I was doing an informal survey, for myself, trying to determine who were the classmates who seemed happiest, seemed most satisfied with how their lives had turned out

72

so far. Were there any patterns, warnings, clues? I was also trying to decide what I thought constituted a "success." Happiness? Achievement? What sort of achievement? So far I had concluded only that it had something to do with honesty, with a lack of pretentiousness, with some quality of warmth, and . . . interest in others, was it?

I pursued my inquiries through brunch, but all too soon it, and a lot of fond farewells, became a part of the past, like the rest of the weekend, and it was time to go meet Pudgie and her friends. I walked back to Main and took the elevator — a tiny shaking thing dating back to perhaps the *Quattrocento* — to the fourth floor, then walked up the separate flight of stairs that led to the tower.

Main's two towers, called North and South, each consist of a set of small bedrooms arranged around a central living room and they accommodate groups of nine or ten roommates each. They were greatly sought after in the drawing for rooms for senior year; my roommates and I had drawn South Tower our year, and returning to them was like returning to a part of my own past. The living rooms were smaller and shabbier than I remembered, and darker, but I didn't have time for more memories because the people waiting there looked both expectant and agitated.

Molly offered coffee from an electric percolator someone must have brought from home, and I accepted my fourth cup of the day as Cinnie introduced a short, dark, good-looking man as Pudgie's husband, Hayden Brown. She said Alice had gone off somewhere but would join us shortly. Then Molly burst out, "Pudgie's been *arrested!*"

"Did they say why?" I asked.

"They searched here this morning," Cinnie answered. "It was after that. They came as we were leaving for the brunch; they had a warrant. And they found the rings — I still can't believe it!" She raised an elegant hand to her sleek blond head and ran her fingers through her perfect hairdo like a rake, leaving her with a slightly surprised, disheveled look as she continued. "I was watching as the man — they were in a little black bag stuck up in the back of that closet shelf over there. He rolled them out into his hand and showed them to that big policeman, the one in charge, then asked Pudgie if she could identify them. Pudgie's diamond sapphire was with them and so was a huge rose-colored diamond of Mrs. Warren's — it's a very rare and unusual piece. Of course Pudgie identified them."

"I went down with my wife to the jail,"

Hayden Brown interrupted. "They let me stay until she was booked." His weary, good-looking face drooped even more; he looked ill, really. "'When with intent to cause the death of another person . . . you cause such a death' — I don't think I'll forget those words as long as I live."

"Yes," I murmured, "they are somber, aren't they? But what's happening about a lawyer?"

"We called someone Alice Worthington found here in Poughkeepsie," Hayden answered. "He's still down at the jail. He said working out something about bail will take a little time."

"So she'll have to stay there at least to-night," Molly said. "Probably longer, I'm afraid."

"And we've all talked it over, Maggie," added Cinnie, "and we want to hire you to find out what the *hell* is going on."

"Right," Hayden said, looking numb and groggy, as if his thoughts were somewhere else, "right. If those rings were *here*, someone must have put them here. I want you to find out who."

"I couldn't spend all of my time on it right now," I answered, hedging. I really didn't want to take the case if I couldn't count on

O'Reagan to help; I really wanted a vacation. . . . "I have a couple of other commit-
ments that will take a good deal of my time."

"Other investigations, you mean?" Cinnie
asked.

"No — private business. You might be better off with someone else. I'm sure there are
a lot of excellent people in New York who
could devote full time—"

"Could you give it at least half time?"
Hayden interrupted.

"That should be no problem, but still you
might be better—"

"No, no, we'd like to have you. You know
the set-up, you're the sort who can blend with
the kind of people we know. Alice said she
knows someone out on the West Coast you
did really outstanding work for."

"All right. I'll have to talk to your wife
before I can say for certain, but let's assume
I take the case. Who is it exactly that is hiring
me?"

"We all are," Cinnie said. "Those of us here,
that is, and Alice, also. We roommates will
put up a retainer while Pudgie and Hayden
are getting the bail straightened out."

I told them what our fees and the usual retainer were, and Molly handed me a check that
she'd apparently made out earlier; it was

for four thousand dollars, double the usual retainer. I put it away in my purse and said, "Why don't you start, Mr. Brown, by telling me what your wife told you about the murder?"

"Hayden, call me Hayden. All right. Let me think." He got up and absently poured himself another cup of coffee, then forgot to drink it as he described the murder as he had heard about it from Pudgie — the two women walking down the path, the man in a rubber mask demanding their "jools," then shooting the old lady when she objected.

I took notes and jotted down questions that I'd want to ask Pudgie later. Cinnie said, "Pudgie tried to tell her aunt to go ahead and give him the rings, she lives in New York after all and knows if you do everything they want they probably won't kill you. But he just shot Mrs. Warren anyway, isn't that odd?"

"I assume, from what I remember of where Mrs. Warren lived, that she had a lot of money?"

"You've been there?" Hayden asked, surprised. "The place on the Hudson?"

"Years ago, in college. I used to visit Lee Warren there. I met your wife then, too. *Is* there a lot of money involved?"

"Well!" said Hayden, "yes. Yes, there is."

"Who inherits?"

77

"My wife, unfortunately. Never seemed unfortunate before, of course."

"Was it known, then, before her aunt's death?"

"Oh yes. There are some other bequests, but the bulk goes to my wife."

"If she were convicted of the murder and therefore couldn't inherit, who would inherit?"

Hayden looked uncertain. "I don't know," he answered slowly. "No one else is mentioned in the will . . . I don't think." He ran a hand across his brow, rubbing it slowly, and sighed wearily. "I guess the lawyers would know."

"What do any of you know about the fingerprints on the gun?"

"They came up here yesterday," Cinnie answered, "after the AAVC meeting, and showed her a gun and asked her if it was the one her aunt was shot with. She said she couldn't be sure. Then they asked if she'd grabbed for the gun at any point, and she said no. And then they said how could she explain the fact that her fingerprints were on it? She said she guessed she had grabbed for the gun, and had forgotten."

"She didn't remember, or was she just saying that?"

"After they left she said she was sure

she'd never touched the gun, she'd never been that close to it."

I switched subjects. "Did you know there's been another murder? A student here named Deborah Marten?"

They nodded, and Molly asked, "Are they connected, do you think?"

"Almost impossible to believe they aren't. Did any of you know her? Ever hear the name? Know of any connection between Deborah Marten and Pudgie, or Mrs. Warren?"

They all shook their heads.

"What *do* you think is going on, Maggie?" Cinnie asked. "The rings . . . the finger-prints . . ."

"*Do* you think you can do anything?" Hayden asked.

"It seems to me," I said slowly, "that there are basically three possibilities."

"Ah," said Cinnie. "What?"

"Since they found the rings up here, that kills the idea of some random robber who wasn't connected with Pudgie or Mrs. War-ren, who just happened by and did the shoot-ing and the robbery, right? Which leaves pos-sibility number one, that Pudgie did shoot her aunt—"

"Now wait just a minute!" Hayden inter-rupted, with more energy than I'd seen from him up to now. "My wife is an innocent victim of some horrible scheme to incriminate her and I don't think—"

"Let me finish. I'm talking about what's possible as far as the evidence goes, and we have to look at all of it. All right?"

"All right," he murmured, though none too graciously.

"Possibility one, then, is that Pudgie shot her aunt, was careless enough to leave her fingerprints on the gun, and stupid enough to hide the rings here where they could be easily found. She made up the story of the masked man. Possibility two is that someone who had a reason to kill old Mrs. Warren did so, and has laid a frame on Pudgie."

"That's more like it," muttered Hayden. "What's number three?"

"That someone murdered Mrs. Warren in *order* to hang the frame on Pudgie. Someone who wants Pudgie out of the way, who hates her, who would benefit. Can any of you think who that might be?"

"We-ell," Cinnie murmured, looking at Hayden. "It seems a bit farfetched, but what about Corinne?"

Hayden winced and said tightly, "No. Not Corinne. She's still a little upset, yes." He paused. "But not Corinne. Anyway, it's me

Corinne hates now."

"Possibly, but certainly not exclusively; don't be a ninny, Hayden," Cinnie said firmly. "And then there's Edward; Edward hates Pudgie also, I'd say."

"Who are Corinne and Edward?" I asked.

"My ex-wife," Hayden answered, "and my wife's ex-husband."

"And they hate you because. . . ?"

"We'd all known each other such a long time, you see," Hayden began, then seemed uncertain as to how to continue.

"When Pudgie and Hayden decided to get married," Cinnie explained, "they were still married to Edward and Corinne. And Edward and Corinne didn't take very kindly to their decision, naturally."

"How long ago was all this?" I asked.

"Couple of years," Hayden sighed. "Pudgie and I married a year ago; the year preceding that was . . . we were involved in implementing our decision to marry."

"Getting their divorces," Cinnie put it more crudely but a lot less vaguely.

"Corinne was in our class, too," Molly added, "although she wasn't a roommate. She and Hayden married at the end of our junior year. She's my next-door neighbor, as a matter of fact, so I happen to know she has been —

she hasn't really gotten over the divorce yet."

"Putting it mildly," Cinnie said.

"Neither marriage had been any good for a long time," Hayden said defensively. "Corinne, well, Corinne unfortunately felt . . . somewhat abandoned . . ." He sighed deeply, shifted his position, rubbed his hand back and forth across his forehead as if it hurt. It probably did, every time he thought about his ex-wife.

Molly shook her head sadly. "I wish it could have been that townie."

"Any other candidates?" I asked.

All three shook their heads.

"Back to possibility two, then. Who might want old Mrs. Warren dead?"

They thought about it for a while, then Cinnie said, "Just all that money. As you said, it will be interesting to see who would inherit with Pudgie out of the way — or why frame her?"

"Or the murderer might be one of the other beneficiaries," I pointed out, "desperate for money for some reason. Or have some other reason to want Mrs. Warren dead, but be a nervous type and want someone else quickly arrested and convicted. That would make it someone with an obvious motive, someone else who inherits a lot, perhaps. The way it is now, the police won't have much interest in anyone else."

"Why not, why won't they?" Molly exclaimed indignantly. "They don't *know* Pudgie did it!"

"Having got to the point of arresting her, it'll be because they think they have the evidence to convict, or can get it. Now they'll just be interested in getting more of the same; they think they have the person who did the horrible deed, so why waste time looking any further?"

"Well, but if we explained to them about these other possibilities," Molly said softly, "then they'd look into it, surely?"

Cinnie gave a sort of snort, but didn't say anything.

"What will you do next, then?" Hayden asked. "How will you proceed from here?"

I looked at my watch. "I'll want to talk to Pudgie tomorrow, at the jail if she isn't out. Then it's a matter of talking to all the other people. Finding out what I can about the other victim, the student. Talking to Edward, to Corinne. Did you say Mrs. Warren had a secretary?"

I started a new list. Names, phone numbers, addresses of the people I'd want to see. Hayden said he'd talk to Pudgie and find out

83

when I could see her the next day. Molly said, "Corinne and I are neighbors in Darien. I'll talk to her about seeing you."

"I can't promise you Edward," Cinnie said, "but I'll give it a try."

"Will you stay on here, then, tonight?" Hayden asked.

"Yes. I'll be at Alumnae House, hopefully see Pudgie tomorrow, and then come down to New York."

We exchanged phone numbers and agreed to meet later in the week to assess our progress.

SEVEN

I didn't have any change, so I walked down the five flights of stairs to the Message Center and got some, then found a phone booth and fed in the first two dimes, which got me the operator, who got me our answering service in San Francisco. I left a message for O'Reagan saying that I was probably taking the case and to call me in a day or so. I wouldn't cash the check Molly had given me, though, until after I'd seen Pudgie. The next two dimes bought me the Dutchess County Jail, which said visiting hours were between one and three and told me how to get there. Four nickles got me Alumnae House, which asked if I wanted a room on the second floor for fifteen dollars or one of the smaller rooms on the third floor for seven? I didn't know you could get a room for seven dollars anywhere except maybe in Appalachia and I said to reserve me one of those.

When I got back to my room on the third

floor of Main I found the door unlocked and Alice Langley Worthington sitting comfortably on my bed.

"Your friend just left," she said, "but I waited because I wanted to see you right away. I was sorry to miss the meeting upstairs but I've been busy. You *are* taking on the job of clearing poor Pudgie, aren't you? They told you about the rings? Honestly, these flat-headed small-town police! But just after the brunch I ran into the mother and the fiancé, so I've been busy setting it up for you to see them." She exuded energy and well-being to an extent that made me feel a little tired.

"The mother?" I said blankly, "and the fiancé?"

"Deborah Marten's mother. The student who was killed. She and the boyfriend flew in from Minnesota; that's where they live, poor things. I thought while you were talking with the others, I'd see what I could do on the Deborah Marten end, because they're bound to be connected, don't you think? The two murders?"

"Oh I do, yes," I murmured, feeling a little bulldozed by her incessant managing, although not ungrateful.

She looked at her watch. "Four o'clock. I told them to expect you this afternoon, so we could go now if you want."

"Why don't you tell me what you've found out while I pack? I only know the little they had in the *Times* this morning. Then I'll check in at Alumnae House and see them. When are you going back to New York?"

"Tonight, unfortunately. I would like to stay over to help you, but I have a St. Luke's Women's Auxiliary first thing in the morning. I'm chairman and of course they always get me to do everything. I could come back after tomorrow, though. I'm frightfully interested in all this and I'm *awfully* good at finding out things. Always have been. Really, I should have been a detective myself."

"Thanks. But I've a feeling you'd be more useful in New York than here. You must know a lot about the people I want to talk to — Edward Corliss and Corinne Brown, for instance."

"Oh, yes. I know everybody, I sometimes think. Everybody of any importance. I suppose it can't have been that townie now, can it? With the rings found upstairs?"

"No, not likely. But tell me what you've found out about the student while I pack."

"Right." She sat up and took the limp pillow from behind her, vigorously fluffed it out, and put it behind her again. Settling back comfortably, she lit a cigarette and then talked steadily as I wandered about the small, threadbare room folding dresses, wrapping a pair of beautiful but uncomfortable new shoes in a paper bag and putting them in my case, taking the few things I'd put in the closet off the hangers and folding them. The white dress, I saw, needed washing, but the red silk could be worn again.

"She was a junior — that is, she'd just finished her junior year. A scholarship student, drama major — they say she was a dancer. Quite outstanding, apparently, which is how she got here; she got a very good scholarship. The family are nobodies. Even in Minnesota, I mean. She had to work to stretch out the scholarship; apparently these grants aren't enough to cover everything. She had a job in the bookstore off and on, which is why she was still here — normally she'd have left in May."

"She worked in the bookstore during the year?"

"Right. And was supposed to go on to New York this week — she had some theater job lined up in New Jersey somewhere and was sharing an apartment with three other students from here until it started. They were all friends of hers, or maybe roommates, so I got the address. It's here somewhere." She felt around in her purse, which was large and of a dark purple color — not quite a pretty color — in some heavy native weaving, with little pale-yellow bobbles hanging off the shoulder strap. "Here you are." She handed me a piece of paper with three names, a phone number, and an address on West 106th Street.

"Thanks. I suppose the police have been talking to the mother?"

"They have communicated to her their idea that Pudgie murdered their daughter after she saw something or other that would have incriminated Pudgie in her aunt's murder, yes. Of course, then I had a talk with them and explained the whole thing properly and told them that we have hired you to find out the real truth of what happened. I emphasized quite strongly that the two were surely connected, the two deaths, and that their daughter must have seen something that would have incriminated somebody — the question is, what, and who?"

"Those are the questions, all right," I agreed. "I'm ready to go — you can finish as we walk over."

"Well, there isn't any more, really. The father didn't come because they're farmers, of all things, and this is apparently a busy time of year for farmers."

It was rather cold again and raining quite hard outside, and I was glad for the last-minute impulse that had caused me, in San Francisco, to make room for my old full-length trenchcoat instead of the windbreaker I usually wore. There were several cars pulled up in front of Main, and most of them were having luggage put in their trunks as the last remaining reunion people got ready to leave. They all looked hurried, harried, and wet, but the pink-and-white peonies lifted wide happy faces to the rain, and the leaves and branches of the huge old trees seemed to dance to a tune I could almost hear — Beethoven perhaps, da-da-da-*dum*, da-da-da-*dum*, was that the Fifth? I intermittently hummed what I could remember of that giant beginning as we drove over to Alumnae House and Alice told me about a wonderful novel she was reading, all about an aristocratic German girl in the 1920s. It sounded pretty awful, and then I caught myself being picky and critical and tried to widen the space between my ears to allow Alice to read whatever the hell she wanted to without negative comment from me.

There was a substantial fire burning in the big stone fireplace in the lobby, and several old ladies — the few survivors who had made it to their sixty-fifth reunion — were sitting on the couches in front of it, all looking remarkably fit for women just a few years short of ninety.

Alice said she'd find Mrs. Marten and the boyfriend while I registered. "There's a little sitting room off the second floor landing," she added. "We can meet there. If anyone's using it, I'll make them leave."

She went off to round up what I couldn't help thinking of as her victims, which was hardly fair since they were just as much my victims. I got the key to my seven-dollar room. Then I walked up to the third floor, and when I opened the door I saw that when they'd said on the phone that the rooms were small, they'd been telling the truth. Still, there was something cozy about the smallness; with the slanted ceiling tucked under the eaves of the big old house, the room had the comforting feeling of a tiny garret. I put my bag down at the foot of the bed and walked the remaining two steps to the window and opened it to let some air, cool and fresh from the storm, come into the room.

There was a small mirror over a narrow shelf on the wall opposite the bed, and I took a quick look into it, smoothed down hair that had become a little flyaway and curly in the damp weather, thought I otherwise looked presentable, changed from my wet shoes into, alas, the beautiful but uncomfortable ones, and went back downstairs. I put my sandals on the hearth in front of the fire, where I hoped they'd dry before my feet were wrecked by the new shoes, and then I went back up to the sitting room.

Alice was already there, along with a fat, big woman and a thin, tall, blond young man who was very good-looking, just missing being beautiful because of an overly sharp nose and a somewhat receding chin. Right now he looked unhappy, and the woman's face was shiny and tear-streaked. She dabbed at it with a large blue-and-brown handkerchief, held in big, clumsy red hands that had seen half a lifetime, so far, of hard, physical work. The young man, on the other hand, looked considerably more citified in a good suit and with slim, well-kept hands.

Alice introduced us, and I told the two sad-looking people that I was very sorry about Deborah's death and would be doing what I could to find out who caused it. Mrs. Marten said, "You don't think it was that society woman, really? You really don't think so, or are you just working for her?"

The young man, whose name was Herbie, looked a little embarrassed; Mrs. Marten was the kind of hard-worked old farm woman — old by middle age — that twenty-year-olds headed for the city would always be embarrassed by; only later, looking down at the big red hands folded and at rest at last, in her coffin, would he suddenly realize something sustaining had gone out of his life, and feel ashamed, and wish he'd been nicer, and more patient.

I answered her question. "There's no way to know for certain at this point, Mrs. Marten. But for what it's worth, no, I don't. I don't think Pudgie Brown killed either your daughter or her aunt. The evidence, the clues that the police found, were awfully obvious, for one thing. But if I *should* find evidence that she is guilty, I'd naturally give it to the police. But I'm—"

"I never did want Debbie to come here!" Mrs. Marten broke in, dabbing at her watery blue eyes. "But she wanted to so much, Dad and I gave in. Oh, why did I ever let her come to this place?"

"Why *did* she choose Vassar? I understand she was a very gifted dancer. I'm surprised she didn't choose a school where she could get top training as a dancer."

"She said she could do that later. Her best friend was planning to come here, and Debbie had her heart set on their coming together and being roommates. Her friend didn't get in, as it turned out — she's a nice girl but never was as smart as Debbie. I can't help thinking if I just hadn't let her come here. But she didn't just want the dancing, she wanted to go on the stage. Well, her teachers and all said she had great ability that way, and when she got that scholarship, why Dad and I didn't want to stand in her way.

"Do you have other children?" I asked.

"Yes. But none like her." She sighed. "Perhaps it's as well."

I turned to the young man. "You were Debbie's fiancé?"

His pale face was washed suddenly with red, and there was an awkward silence before he mumbled, "No . . . yes . . . well—"

"Had been — would be again was *our* hope, Dad's and mine," Mrs. Marten answered for him. "Debbie broke it off this last Christmas, without giving any good reason. I thought it was just some lovers' tiff, maybe, that would blow over. But then she got another summer job here in the East and it didn't hardly look like she would ever be coming back much."

I asked Herbie, "Did she give you any reason?"

"Not really." His sensual lips pursed tightly above the weak chin. "Just said her life was going to be in the East. I did think there was someone else she'd fallen for, but she said there wasn't."

"Did you keep on thinking there was someone else, even though she denied it?"

"Well, I did. Though I had nothing to go on, it was just a — just a feeling. I took the ring back, but I told her I didn't accept what she'd said as final. I hoped she might, well, have a harder time with all this theater stuff than she expected, to tell you the truth. Get it out of her system. I mean, she came home Christmas. I thought she'd met somebody else, maybe, at that theater place."

"What made you think so?" I asked.

"Well, I've thought about it a lot, naturally. And you see, she was real carried away, real enthusiastic, about all the people she was working with. The star, Miss Hope, she's a famous actress in New York, I guess, and, oh, the whole bunch of them — she talked about them all the time, in her letters. And I kind of got the feeling she was thinking maybe these were the kind of people she wanted to be around — instead of me, maybe. So I took the time off from work to come back here and see what was going on. And like I say, she was different toward me, but nothing I could put my finger on. She *said* nothing was wrong, so . . ." He spread out his arms and shrugged.

"Well," I said, "the assumption is that Debbie saw something, saw someone, that would have connected them to the crime, or at least they thought so. So I'll be talking to her friends, the roommates in New York. Maybe you'd tell them I'll be calling, Mrs. Marten? And I'd like to see the letters you both have. And I'd like a good picture of Debbie."

"I have a good clear one," Herbie said. "I'll send it off right away with the letters."

We talked a bit more about Debbie's friends at college, her general interests and likes and dislikes, and I asked them to call me collect if either thought of anything different or special about her life in the past year or so.

"I'll be looking for anything, any people in her life, that are also connected with old Mrs. Warren or Pudgie Brown. It's a kind of rummaging around in the dark, a long shot, but it is, at least, a place to start. Will you help me?"

"Yes, oh yes," said Mrs. Marten.

"Anything," Herbie said.

The situation didn't seem to be waiting for me to talk with Pudgie before making up my mind. I seemed to have a case on my hands now whether or not I felt very confident about my ability to solve it.

EIGHT

I sat in a very hot bath in a large white-tiled bathroom down the hall from my tiny room, making mental lists: I hadn't heard from Hayden about seeing Pudgie in jail/I really should have a talk with the police, even though they'd probably hate me on sight or principle/ tomorrow early I'd go through Deborah Marten's room at college/I'd be in New York Tuesday so I could see her New York roommates then. . . .

I lay there soaking and only realized when the water cooled off that I'd fallen asleep. I turned on the hot, but it wasn't running very hot anymore, so I reluctantly got out. Back in my room I wrote down all the things I could remember from my bathtub list, then focused my thoughts on the evening ahead as I dressed.

Peter Warren, great nephew to Chloe Warren and friend of Pudgie, should be able to fill me in on the family. My mind went back to the weekends I'd spent at Chloe's mauso-

leum on the Hudson all those years ago —
sixteen, seventeen? But the images were hazy
. . . huge old house, tennis courts, lawn down
to the river, lots of flowers, and gorgeous hot
weather . . . old Mrs. Warren with piled-up
white hair and prune-dark, malicious eyes
presiding in the grand manner at a giant
mahogany dinner table but otherwise not seen
. . . ditto for Pudgie, who'd been married to
her other husband then, but I had no memory
at all of him . . . a big swimming pool, and
plenty to drink . . .

I realized I was standing in the middle of
the room, staring unseeingly out the window
and making no progress in getting dressed. I
put on the red silk again, and the uncomfortable shoes, with Band-Aids protecting my blisters. As I brushed my hair, I ran down what
I knew about Peter Warren, a list supplied by
Muffy, who knew him socially in New York.
Lots of money, ran a family company that
made something for computers; Peter himself
had developed the computer part of the business and it had paid off like Midas. Hotchkiss,
Princeton, Cottage Club, New York and big
business, and early success. Rather active,
Muffy thought but wasn't sure, in the Republican party, possibly interested in running for
Congress or something. Republican, I

thought; God, we'd have nothing at all to talk about beyond the murders. Although he had seemed awfully human and attractive — for a Republican. There had been no visible rocks in his path so far except for one broken marriage. He'd traveled a lot, with a rapid turnover of women since the marriage (Muffy had warned). Was he interested in my becoming one of them, or interested in me only as a detective? I wondered. Was *I* interested in becoming one of them, one of Peter Warren's many women? Put like that, the prospect was not terribly appealing. In fact, how could I even be considering such a thing, after Richard? *After* Richard? Was that settled, then?

The face that looked back at me from the mirror gave no answer but was otherwise satisfactory. I look better sometimes and worse others; I'm never quite sure what causes the difference. Tonight, at any rate, I was looking my best. Good!

I went downstairs and waited in a big overstuffed chair in front of the fire. Two of the old ladies who had been there earlier were still sitting on one of the couches. I thought about introducing myself and getting their names and addresses in case I wanted to ask them later about Chloe Warren, but realized I really didn't want to right then, so I just relaxed in my chair and idly listened to their conversation.

"A rather loathsome painting of a field of daisies," one of them was saying, "with a man and woman in it who were looking toward the sun, which for some reason was in a sort of window frame, I don't know why."

Her companion nodded. "Why on earth do they keep it, do you suppose?"

Then they fell silent, and I listened to the snapping and hissing of the fire, looked into it and tried to use it as a mantra to empty my mind, for a while, of all it contained. I was succeeding pretty well when a hand gently shook my shoulder.

"Maggie?"

I looked up to see Peter Warren, suntanned and smiling, in a different beautiful suit, a beige one. His light gray eyes were warm and friendly, and I felt an unexpected connectedness with him that I'd not felt when we'd talked at the party.

"I was trying to not be anywhere for a while," I said, "or maybe in the still center of that fire. Hello, Peter."

He stood there smiling down at me, saying nothing, and I smiled back. "You're looking as good as ever, I'm glad to see." He paused and then asked, "Hungry?"

"Starving," I answered, feeling uneasy for some reason at the compliment and side-stepping it. "I seem to have taken on your cousin's case, by the way, unless an interview with her tomorrow gives me some reason not to. Did you know she's been arrested?"

"I heard. But let's think about dinner first — there's a place out on Route 376 that's supposed to be pretty good, sort of Americanized French, I think. Want to try that?"

"Sure. I think I'd like to get away from here, get away for a while from everything connected with the college, broken-hearted mothers from Minnesota . . ."

"I'll do my best" — he grinned — "to put your mind on something else. But who are the broken-hearted Minnesota mothers?"

I smiled but didn't answer. As we left I remembered to ask the desk if I'd had any calls — neither the seven- nor fifteen-dollar rooms had phones — and was given a pink while-you-were-out slip that said Mr. Brown had called and that I could see his wife the next day at one o'clock.

Outside it was no longer raining, but the wind was tossing the tops of the trees about as if they were playthings and there was the strong smell of more rain to come. Peter's car was a squarish black sedan that I couldn't identify. In spite of its rather klunky appearance, it gave off a strong aura of power and money and I wondered what it was. I'd have to reveal my ignorance and ask.

Peter got to my side of the car before I did and held open the door. I hesitated, then got in. When he slid in behind the wheel I said, "Having tried it both ways, I've found I prefer opening my own doors."

"Oh, okay, sorry." He turned the key in the ignition and the engine responded instantly with a muted roar. "If you want to lock the door in question, push that farthest button over there."

"Thanks," I said, but didn't. "What kind of car is this?"

"Ferrari."

"Ah. I've never been in one. I edited a film once where they were being raced. They won, too."

"Where was the race?"

"Le Mans, but this was years ago, about ten years ago. Are you a fan?"

"Used to race some. Never there. Quit after a second bad smash in a year. No guts, or growing intelligence — take your pick."

"No thanks. Were you afraid after the crashes, then? Differently, I mean, than before?"

"Yeah. That's right. Driving became — after the first one — a big effort. I got back on the horse, but cringingly. Gave up after the second one."

"You blame yourself? For being afraid that way?"

"Yes and no; I miss it, but I'm glad I'm not doing it anymore."

We drove down Raymond Avenue past faculty housing and the southern tip of Vassar Lake, then past more faculty housing to the intersection with Route 376. Just ahead on our right was a cluster of old, well-kept white buildings.

"Oh, damn," I said, forgetting my resolve to think no more of the murder for a while. "There's that convalescent hospital; I forgot to put it on my list of things to do."

"You've decided to arrange for your senile old age while still able-bodied?" Peter joked.

"Don't you think that's wise?" I responded in kind. "So many people get into such a panic about it at the last minute — and I don't have children to do it for me. Seeing all the old ladies at the reunion, you know, I thought Poughkeepsie would be as good a place as any — it's probably a lot cheaper than California. Anyway, I thought I'd just check it out while I was here."

"Very wise," he agreed. "Never too early to think about those declining years, as I am constantly telling the people who work for my company, but do you think they'll listen? You'd be amazed, no, they won't. Now I, on the other hand, have reserved a place in a home, uh — outside Kansas City. The scenery won't matter since the brain cells to appreciate it won't be there either, and the rates are quite agreeable. Perhaps you'd be interested in seeing my place in Kansas on your way back to California? And maybe I should look at this place here."

"It would be a lot cheerier," I agreed, "knowing someone else there, wouldn't it? Even, do you suppose, if you no longer remembered them?"

"I'll look into your place, but then you must go to Kansas City."

"All right."

Now what, I wondered. Now that the borderline humor about a really creepy subject had run its course, what could we talk about? We hardly knew each other. I started getting a tight, uncomfortable feeling around my solar plexus and remembered it from the first year I was at college and the awfulness of blind dates. It would pass, I reminded myself. Probably. I resolved, in any case, not to try and force it away by making conversation, but to let the silence roll a while and just see what happened. Peter must have come to the same decision, because for a while neither of us spoke. Many men — or women — would have turned on the radio at that point, but he didn't, just kept peering ahead into the headlight-streaked darkness and whistling a ragged, thin little tune between his teeth. I thought it was that old Calypso song, "All day, all night, Marian," then it changed and I couldn't make it fit a pattern or put any words to it.

We drove on into the lush, summery, green countryside passing the occasional well-kept "gentleman's farm," which were probably owned by men who worked for IBM. Pough-keepsie was the original home of that giant and its founder, old man Tom Watson.

"I'd be interested to hear," Peter interrupted my scattered thoughts, "your thinking on that door business."

"All right." I gathered together the swirl of impressions his question brought to mind. "Frailty. Uh . . . you know, messages — you're big and strong and I'm weak and need help. I don't need any more of those, I'm not accepting any more of those than I have to — not that I like ranting and raving about it, either."

"I didn't accuse you of ranting," he said equably. "I assumed you meant something like that. But I wanted to be sure, that's all."

We lapsed into silence again. The uncomfortable blind-date feeling seemed to dissipate with the little exchange about the door. I was feeling surprisingly relaxed and thinking about how I enjoyed being driven through the night to I didn't know where, when we got there and turned in. There was a softly lit two-story Colonial, with a widow's walk on the roof. A discreet sign in black gothic script by the edge of the small gravel parking lot said *Edward's*.

Inside, a birdlike elderly lady with frizzy gray hair and lovely sky-blue eyes came forward with menus. We followed in the wake of the soft rustle of her dark silk dress to a candlelit table in the corner. The room was smallish, with an open-hearth stone fireplace in the center and ten or so tables scattered around it. Most had couples eating and talking quietly.

"Why are you limping?" Peter asked after we sat down.

"It's my shoes. They're new and too tight and I thought Band-Aids would help with the blisters, but they *haven't*."

"Hand one of them over after we order.

Maybe I can fix it."

The restaurant was one of those places with a small set menu, which means that the food comes pretty quickly. Peter ordered steak and I went for the *canard à l'orange*. My French is nothing to write home about, but I'm extremely fond of orange duck and it's a lot of work to make, so the words just roll off my tongue automatically in places like that restaurant. Peter ordered a martini and I ordered orange juice that was claimed to be fresh.

"You don't drink, do you," he commented. "This place seem all right?"

I hesitated. Did I really want to say anything about the alcoholism business just then? "The place is fine," I said, "peaceful-feeling. I like it."

He took five or six black olives from a crowded antipasto plate and ate them. "Hand over a shoe, while we're waiting. Where's it too tight?"

"This front part by the toes, along that ridge."

I handed it to him and thought of the unusual combination of characteristics he'd displayed: Drove a very fancy car (pretentious, wasteful, but also awfully comfortable); ex-race car driver (aggressive, self-destructive, elitist, but also, I had to admit, something of a turn-on); and yet also observant of my slight limp in the dark restaurant and willing to try and do something about it right then and there. . . . Pick, analyze, judge, as usual: it was a habit that came in handy as a detective but wasn't so great for relations with the other humans on the planet. I sighed.

Peter pushed back and forth along the inner edge where the shoe was too tight with the handle of his dinner knife for a while and then said, "Try that. I think I've got it stretched now so that ridge will go back the other way. Both too tight?"

I gave him the other one, put back on the shoe he'd worked on, and found that it was no longer binding across my toes. "Wonderful," I murmured gratefully. "You *have* fixed it. How nice of you and how . . . competent. I've been pulling at it off and on, trying to stretch it, but it wasn't doing any good."

"I enjoy fixing things, always have. Meanwhile, how about the story of your life, while we're waiting for dinner?"

"I'm not that young," I countered. "It's not that short. How about yours?" I helped myself to a piece of celery and loaded it with chicken-liver pâté.

"I told you some of mine coming over. Your turn." He helped himself to more olives.

"Requesting any particular chapter?"

"Well, how did you get to be a private detective? Do you like the work? That sort of thing."

"Leave me some of those olives," I suggested, "and I won't eat all the pâté. All right. Detection. I haven't been doing it for very long, about a year." I told him about my half-sister Celia, who'd been murdered three years before, and about working with ex-cop O'Reagan on the case just to satisfy ourselves but succeeding, finally, in finding the murderer. "Afterward, O'Reagan and I decided to set ourselves up as private detectives. It was something we both wanted to try; he had the experience necessary for getting a license. We've worked on several cases now; we work well together. I got my own license just before I came East."

"I'm a big reader of all that sort of thing, murder books, spy books, but in real life it must be a lot more routine. Do you like the work?"

"Mmmm, some things. Talking to all sorts of different people, trying to figure them out, trying to sort of, uh, *sense* where the pieces of a case fall together, and where they don't. And I don't mind the routine, really, looking things up. That's a kind of following the trail in a different way. And it can be exciting when you come up with something."

"And are you a confirmed loner, as all good detectives seem to be? Sam Spade, Marlowe, Lew Archer? Living alone in your skimpily furnished apartment, the chess set laid out with the game that is never finished . . . the romance that always falls through in the end?"

I laughed, a rather strained laugh, and didn't answer. "Here's dinner," I said, instead.

We turned our attention to the food. When Peter lit a cigarette afterward, I said, "You said you were concerned about Pudgie and want to help?"

"Absolutely. Anything I can do."

"How about starting with a brief rundown on your family? As it relates to Chloe Warren and Pudgie."

"A brief history of the Warren family? All right. How far back?"

"However far back you know, I guess. Where does the money come from? Who else is in the family? How exactly are you all related?"

"Okay. Let me think." He put out his cigarette and steepled his fingers together beneath his chin. "Once upon a time there were three brothers: Matthew, Mark, and John.

111

There was a Luke who died as an infant. Matthew was Aunt Chloe's husband, Mark was Pudgie and Lee's father, and John was my father's father. The family was in farming, prosperous but not big-time rich. Then the three boys started branching out into various business ventures that eventually included, for Matthew, railroads and oil. Pudgie's father and mother were killed in a sailing accident when she was in her teens and Lee was about five, and they went to live with Chloe and Matthew, who were childless. Matthew died about eight years ago, super rich. Mark was doing all right when he died, but nothing like Matthew's league, and that money of course went to Pudgie and Lee. My grandfather also did all right but wasn't the spectacular money-maker that Matthew was—"

"You're second cousins, then," I interrupted, "you and Pudgie."

"That's right. And, of course, she's years older, but she was very good to me when I was a child, during our summers in Maine; she taught me to sail, for one thing. I always liked her enormously. But back to the brothers. Who's left? My grandfather. He developed a small but lucrative machine parts company that was passed on to my father, but my father was never very fond of working, so when it turned out I was interested — and competent — he turned the whole thing over to me. He takes a good whack of the income, of course. He and his wife live in Europe, which they greatly prefer."

"His 'wife'? Not your mother?"

"No. She ran off — with a race car driver, oddly enough. When I was quite small. She lives in Monte Carlo now; I don't see her very often. But back to Chloe — where was I?"

"Did she legally adopt Pudgie and Lee, she and Matthew?"

"No, but they had no children and the two girls became their daughters in every way but legally."

"And Pudgie inherits, right?"

"As far as I know. I don't think they've made the will public yet."

"If Pudgie *were* convicted of the murder, who would inherit then, do you know?"

"Nope. But I'd be very surprised if it was either me or Cici. Or my father; Chloe's never been very friendly toward our part of the family. Cici made a point of visiting her, and wangled a party or two out of her, but I don't think she ever stood any chance at all. It's always been Pudgie all the way. Even when Lee was alive, Pudgie was clearly the favorite."

"What was Chloe's background?"

"I don't know much — rich girl from New York City, I think. She has some relatives out in California, but she liked them even less than my side of the family. I've never heard why. She made an exception of her nephew's daughter though. That's who she and Pudgie went to see in the nursing home — she's only twenty-five, poor kid, and I guess pretty much a vegetable: car wreck when she was at Vassar. Before that, according to Cici, the old lady had got almost as fond of the California niece as she was of Pudgie. After the accident, she visited the girl often. Pudgie usually took her there. Chloe hasn't driven for several years now, though of course she had someone to drive her wherever she wanted to go."

While he'd been talking we had been served one of those fancy desserts that comes in a small ice cream soda glass and involves ice cream, nuts, chocolate, little pieces of mint candy, strawberries, and whipped cream. Peter went to work on his and I sipped coffee, having already polished mine off as he was talking. He finished and said, "I'm very lucky in having — I mean, money is not a problem for me. If Hayden hadn't hired you, I was going to, if I could. You and your partner have a good reputation, by the way, on the

West Coast. Anyway, I happen to know that Hayden and Pudgie are short of cash just now. So I'd like you to consider me an interested party, if you would, and if there's anything I can do, anything you need, more money or whatever, call on me for it, all right?"

"All right."

We talked about other things then, in unspoken agreement to drop the subject of the murders for a while, and he invited me to come with him to the current very special Broadway production of *Peer Gynt*. It was supposed to be impossible to get tickets, and I accepted gladly. And in spite of my earlier conviction that there'd be nothing I could possibly talk about with a Republican, we talked easily and comfortably about a number of subjects (politics wasn't one of them). Furthermore, he certainly didn't seem like the Don Juan type, vain and self-satisfied. Maybe Muffy's information had been wrong on that. Maybe he wasn't a Republican either? He didn't seem closed-minded and interested in nothing but money and power regardless of who suffered and paid for it. I had to smile at my own closed-minded thinking then, and when Peter asked what I was smiling at, I merely said, "I'll tell you someday, maybe."

Eventually we got back into the extravagant, ostentatious, but comfortable car and, at the entrance to the parking lot, turned not back toward the college but right, deeper into the unknown night. It wasn't late, only about eleven.

"I feel like driving for a while. Mind?"

"No. I'd like it." The night was cool, and I started putting my window up.

"There's a sweater on the back seat if you want."

"Don't you want it?"

"No. I have another, if I do."

I put on the sweater, which was light and soft, and rolled the window down. The air felt wonderful; the headlights caught the edges of huge, thick-leaved trees; the sky was moonless and black except for the thousand million tiny cracks where the glitter of the stars showed through; the air smelled sweet and new.

We drove and drove and eventually pulled in between time-softened stone posts that I remembered along with a certain Yalie. It was the entrance to some long-dead robber baron's place that had been given to the state, a little-known spot for college dalliances in the old days, as I remembered quite well.

"How'd you know about this place?" I asked. "Your friend recommend this along with the restaurant?"

"I didn't go to Princeton for four years for nothing," he replied loftily. "But if you feel it's too early in our relationship for sex, we can walk around and look at the stars. I won't be offended. My plan of attack calls for more than getting my hands on you in bits and pieces, anyhow."

"Plan of attack? That sounds ominous. Organized, premeditated — cold-blooded, even."

"Organized and premeditated, perhaps. But not cold-blooded, I assure you."

NINE

Next morning bright and early — about eleven o'clock, that is — after sleeping like a stone and then downing some bacon and eggs at Alumnae House, I stood before Deborah Marten's door in Main and unlocked it with the combination her mother had given me the day before.

The room was a single and the long, narrow railroad shape of many of the old dormitory rooms at Vassar, with two tall windows at the far end that didn't let in much light. There was the usual minimal brown-painted college furniture plus an overstuffed chair covered with a bright magenta cloth. Several dresses and a bathrobe, also bright colors, were strewn across the chair, the bed, the chest of drawers. Dungarees and running shoes and sandals, green and pink and white, were piled in a corner on the floor. A bookshelf with several books sat beneath the window.

I knew the police had gone over the room

far more carefully than I could, but I thought we might be looking for different things, and in any case I wanted some sense of the sort of person Deborah had been. Apparently, the police had left the room as they'd found it, leaving, as well, a general impression of energy and chaos, of a personality with traits like color, motion, a little spacey . . . an impulsive sort of person. . . .

I opened the closet door and saw that there wasn't much there. Most of Deborah's clothes had been packed and sent on to Minnesota, I supposed, for that large, red-handed woman to wash, iron, sew buttons on, and give to the younger daughters.

The drawers were mostly empty too, with just some underthings in the top one and nothing underneath them — no old, yellowed newspaper clippings (unless of course the police had taken them), no thin bundle of love letters tied with a robin's-egg-blue silk ribbon. I sighed. The pockets of the few clothes, the ones strewn about and the ones in the closet, yielded nothing either; there were books of matches, but they all said Vassar College; there were lipsticks, compacts for eye make-up, rouges, a pair of stick-on false eyelashes unexpectedly in the pocket of a tweed jacket, but I couldn't see that any of it got me any further. At the moment I felt about a million light-years away from the slightest clue as to how to proceed. If Pudgie wasn't the murderer, and if whoever *was* just kept quiet and did nothing more, how in the world would I ever discover their identity, much less prove it? Of course I'd found *and* helped convict a couple of killers before, as well as a few big white-collar crooks — but always with O'Reagan there to bat it all back and forth with, working it out together. . . .

I sighed again and turned my attention to the books. On the top of the pile was a paperback *Collected Lyrics* of Edna St. Vincent Millay, who was, I remembered, a long-ago Vassar graduate. The preface, written by her sister, was heavily marked, so I put the book aside for the moment and looked through the others. Two — Spanish and astronomy texts — were new and unmarked. My heart quickened at the sight of a red leather book with *Diary* stamped in gold across the front, but it was empty.

I took the Vincent Millay over to the chair, pushed aside the clothes, and sat down. The poet had certain things in common with Deborah Marten, and these were the places that were marked. She'd come from a relatively poor family, for instance, and been offered a college education by summer visitors to her town in Maine who were impressed with her prize-winning poetry. She'd chosen Vassar, graduated in 1917, and then gone to live in Greenwich Village, where she'd been involved in the theater — acting, writing, directing, none of it bringing her very much money. The introduction continued for another four or five pages, but the markings stopped after the discussion of Millay's early theater years in New York and New Jersey.

I looked through the poems and found a heavily penciled line in the last verse of a poem called "Souvenir," along with the letters *C. H.* This was more like it. I read the marked verse:

> *Just a rainy day or two*
> *And a bitter word.*
> *Why do I remember you*
> *As a singing bird?*

I went back and read the first three verses, thinking they might provide further information:

> *Just a rainy day or two*
> *In a windy tower,*
> *That was all I had of you—*
> *Saving half an hour*

Marred by greeting passing groups
In a cinder walk,
Near some naked blackberry hoops
Dim with purple chalk.

I remember three or four
Things you said in spite,
And an ugly coat you wore,
Plaided black and white.

And then the final verse — bitter word, singing bird.

I looked through the rest of the poems but nothing else was marked, so I scribbled the name of the poem and the initials into my notebook and put the collection back on top of the pile. Then I leaned back into the chair and thought over what I knew about Deborah Marten's murder.

It wasn't much.

She'd been found in the costume room a couple of hours before Muffy and Caroline and I had been shown her body, found by a maid named Wilma Alleylon (so had said *The New York Times* in print, and over the telephone later after an introduction to the appropriate reporter by Muffy). Medical evidence said she'd been there five to seven days. She wasn't pregnant, she hadn't been raped, but she had had sex shortly before she died. With the murderer? There was nothing to indicate the sex had taken place where she'd been found, but nothing to show that it hadn't, either. She had had a rather clumsy abortion in the past year. She'd been strangled with the belt of a bathrobe that had been hung on the costume rack above her. There were no fingerprints at all in the immediate vicinity of the pile of costumes her body was sprawled upon, or on the costume room door, except for those of the maid who'd found the body. And, of course, there should have been.

The cleaning woman had kept her head, closed the door, and, when she'd finished vomiting, gone to a pay phone down the hall and called the police, who'd arrived promptly. There was no reason to think the woman had anything to do with the murder other than the discovery of the body; she said she did not recall ever seeing the girl before at college.

Deborah had last been seen by classmates who'd also stayed on campus to work the reunions. She'd had breakfast at Student's on Monday morning, had seemed in a hurry and eaten alone. They didn't know what plans she had until her reunion job began but thought she'd been planning to do some research in the library. However, they said she often spent nice days sunbathing or reading outdoors when she had time off — sometimes in the Shakespeare Gardens. I recalled that they were about halfway between the lake where Chloe Warren had been shot and Avery, where the girl's body was found. Deborah had had a key to Avery because she was a theater major and a lot of theater work was done there.

The reporter said he thought the police had little or nothing to go on other than their conviction that Pudgie Brown had murdered her aunt and had subsequently — presumably because she'd been seen — murdered Deborah Marten as well. But it seemed obvious to me that if the girl had actually witnessed the murder, her body would have been found down by the lake. Since it also seemed out of the question that her dead body would have been carried from the lake to the costume room in broad daylight, it seemed a reasonable assumption that she'd willingly taken the person in there with her. Or if not willingly, if it had been at gunpoint, then it would have been someone who knew her well enough to know she had a key. So . . . the most likely assumption, it seemed to me, was that she hadn't seen the murder, but had seen the murderer coming up from the lake afterward — on his way to South Tower to hide the rings? — knew him, and knew of some connection between him and Chloe Warren that would make her realize or at least suspect that he had killed the old lady, once the body was discovered.

It was getting to be time to get myself down to the jail, so I took another quick look around and then left, leaving the door locked behind me. I continued to mull things over as I walked back to Alumnae House to get my car. Since Deborah had recently had sex, it was probably worth my while to try and find out with whom. The same man who'd caused the aborted pregnancy? The one of the poem, singing bird, bitter word, with the initials *C. H.?* A man she was still crazy about whom she'd seen coming up from the lake and invited into the costume room to have sex with — who had made love to her on the hastily created pile of costumes and then pulled the blue belt tighter and tighter around her neck until she couldn't get any air into her lungs and her eyes bulged out and her face turned purple and she was dead?

I'd have to find a "blackberry hoop," whatever that might be, and a man who owned a black-and-white plaid jacket. Would it all lead me to the murderer? Or just to some brief love affair of no importance at all as far as the murder was concerned? I hoped her New York

125

roommates would know who and what the poem referred to, and whom Deborah might have been having sex with. And I had to remember to ask her ex-fiancé Herbie what he knew about the abortion — but not in front of her mother.

TEN

The directions I had to the jail took me into downtown Poughkeepsie and then, turning left at an elderly-looking deserted city park, down North Hamilton Street. I drove through a run-down residential area of old, small, two-story houses of wood and brick surrounded by medium-sized yards dotted with old spreading trees. The rain had stopped, but the leaves hissed and rumbled with the hint of more to come. The few people on the street were young and they were black, moving with energy down the sidewalks toward destinations I couldn't guess at — except for the handful of dilapidated winos lounging outside the corner store with flashing neon that said *Liquor* over the door; they'd stopped moving years before and their lives held no more destinations but one, the cemetery.

After a few blocks the Dutchess County Jail loomed up on my left, a solid brown brick building with fifteen or twenty tall antennas sprouting from the flat roof like the feelers of a group of giant insects swarmed.

Inside, an officer came to the usual chained glass window. I told him my name and what I wanted; he said to wait at the end of the hall and pushed the buzzer that unlocked the heavy metal door leading to the rest of the building. I went down a corridor of two-tone green concrete, neither tone nice, and dirty-looking linoleum to a waiting area where institutional oak benches with stiff backs and fat arms lined both sides of the hall. The rest of the corridor was shut off by locked metal gates.

I sat down on one of the hard benches and waited for someone to come and let me in. Three large men in dark suits came out of a room at the end of the corridor with a thin young kid in jeans and a shirt with a rainbow on it. The cops' hair was cut short and the kid's hung down to his shoulders. His hands were cuffed together in front and holding a white Styrofoam cup. The three cops took him into one of the rooms at my end of the hall and shut the door. No one else was around; a sign on the wall opposite quoted St. Francis:

It is in serving others that we live

in ornate gothic script of red, gold, and black. After a while the cops and the boy came back out, the cops shaking their heads.

"The car keys were in the door," one of them said.

"Why was he arrested?" a second one muttered. Both sounded disgusted. Then they all marched back to the room at the far end of the corridor.

Just as I was about to go back to the front desk and remind them of my existence, a thin man with a bony face with tight-stretched skin that made me think of Don Quixote unlocked the metal gates. He was wearing flashy clothes, a salmon-and-navy striped jacket, dark green pants, a lemon yellow shirt, and shiny black boots.

"You're here for the women's jail?" he asked mildly, as if he didn't much care or was thinking about something else.

"That's right, to see Mrs. Brown."

"Follow me, then."

We went down concrete stairs past a large brightly lit room he said was the booking office and through another metal door into a much older part of the building.

"Split-level jail," my guide muttered over his bony shoulder. "Old section here, where we keep the female prisoners."

I followed him into a musty self-serve elevator with round porthole windows covered by wire mesh. We got out on the third floor and he rang the bell by another green metal door with a window in it. A uniformed woman stepped around a disheveled woman leaning against the wall and unlocked it.

"Here to see Brown," my guide mumbled.

"Thanks," I said to his disappearing back. He waved a hand without turning around, got back into the elevator, and was gone.

I walked into the jail and heard a loud and depressing series of clicks behind me.

"I'll go and get Brown; you can wait in there."

She nodded to a small room on the left. Farther down the hall I could see through glass-topped steel-meshed doors into another small room where about ten women sat around listlessly. The cop walked on past and I went into the interview room. The dark brown linoleum on the floor reminded me of Vassar. Perhaps a local linoleum magnate had sold the stuff to every institution in the area a hundred years earlier?

There were two folding metal chairs, unfolded, and a weary-looking card table standing next to the room's only window, a tall old-fashioned one with elaborate molding and more wire mesh. A bare sixty-watt bulb dangled from its own cord like an inmate who had hanged herself. Rain rattled against the tall, beautiful window as the storm gathered in strength; the wind swooshed by, the skies darkened, and the room inside got darker and cooler, too.

Pudgie Brown appeared in the door, hesitated, then slowly walked in.

"You are Maggie Elliott?" she asked in a voice so low I could barely hear her, and then cleared her throat.

"Hello, Pudgie. I was a friend of your sister, Lee — do you remember me from when I used to visit her at your aunt's? When we were at Vassar? I'm glad to see you again, and I'm sorry that it's here. Let's sit down."

She looked distractedly at the splay-legged table and then sat, like an obedient little girl responding to one of the grownups. "Oh," she said slowly, brushing a limp hand across her forehead, "of course . . . Maggie . . . forgive me, I'm just not very . . ." She hesitated, looking for the right word and apparently not finding it.

The cop cleared her throat and said, "I have to leave this door open a little so I can look in every now and then to check on the prisoner, but otherwise you'll be perfectly private."

131

She left, and I asked, "Do you have any idea how this happened to you?"

She shook her head slowly, wearily.

"I told your husband and your friends I wanted to talk to you before I made a final decision whether to take the job, finding evidence that would clear you, that would lead to a charge against someone else. Are you with me so far?"

She nodded her head slowly.

"All right. They told me everything you told them about your aunt's murder. Now I want you to tell me. I know you must be sick of talking about it, but I'll have to hear it from you. This is a tape recorder" — I pulled a small Sony out of my purse — "and I'd like to tape what you say. If I end up not taking the case, I'll give you back the tape. Otherwise, I want to have a record of what you say, because later something you mention that doesn't seem important now, that I might not remember, might turn out to *be* important. Is that all right with you?"

She nodded again, then finally found her voice. "I keep thinking this is all just a mistake. And that they'll realize it, and let me out. I didn't do anything wrong, so I shouldn't be here." She swallowed and continued. "But I am. Here. And now they've found our rings, the rings that horrible man took, found them in the tower where I — they told you that, didn't they? Hayden and the others? It's just like a nightmare — it's just like a nightmare except *I'm not waking up.* Do you think you can do anything?"

"I can certainly try. Would you like me to?"

"Oh, yes. Yes I would."

"All right. Somebody put those rings there, and if it wasn't you then it was somebody else. It'll be my job to find out who." I pushed the red record button. "Let's start. I want you to tell me everything you can about what happened. Don't leave anything out, even if it doesn't seem important. Why don't you start with when you picked your aunt up at the hospital?"

She repeated the story of their walk along the path, the masked robber, the murder. I asked, "You keep referring to the masked person as 'he.' Why?"

"Why? Well, because . . . I just assumed . . . it *seemed* to be a he. . . ."

"Because of the voice?"

She put her elbow on the table and her hand underneath her chin and thought about it. "I see what you mean. It *could* have been a woman, I guess."

"Young or old?"

"Young, I thought. I don't know why. But like a townie, a young thug."

"Tall, thin, what?"

"Fairly tall, well, quite a bit taller than me, but then I'm rather short. Maybe five-ten or so. But I'm not good at that sort of thing, I'm afraid. He was bulky-looking but then he had that cape down to the ground, so I really couldn't tell."

"Tell me about the cape."

"All right. Long, down to the ground, black, cotton. A sort of collar, a rolled collar. And it was torn, ripped up one side."

"Which side? How big a tear? Visualize it."

"Ummm," she murmured, "right side, about, oh, eighteen inches, I'd say. Jagged. I could see jeans underneath, and plain black boots, cheap-looking."

"So you could identify the black robe, if you saw it again, by the tear?"

"I suppose so, yes."

"And the mask?"

"Oh, yes, I'd recognize that if I saw it again."

"Anything distinctive about it, like the tear in the robe?"

She searched her memory again, then shrugged. "Sorry, not that I remember."

"What about the voice?"

"I thought it was a man's, but again — it could have been a woman's. A kind of — hissing whisper. It was a horrible voice, horrible."

"Who else knew you'd be walking down that path after you left the convalescent hospital?"

"The people in the hospital, some of the staff, they must have heard us discussing it rather heatedly. I wanted to call a cab because it looked like rain — oh, if only I had! Now the police are saying we had a violent argument." She sighed.

"Which staff?"

"The head nurse, on the floor where poor Sally Steele is, Chloe's great niece. Do you know about her?"

"A little. But right now I'm interested in who knew you'd be on that path, knew and was capable of getting out there ahead of you. Was this something you did regularly, walk back to the college after you'd been to the hospital?"

"Well — I guess — usually we would. We would go see Sally, which seems quite futile because she doesn't know anyone. Then, after, we would generally walk over to the college. Aunt Chloe liked to browse in the bookstore — oh, poor Aunt Chloe! I feel so

sad about her, all . . . crumpled . . . up . . ."
Pudgie was fighting back tears now. "Crumpled, and blood, ooh . . ." She rubbed her fists into her eyes, took a deep breath, and then continued. "Sorry. Anyway, then we'd have coffee in the Retreat. So the whole thing, the drive down, seeing Sally and so forth, was a nice little outing for her. She'd always taken a walk in the morning, at home; this way she didn't miss her walk. I'd drop her off at the hospital, then drive over to the college and park, say hello to one or two people, then walk over to the hospital."

"So lots of people could have known ahead of time that you were likely to walk back?"

"Yes, I suppose so."

"Who, for instance?"

She lowered her eyes and looked at her hands clasped in her lap, unclasped them and turned them palms up, looked back at me. "My husband knew; I can't think of anyone else I talked to about it, but I wouldn't necessarily remember mentioning it. Stony would have known — Aunt Chloe's secretary. And probably lots of others, too."

"How long have these outings up here with your aunt been going on?"

"Ever since poor Sally was in the accident, about three years ago, or maybe four — no, five years now. Oh, Maggie — you can't imagine what a relief this is, to be asked questions aimed at getting to the bottom of this horrible thing! I've felt so trapped in here, as if a noose was tightening around my throat. I was against the idea of hiring you at first. Hayden and I have been — our cash flow isn't very good right now, and I didn't want to spend the money. Of course, that was in the beginning, too, when I didn't think I'd be arrested. Now I'm so glad they all insisted on bringing you in. And that I listened. Jail has given me better ears."

She did look, suddenly, better. Her eyes were brighter and her beautiful skin pale but not so sallow-looking.

"I'm glad," I said. "I'm glad to hear you coming back to life. I'm going to need a great deal of help from you. Because if anybody has the information that can tell us who murdered your aunt and framed you for it, it's you."

"But I *don't* know, Maggie. I've wracked my brains and it just makes no sense at all," she said in dismay. "That's what I want *you* to find out—"

"And that's what I'll do, with your help." I wasn't at all sure of my ability to do what I said, but it wouldn't help to let Pudgie know that. "But you do know a lot, you must, about

137

all the people involved with you or your aunt who could possibly have done this. That's who I want to know about, everything you can tell me. And then I'll start poking around until I find out which one of them it is." I smiled with more assurance than I felt.

"All right, but who, exactly?"

"Who benefits from your aunt's death? Besides you? That means financially, but not *only* financially. Who would inherit if you were convicted of your aunt's murder? Or who might hate you enough to set you up for a murder charge?"

"I notice you don't say *does* anyone hate me."

"That's right. I gathered from Cinnie and Molly that there are at least a couple of good possibilities."

"Corinne?"

"Corinne. And Edward. Corinne first."

Pudgie sat and looked at me without answering. Finally, she said, "All right. Corinne does hate me. At first I felt very guilty, of course, and wished she'd get run over by a taxicab so I could have Hayden without any fuss. I admit that. But she's dragged her wretchedness on and on, made such a song and dance of it, that lately I've felt mostly — annoyance. Impatience. And — disgust. Disgust at what she's put their children through. She hates me, all right. She blames me, you see, for everything that's wrong with her life. And of course I'm not responsible for *all* of it, but she's chosen to think I am. Yes, she hates me, all right. Funny, I never even thought of her in all this."

"She would have known, for instance, that you'd be spending the reunion weekend in South Tower. Or could easily have found out, from Molly. What about your ex-husband?"

Pudgie frowned in thought, then said, "I haven't been accustomed to think about people in terms of which one hates me. But I suppose Ed Corliss probably could be said to hate me."

"You're not sure, or you just don't like to think it?"

She sighed heavily. "Don't like to think it, I suppose. He does appear to hate me." She sighed again.

"Would he know of your practice of walking back to the college?"

"Yes. Oh, yes. Until about two years ago he knew every little thing I did, until I left him for Hayden. Actually, I had dated Hayden in college; he went to Yale, before Corinne waltzed off with him — literally — at the Junior Prom. He was my date; we were friends from Blue Hill. That's in Maine, a summer place. There was nothing exactly serious, all those years ago, but I really liked him and sort of hoped it might get serious. But then someone introduced him to Corinne and they went swooping off down the length of Student's — that's where we had the dances then, that huge room where the central dining area is now. Anyway, they went floating away to the very romantic strains of an old-fashioned waltz, and that was the last I saw of Hayden, in any real way. Corinne was very, very beautiful in those days. They got engaged almost right away, then they married. I put him out of my mind. I met Ed and married him the summer after graduation. Then, years later — we'd all seen each other over the years at Blue Hill but there'd been nothing special — I don't know, the summer before last it all changed very suddenly and Hayden and I found ourselves, well" — she cleared her throat — "in love. We had an affair. I'm somewhat ashamed to admit it, but the truth is essential now, isn't it? We met in New York and so forth, very sordid, and I'd forgotten what it was like to be so happy. If I'd ever known."

Staring dreamily out the window into the dark June afternoon, she reached into her pocket and fumbled around, then pulled out a package of Kent cigarettes and lit one. She blew a long puff of blue-gray smoke into the dreary little room, looked at me, and said, "Isn't life the strangest thing?"

ELEVEN

As she talked of her love affair, her face took on a rosy glow that made her look twenty years younger than the woman who'd walked into the room fifteen minutes before. A woman, definitely, still in love.

I got back to why her ex-husband might hate her.

"I tried to remain friends at first. But he would hardly even speak to me. All our business was handled through lawyers; the children go back and forth as they please between us. I left him with the house in Stamford and everything in it. It's a big, a huge, house; it's worth quite a lot of money. A lot more than the New York co-op that I kept. And the contents of the house, there's an extensive art collection, all that's pretty valuable, too. But Edward was so very unpleasant, and after all I *was* the one 'breaking up the home,' and he was so threatening, and I did feel—"

"Threatening? What did he threaten?"

"Well, not threats exactly, it was more his manner. He rather . . . emanated a feeling. That I'd be sorry, that something terrible would happen — I don't know exactly how to describe it, but it frightened me even to be around him then. And I did feel guilty, too, so I just let the house and all that go without much fuss, though it had been mostly my money from my parents to begin with. That bought the house. And the things in it. My lawyer was horrified, but it didn't seem worth a nasty fight — which would have eaten up a lot of the assets anyway, in legal fees. And the house will go to our children, eventually. I did feel rather frightened of him at one point, as I said; I just wanted to placate him, if I could. I was always placating Edward, throughout our marriage. I thought if I gave him all the material things we had left . . ."

Her voice trailed off as she thought about the years of placating Edward.

"And it isn't as though he loved me," she continued. "I don't know that he ever did, really. But I was very handy, I waited on him hand and foot, and I had a good deal of money from my parents that provided us with a very . . . comfortable standard of living — until it was gone, which was three or four years ago. I even thought he might *like* being free to go find another rich wife. He can be extremely charming when he chooses. But he wasn't pleased, he wasn't placated, he was furious. The — I think it's his vanity. He was absolutely outraged that *he* could be *left*. He'd had little affairs throughout the marriage, but that was different. He was furious that for once I wasn't going to do what he wanted, which was to stay married to him. I don't know why he wanted that, except, as I said, for vanity. There'd been nothing real between us for years and years. If there *ever* had been. I gave the appropriate parties, we saw the appropriate people—"

"What does he do, by the way?"

"He's an art critic. Has a couple of books out, but they never made much money; those sort of books don't, usually. He's had newspaper columns from time to time — right now he has one in the Stamford paper, but that doesn't pay much either. He's supposedly been writing the Great American Novel almost since we married, but I stopped believing in that years ago. For a long time it didn't seem to matter that he didn't make money. It never occurred to me, for years, that I'd ever come to the end of the money I'd inherited from my parents. Lee's share came to me, as well, after she was killed." She paused. "And I knew I'd have Chloe's money someday. She paid all the school bills for the children; my two daughters are at Madeira, and of course that's way beyond our means now. Our son is in school in New York . . ."

"He lives with you and Hayden? How old is he?"

"Eleven; yes, he's usually with us and then with Edward in the summers, if Edward isn't traveling, which he often is. I'm so worried about them, my children. Imagine having your *mother* arrested for murder! Especially at their ages, when the last thing in the world you want is to be even the tiniest bit different — and that goes for your parents, too! I almost hate that the most, what this must be doing to them. I could kill whoever's done this to me."

"Best leave their punishment to the state of New York, once we find them. Are you going to try to raise the bail, by the way? Molly said it's two hundred thousand and your lawyer is trying to get it reduced?"

"Yes. At first I thought I should just stay here. That was when I still thought it was all just a mistake and they'd soon let me out. My husband recently switched careers — he'd been in advertising, had done very well, but hated it, hated it. He quit when we married and started his own business, a video firm that documents things important to families — interviews with old grandmothers before they die, bar mitzvahs, things of that sort. He loves it and is doing quite well, but the investment in equipment has been astronomical — he's set up branches in several of the big cities. In fact, I was trying to get Chloe to loan us some money or invest in his business, but she was still angry at me for divorcing Edward. She was always very fond of Edward. Of course, he made up to her disgracefully because of all her money — you see, I can't be fair when talking about him. Maybe he really cared for her, but I am bitter."

"You were starting to say about bail?"

"Oh. Yes. At first, when Hayden said he'd raise money on the equipment from the business and get another note on the co-op, I thought in some muddle-headed way that I should wait it out here. But I *hate* this place. It's totally demoralizing, and I realize I have to get out if I can, no matter what it costs."

"When does he expect to have the money?"

"Possibly today or at the latest by tomorrow, he said. Of course when he and Corinne divorced, everything went to her. So we haven't had much spare cash. But probably tomorrow. He went back to New York last

146

night, to work on raising the money. And to try to find a good criminal lawyer for me. The lawyer here, Robert Shaw — he's not criminal — he's working on that also." She lit another cigarette, then continued.

"Oh, this is so humiliating. Sometimes I actually pinch myself, sitting in my cell" — she raised her right arm to show me and there were indeed black and blue marks along the inner forearm — "trying to pinch myself awake and find it was all just a bad dream. Sitting in my *cell*. And it just goes on and on."

And could turn out to be more than humiliating, I thought; it could turn out to be life imprisonment if I didn't come up with something good. I asked, "You'll go back to New York, when you get out?"

"Yes. The children are staying with some friends in Virginia right now, but they can't stay there forever. Of course, there are a million things to be done at Aunt Chloe's, but I don't know if they'll let me."

"Her secretary could start taking inventory, I'd think. I'd like to go out there later today and talk to her. Is she there, do you know? Do you and she get along?"

"Stony? She's always been very fond of me. Yes, she should be there. But you better call first."

She gave me the number and directions, and then I said, "I'll also want to see Mrs. Warren's lawyers. You haven't gone over the will with them yet, Hayden said."

"Just the gist, over the telephone — Swarthmore, Gibbons and Rudleigh, on Wall Street. Old Mr. Rudleigh has handled her affairs forever; he was Uncle Matthew's lawyer. His son does most of the work these days; the father is *very* old. But the son's in Europe right now."

"And it's mostly you who inherits?"

"Yes. The bulk of it. There are several others and some fairly large amounts, but I don't know the details. I was waiting until I got back to New York and then we were all going to meet with Mr. Rudleigh, but then I was arrested. . . ."

"Who else inherits?"

"Well, Aunt Chloe added something for Edward last year. She always liked him; he was unfailingly charming to her and she was positively livid about the divorce. She told me at the time she was making some changes in her will to compensate for what she called my atrocious behavior to Edward. She didn't know, of course, the extent to which he'd gone through almost all of my money over the years adding to his art collection or she might have been a little less charmed. Though perhaps not; she really thought he was just *it* as men go. I don't think she ever really understood why he married *me!* In fact, the way *she* felt about him had a good deal to do with why *I* married him, I've just this minute suddenly realized."

"When did she change the will?"

"About a year ago. When I married Hayden she told me she'd changed her will. Made it sound quite dire. Then after a few months, when she'd gotten more used to the idea and we were on better terms again, she relented and told me that I was still the principal heir, as I'd been since before I went to live with them. But she didn't ever say how much she was leaving Edward."

"I'll want to talk to Mr. Rudleigh, tomorrow if possible. You'd better call him, if you can from here. I doubt he would tell me anything unless you asked him to."

"I'll call him when we finish. If they'll let me. I talked to him briefly just before I was arrested and he offered to come up, but he's so old and I told him Hayden had found someone and not to bother. But he knows what's happened."

"Good. Anyone else you can think of that I should know about? Who stands to gain by your aunt's death or your conviction for it, or who might have hated or feared her? If you were convicted, who would inherit instead of you?"

"I don't know . . . Sally Steele's father would perhaps be the next of kin. He's Chloe's nephew, but she never liked him much. She paid for his children's schools, too; the son is at Princeton now and I'm sure she paid for that, but she always said she wasn't leaving much of anything to that side of the family. Some old family quarrel with Franklin's mother, who was her sister. I don't know the details. Franklin, in any case, is a perfectly nice man. He tends to be a little—"

"Visiting hours are up in a couple of minutes," interrupted the policewoman who'd let me in.

"Let's see if you can call Mr. Rudleigh," I suggested.

Pudgie asked, and the guard said she could call later. I told her to set up an appointment for me for the next morning or any time Wednesday, and to let me know at Alumnae House. I stood up and smiled what I hoped was an encouraging smile and held out my hand. She accepted it and pulled her rather heavy body out of the chair; she had that pinched, exhausted look again, but it wasn't as noticeable as when I'd arrived.

150

"I may see you in New York, then. Tomorrow," she said, in a voice that sounded as if she was afraid she might never see New York again. Then she trailed off forlornly behind her guard.

TWELVE

I telephoned Chloe Warren's secretary from the jail and then, following my hazy memories and Pudgie's directions, headed north out of Poughkeepsie on Highway 9. A few miles past Hyde Park I followed a tall, white stone wall on my left for about two miles, came to the painted iron gates I remembered, and turned in. A big elderly man in a gray uniform came out of a stone gatehouse that matched the wall, and when I gave him my name he said I was expected and waved me on.

I drove for what seemed like a long time through well-kept grounds liberally spotted with beautiful trees and tall, old flowering shrubberies, the road winding through gently rolling land and taking me out of sight of the highway before I saw the house. It was as monstrous in size as I'd remembered, built of soft, cream-colored stone that absorbed the late afternoon light so that it almost glowed. I drove past a small pond that didn't cover more than a few acres through bright formal gardens, up the circular drive to the front door, and got out.

A maid in a black uniform and white starchy apron and cap answered the door and led me through several huge, richly furnished rooms to a smallish sun room in back that overlooked the Hudson River. A tall, thin, serene-looking woman with faded blond hair pulled up in an elegant French twist introduced herself as Claire Stone — "but call me Stony, everyone does." The room contained a large, cluttered desk, a number of filing cabinets, some bookshelves, and several overstuffed chairs, one of which I sank into. She offered me a choice of cocktails or tea and sent the maid off for them.

"As I said on the phone," she began, "I want to help you in any way I can. I know, as well as I know anything in this world, that Pudgie would never have harmed her aunt. What can I tell you?"

"I'm working on the assumption that whoever murdered Mrs. Warren deliberately framed Pudgie for it. So, who benefits? Either from the death of Mrs. Warren or from the conviction of Pudgie? Any ideas or intuitions you have on either?"

"As far as financially benefiting, I know Pudgie is the main heir; I myself benefit by seventy-five thousand dollars. I was here at the time Mrs. Warren was killed and the cook and one of the maids have sworn so to the police. As far as who else benefits, and for what amount, I don't know; she called me her confidential secretary, but there were certain things she didn't confide. Mr. Rudleigh called earlier in the week and told me about my seventy-five thousand and also asked me to inform the servants of the various amounts they will receive: three months' salary for most of them and nine months for those who've been here over ten years."

"How long had you worked for her?"

"Twenty-five years." She gave me a slight smile. "That's most of my adult life, if you're wondering: I am fifty-two years old and came here when I was twenty-seven."

"Did you like her? Did you like working for her?"

"Let's say I could handle it. She was a complete tyrant, but I let a good deal of that roll off my back and simply proceeded with my job. I didn't plan to stay all these years, of course, when I came. It just happened. We suited each other and the pay was excellent."

"You must know a lot about her. Any idea at all who might have wanted her dead? Enough to kill her?"

"Other than the ones who benefit financially, you mean? I've certainly thought about it. She was very secretive about certain things, and there might be some sort of answer there. But I don't know enough to do more than speculate. I can indicate two or three areas that might be worth looking into, though."

"Did you tell the police about them?"

"Yes. They weren't interested, as far as I could tell."

"Try me. What are they, these areas?"

"Well, there's the seed man. I don't remember his name, but he was biology or something at Princeton and was a protégé of old Matthew Warren. Mr. Warren became ill and died unexpectedly and rather quickly. A few days before he died he called me in and dictated a couple of letters. One was to his broker, and that seemed routine to me. It was the other letter, the one to the professor, that I think might be something for you. Mr. Warren wrote the professor telling him he was ill and that he'd arranged for his wife to take charge of the fund set aside for their institute, in case he did not survive his illness — that Chloe would take care of it and the fellow was not to worry."

"And did she take care of it?"

"No. Several letters came from the man over

the next few months. The fact is, she didn't like him and thought the institute was a waste of money, money just hoodwinked, as she called it, from an ailing old man. It was for some sort of research having to do with seeds. At first she just put off doing anything about it, but then the professor got a lawyer on to it. Mrs. Warren tried to legally have the fund canceled, but couldn't. But he couldn't get the money without her signature, so it was a stalemate. I don't know if he'll get it or not, now that she's dead."

"How much is it?"

"I never knew. A lot, I believe. But Mr. Rudleigh, the lawyer, handled all that for her and I never really knew much about it except what I picked up from her occasional grumbling. Mostly she didn't like to talk about it; the subject irritated her. One of her few defeats, that's probably why. Or partial defeat. But Mr. Rudleigh will have the man's name and so forth and can tell you more about it."

"He must have felt like killing her, whether he did or not. You said two or three areas?"

"Yes, well, there was something funny about the convalescent hospital, where Sally Steele is, the great niece. You know about her?"

"Yes. What do you mean, something funny?"

"I don't know exactly. In fact, it might be nothing; it's more accurate to say Chloe *thought* there was something wrong. It had to do with the sister of an old friend of hers, a very old lady, older than Chloe, who was there at the hospital. A few weeks ago Chloe had me write and make an appointment with the head of the place, a Dr. Horton, saying she wished to discuss the matter of Emily Strong."

"And why do you think she thought something was wrong?"

"She wrote, and I quote, I have the carbon here, 'Information has come to my attention about this patient that will require an explanation.' Unfortunately, particularly during the last few years, Chloe had become terribly secretive — it was almost like an illness. Secretive about little, meaningless things, I mean, like whether or not she'd read the newspaper that morning, or how many cups of tea she'd had, as well as about business matters, her correspondence, and so forth. So while she had me take down most of her letters, type them up, and send them out, she tended to word them in a way that made it hard for me to know exactly what was going on. I didn't mind, I just went along with it, was even a little amused by it, in fact. But there was something at that hospital that bothered her, having

157

to do with that patient. Whether it was imaginary or real, I don't know."

"I'll look into it. Is that all you can tell me about it? May I see the carbon of the letter?"

"I've made you a copy," she said as she handed it over. "You can keep this."

"Thanks. What's the third area?"

"Probably nothing, but I thought I'd let you be the judge. Chloe had a great nephew, Peter Warren."

"I've met him; his sister was in my class at Vassar. And?"

"Shortly before she was killed, Chloe wrote asking him to come and see her, which was very unusual. She had very little contact with that part of the family, and no fondness for either Cici or Peter, though Cici kept trying. At any rate, the letter said that in going through some old papers she'd come across something that he would be wise to come and see her about, something that might affect him greatly. Here's the carbon for that one. I mailed it off a few days before she was killed, so, who knows, he may not even have received it by then. He seemed a nice enough young man the few times he was here, not grasping like his sister, at least not obviously so."

"Any idea what it was about?"

"She always claimed there was a mysteriously missing promissory note — owed by Peter's grandfather to his — and her husband's — father. I don't know the details. Except that it was supposed to be quite a large sum of money, for those days. Chloe believed that as a result, Matthew's parents' estate was pretty much bankrupt and that, in short, John stole from the other two brothers the amount of the loan. Morally, if not legally, it was why she never cared for that branch of the family. Or so she said."

"And grandfather John's business is now Peter's. *Had* Mrs. Warren been going through a lot of old papers?"

"Yes. She'd been sorting through some old trunks in the attic. Several were full of papers, old letters, that sort of thing."

"But you never saw the paper she referred to?"

"No. She had me send off most of what she didn't throw away to the Dutchess County Historical Society. It's really up to Pudgie to go through the papers now, but after she was arrested I started looking through them myself. I found nothing in the way of an old security note or anything of that kind."

"And did he come out here? Do you know if she saw Peter after she wrote the letter?"

"Not to my knowledge."

As Stony had no further ideas or suggestions, I thanked her, left, and tried to sort out the growing list of suspects as I drove the twenty-five miles back to Poughkeepsie. I was starting to feel a little overburdened, in fact, by their number. But the only thing I could do was plod through them to the best of my ability. Pudgie seemed innocent enough, for instance, but was she? She *could* have committed the murders, perhaps with an accomplice, and I'd have to keep that in mind while proceeding on the assumption of her innocence. But what good was keeping that possibility in mind going to do me? I again felt that sinking feeling, almost a pain in the stomach or solar plexus, caused by my fear of never actually finding out anything of real use, real proof, and wished for the hundredth time O'Reagan was working with me and could take on half — at least — of the many suspects. But wishing would get me nowhere, I told myself firmly. So, what about Pudgie's possible guilt? First, I should find out what husband Hayden had been doing at the time of the murder; somehow, I couldn't see her committing the crime by herself. Of course, I couldn't really see her committing it at all. And what was all this about Peter Warren?

Back at Alumnae House, a message from

Pudgie said that Mr. Rudleigh the lawyer would expect me the next day at eleven and gave me an address on Wall Street. I had dinner in the dining room, then sat on the couch in front of the fire making notes and lists and trying to block out my plans for the next week or so. The sinking feeling came back, but having definite things in mind to do seemed to keep it at bay, I noticed. I thought fleetingly of returning Richard's call but was afraid our conversation would just be a depressing repeat of the last few times we'd talked ("I don't care about Ilsa, that's over, it was a mistake, can't you forgive me, I know now it's you I really want, I'm sorry I lost my temper, I was just under so much pressure, I love you"). The trouble was, a part of me longed to trust all that, didn't want to be alone, or start all over with someone else. Was that it, mainly? Not so much that I didn't want to give up Richard himself but that I wanted to be in a relationship, even a bad one, wanted not to be alone? I wasn't sure, but if it was that — I'd better just get used to being alone, and fast. In the end, I didn't call him.

In my dreams that night I went to work for IBM, then went out dancing with a tall, dark stranger who also worked there. As we were dancing, I asked him why he wore a button-down shirt, and he replied, as though it were the most obvious thing in the world, "for baby bunting." I didn't know what that meant, but for some reason I didn't feel like asking, either.

THIRTEEN

The Taconic State and Saw Mill River Parkways, the West Side Highway, and New York, New York.

People, crowds of people, filled the streets as I drove from the top of that long, narrow city to the bottom, the people all moving and the place resembling a gigantic ant colony that somebody had recently poked a stick into. Added to that was a sort of mellow, anything-goes, summertime feeling that started me wondering why I'd ever left; it was so clearly the center of everything. It felt good to be there again: it felt like coming home.

It was dirty, rather scruffy — especially the West Side and the Village — after San Francisco, but everywhere sunny and summery, noisy and stuffed and overflowing with energy, color, and movement, as if the people on the streets were gathered for some special event, and the big special event was, simply, life in New York, New York.

I drove down streets as familiar as if I'd been on them the day before, across others I'd forgotten existed, and I didn't always remember how it all fit together. Seventh Avenue and Broadway do strange things, for instance, below Forty-second Street that I'd forgotten about, and that was odd after knowing the place like the back of my hand the way I used to when this was home . . . when this was home . . .

As I slowly worked my way down to Wall Street and Mr. Rudleigh, I thought about what the logistics of getting myself back living in New York again would involve, and quickly concluded they were too complicated. But for a few moments I certainly wanted to, and when I closed the door on the idea, I left a tiny crack open for any unexpected wind that might come along and blow it open again.

I found myself thinking of Peter Warren, then reminded myself, not for the first time, that the last thing I needed was any other entangling relationship; I still had to get myself sorted out from the last one. Not to mention his presumed horrid status as a Republican and ladies' man. Not to mention the fact, also, that he might be a murderer. Judging from the mess that'd been my last relationship, I wouldn't have been surprised at all, not at all. . . . And then I was on Wall Street. I found a garage two blocks away and walked back.

I think Wall Street is probably just the current reincarnation of ancient Egypt — monolith, stone, giant, a state religion run by and dealing with values that are not human, that have to do with power in its material and manifest form. Not one of my favorite places physically, and I disliked what it stood for, but there I went again: picking, analyzing, judging. Still, the day was so pleasantly warm and bright that even Wall Street took on the sheen of that energetic New York City well-being and could not diminish the buoyant feeling I'd had all morning.

Number seven-eighty. A tall chocolate-brown building with thousands of small windows and an aura of old money. An elevator silent as a padded cell lifted me in one swoop to the twenty-second floor; the doors slid open, still almost without sound, revealing a sparsely but elegantly furnished hallway with pictures of ducks on the walls and four doors opening off it. The one I wanted was on the left, and I opened it and went in.

The receptionist, young but neither pretty nor sexy, made a quiet call and then led me down a hall to a room at the end. She opened the door, murmured "Mrs. Elliott," and went away.

Mr. Rudleigh was just getting up from a large, gleaming desk which had, however, not much on it. Bookcases full of red and green and blue law books lined the two side walls; behind him a huge floor-to-ceiling window framed a sparkling view of the sunny, wide East River, of ships, and of Brooklyn beyond. As he reached across the desk to shake hands, I saw that he himself was small: short, thin, dapper, and very, very old.

I sat down in an extremely comfortable chair, and after he had reseated himself he said, "Actually, I believe I knew your father." His eyes twinkled from behind the desk, but it was the twinkle of a paper-covered Chinese lantern, very ancient paper that at any moment, should you pick it up, might come apart in your hands.

"George Linden?" I asked, surprised.

"We had a case together many years ago involving some oil leases; he handled the Texas end. Smart lawyer. How is he?"

"Fine, thank you. Still practicing. But I thought I was the detective here. How did you happen to connect George Linden in Texas with Maggie Elliott from California?"

"Oh, well." He smiled and waved his hand

dismissively. "After Pudgie, dear girl, called, I felt it . . . ah . . . probably wise to find out a little something about you. The poor girl's in enough trouble, isn't she?"

"Does that mean" — I smiled, too, but cautiously — "that I passed muster, or that I didn't?"

"My dear girl, of course I'm delighted that you will be trying to help Pudgie. You have quite a good record, though not, er, a very lengthy one."

"Thank you," I said. "Chloe Warren was the one who was actually your client, not Pudgie, is that right?"

"I've known Pudgie — literally — all her life, however," he replied, correctly interpreting my question, "and it's utter nonsense to think she would have killed her aunt. Venal nonsense, of course. Of the two, Chloe was by far the stronger character. If either were to commit murder, it would have been Chloe! Heh, heh. Always *most* determined to have her own way. Successful, usually. Now, how can I help you?"

"In general, any thoughts, ideas, intuitions, or suspicions you have about who might have murdered Mrs. Warren. And, specifically, if you could tell me what her will says. Who inherits as it stands now, and who would get the money if Pudgie were convicted?"

He picked up one of the two thin groups of paper that were on the otherwise bare desk and glanced down at them. "I have the will here. I don't much care for ungrounded speculation, but I can certainly help with the specific side of your request."

I waited as he rustled through the papers, then remembered I'd better take notes and pulled my notebook and a pen out of my purse just as he began.

"The main heir, of course, is Pudgie Warren Brown."

"And is there a great deal of money, as everyone seems to think?"

"Oh, yes, enough to satisfy the wildest fancies, I should think." He laughed, a thin, cackling *heh-heh-heh* that ended as abruptly as it began. "Pudgie's share, that is the main share, will be somewhere in the neighborhood of, um, to be on the safe side, let us say fifty million."

"Good lord. Dollars?"

"Oh, yes. Dollars. Not what they used to be, of course, but still, quite an enormous amount of money. There is also a recently added bequest to Pudgie's husband of many years. Now divorced. Edward Corliss." He paused as he thumbed through to the last page.

His hands were thin and pale and covered with large brown blotches; the veins were dark blue and stood out like small ropes laid just beneath the surface of his skin.

"Here it is, I wanted to be certain. Memory not what it once was, I'm afraid, but as I thought, yes, eight hundred thousand dollars."

"Not peanuts either; he should be able to live quite pleasantly off the income of that unless he has extremely expensive tastes. But why is it eight hundred thousand? Any reason?"

He smiled a small, pleased smile. "You are your father's daughter, I see. The truth is, I wondered also and asked her, quite cunningly, as I thought, because Chloe was rather, ah, close-mouthed about her reasons for doing things, generally. Something of a royalty complex and never to be questioned. That was Chloe." The old face once again creased into the series of sharp planes from which the curiously mirthless *heh-heh-heh* emerged, then relaxed into its polite façade. "I did not receive an answer. For whatever reason, she'd decided on eight, and eight it was."

"Earlier — Pudgie said Mrs. Warren was furious at her because of the divorce — did she think of cutting Pudgie out altogether, do you know?"

"Never."

I nodded and jotted down Ed Corliss's name with a big eight beside it. Not that I was likely to forget the amount, an amount easily worth committing murder for. Good.

"There are a number of smaller bequests, of course. Several to servants, her secretary, a few thousand to some relatives in California."

"The brother in California? I mean, nephew?"

"Franklin Steele, her nephew, yes, and his two children." He turned to an earlier page. "A trust fund is provided to take care of the expenses of his invalid daughter in her nursing home; the sum reverts to Pudgie upon the girl's death. Chloe left her nephew, Franklin Steele, the sum of ten thousand dollars. And she left another twenty-five thousand to his son, her great nephew Carter Steele, with the stipulation that it be used to complete his education. He has two more years at Princeton; twenty-five thousand will just about get him through. And that, for the California side of the family, is that."

"Not much compared to the others. Do you know why?"

"I think primarily it goes back to an old quarrel Chloe had with her older and only sister, Franklin Steele's mother. The sister

170

handled their parents' estate, and Chloe always believed she cheated her of much of her share. Whether it's the truth or not, I cannot say. But she never forgave her, and the animus was extended to her son and grandson. Chloe gradually became quite fond of the granddaughter, however, who visited her frequently, I believe, when she was at Vassar, until the accident that left her . . . more or less a vegetable. They say she will never be any better. Poor girl."

"But there was never any question of the girl's replacing Pudgie as the chief heir?"

"Oh, no, nothing like that. Pudgie's parents were killed when she was fourteen. A smiling couple went out sailing one September day off the coast of Maine and never came back. A very great tragedy. But then she went to live with her aunt and uncle, who did everything they could to be good parents to the child, including loving her very dearly. Oh, no, there was never any question that Pudgie could be replaced in her aunt's affections. Even with the divorce, though Chloe was very, very upset, there was no question of disinheritance."

He said nothing for a moment, looking at me but no longer seeing me, I thought; looking down a very long tunnel into the past. Finally, he said, "It was one of those marriages. One of the few really happy couples I've known, and I am almost ninety. But Helen and Mark were not perhaps very close to their children. The girls may in fact have benefited from the change. Once the shock wore off, of course. I would say without question that Chloe and Matthew benefited, in any case."

"You were Matthew Warren's lawyer originally, weren't you?"

"I was, and his close friend; we shared rooms at New Haven, and at Choate before that. During the First World War, if you can imagine that, young lady."

I smiled, and for a moment felt touched by the elusive wings of time, a feathery being whispering words that I repeated to the old man. "'Things past,'" I quoted, "'and passing, and to come' . . . I can't remember who wrote that. Was it Coleridge?"

"Yeats," he corrected, looking pleased with himself. "'Byzantium . . . of what is past, and passing, and to come.' Ah yes. Which brings us to the other major beneficiary, sufficiently Byzantine if you like: Paul Lombardi."

"The Princeton professor? I saw Clare Stone yesterday and she told me something about that, but she didn't know whether or not he'd get the money now. He will, then?"

"Oh, yes. Chloe was able to stall it off in her lifetime, but the trust fund will now go to the setting up of the research foundation he and Matthew had planned."

"Clare Stone said it was big. How big?"

"The amount" — he picked up the second pile of papers but didn't read from them — "the amount of ten million hard-earned American dollars. Heh, heh. Heh, heh, heh!" He looked up at me from the papers to enjoy what he had expected, and found — a very surprised look on my face.

"Good lord! What is this institute, anyway?"

"It's rather a long story — would you care for coffee or tea? Or, of course, you young people always want alcohol, don't you. . . ." He waved vaguely at a beautiful old wood-and-brass cabinet by the door.

"Tea would be lovely," I said. "Really lovely."

FOURTEEN

Mr. Rudleigh pressed a button, and a young secretary, predictably female, brought in a large raffia tray with a beautiful old Chinese teapot, thin cups, silver cream and sugar bowls. There were also scones and crumpets, and butter and jam to put on them. The secretary didn't say anything, just put the things down on the desk; Mr. Rudleigh didn't say anything either, as if the tea had appeared by magic or been brought by a machine. The cups already had tea in them; he took one and added cream. I took the other and put in lemon and sugar while he ruffled through the papers from the second pile on his desk. Then he started in on the subject of Paul Lombardi in his thin, precise voice.

"It was solely Matthew's interest, of course. He was very, very interested in Dr. Lombardi and his work, and decided shortly before he died to fund the fellow with a sizeable enough sum to create his own institute

— to be named, of course, after Matthew. He set up the fund shortly before his last illness; then, fearing he might not survive it, he put Chloe legally in charge." He took a sip of tea, then continued.

"Matthew did not survive the illness. And Chloe was by no means as enamored of this Lombardi fellow as Matthew had been. On the other hand, Matthew's wishes in the matter were quite clear. Well, Chloe hemmed and hawed. Right after Matthew died she was going to sign over the money. Then, after some time had passed and I'd heard nothing more about it, she stopped by the office one day and said she'd been thinking it over, and she really felt Matthew hadn't meant Lombardi to have the money right away, but only after her own death."

He paused to butter a crumpet, then took a healthy bite. I took a scone and spread on some jam.

"Her own death," he repeated, "which, she intimated, would be quite soon anyway. 'I am old, Philip,' she said that day, 'I am old. Not as old as *you* are, to be sure, but I've had a much harder life than you and I know I am not much longer for this world. . . .'" His thin, old man's voice trailed off as he looked down that long tunnel once again.

"You have a wonderful memory, Mr. Rudleigh."

He pulled himself away from the tunnel then, looked at me with sad eyes, and said, "The old are all memory, my dear child, the old are *only* memory. . . . Where was I?"

"Mrs. Warren came by the office and told you she'd decided Lombardi couldn't have the money—"

"Ah, yes, thank you. A bit later she came by again, with a letter from a lawyer Lombardi had hired, demanding that the money be released. She instructed me to stop them from forcing her to do any such thing, and, as it was legally possible to do so, that is what I did. Lombardi had been in touch with me on a number of occasions, I might add, and I must say when he found he had been legally stonewalled, he was not . . . er . . . pleased. That was ten years ago."

"So he's waited ten years for ten million dollars. . . . What is his work? And where is he now?"

"He is a professor at Princeton, or was. I haven't heard from the fellow in years."

"And his work?"

"I don't know what he teaches but his field is — it is highly technical, but it has to do with seeds."

"Seeds?" I asked blankly. "And what is the institute for?"

"Ah, well, that is another long story and I shan't tire you with it." He picked up one of the telephones and said, "Find the address for Dr. Paul Lombardi and give it to Mrs. Elliott when she leaves." He hung up.

It was he who was suddenly looking tired. He said slowly, "The institute has something to do with preserving the natural variety of seeds, which some people apparently believe is endangered by the, ah, involvement of the large corporations in the seed business. But you can find out all about it from him; in fact, you cannot *not* find out all about it, if you talk to the man, unless he has changed considerably. Miss Coombs, at the desk as you go out, will give you the information you require to find him . . ." He suppressed a yawn.

"I appreciate your giving me so much of your time. Just a couple of more things. First, the money that Mrs. Warren left to take care of her great niece, is it tied specifically to that particular hospital?"

"It is just generally for the girl's care, at any hospital; Pudgie is co-administrator with my son."

"And my final question: Who would inherit Pudgie's share if she were convicted and not eligible herself?"

"Chloe, of course, did specify Pudgie and Edward Corliss's three children to share equally. However, that strategy would not cover the present conditions, I'm afraid, even though the intent—" His voice, his energy, seemed to be running down, like a wind-up toy that starts to slow as its spring unwinds.

"Why wouldn't it apply, for Pudgie's children to inherit?"

"It would if Pudgie had predeceased her. There was no contingency for anything remotely like the present circumstances. Lawyers are trained to expect the worst, of course, but I am afraid I fell down quite badly on this one. Therefore, the bulk of the estate would go to Chloe's next of kin if it did not go to Pudgie."

"Is that the nephew, Franklin Steele? Are there any others involved?"

"No. Franklin was an only child, and his mother was Chloe's only sibling." He coughed and clutched at the ribs on his lower left side with a thin hand. His heart? I thought in alarm. Is he going to have a heart attack? But the hand dropped and he continued. "You will have to find out who murdered my old friend, my dear. So that her real wishes in the matter may be carried out. Please give my regards to your father."

"Yessir," I said, automatically dropping into the idiom of my Texas childhood: for women, it was "Yes, ma'am," and you'd best not forget it. "I certainly will."

The sidewalks outside had even more people walking on them than when I'd gone into the building. It was one o'clock and lunchtime, or perhaps some were finished clipping coupons by then and were leaving the area in search of more entertaining activities. I walked back in the direction of the garage looking for a place to get a little something to eat; the scones and crumpets hadn't done more than whet my appetite. I also wanted to find a telephone to try calling Deborah Marten's roommates.

I found the place to eat first, a small, plain-looking Italian restaurant tucked between windows full of cheap luggage on one side and some sort of occult place on the other. I went in and sat down at a red-and-white cloth-covered table with the obligatory Chianti candleholder, ordered, and then tried the roommates on the pay phone. No answer. Probably, they all worked at regular jobs; Deborah's mother had said they were not "artist types." Maybe after five.

I called Muffy to remind her we were supposed to have dinner and she suggested a place near the *Time* building. I tried Deborah's roommates again for good measure but no one answered. Then my steaming spaghetti with butter and garlic was brought to my table and I went over and sat down and ate it along with lots of garlic bread and three cups of coffee.

I felt like a new woman after lunch — but the new woman couldn't get the roommates on the phone, either. Then I called San Francisco and our secretary, Harry, gave me O'Reagan's number in Reno and said he didn't expect him back any time soon. Harry said that he himself, however, would be delighted to find out what alibi, if any, Franklin Steele had for the time of the murders, and would give it a rigorous check. *Rigorous* was currently one of Harry's favorite words; he was getting a master's degree at San Francisco State in English literature at night, but I'd noticed a growing yen for the detective business in him lately. The few things he'd done for us in that way had been well enough done, so I agreed.

"But can you do it without his knowing you're doing it? I'd rather he weren't put on his guard in case he does turn out to be the one."

"Naturally," Harry replied loftily. "Have no fear, I am ever the soul of discretion—"

"All right, all right, listen."

"Yeah?"

"There's also a son, just finished his second year at Princeton. You might find out whether he was in California or back here at the time, while you're at it. His name is Carter, Carter Steele."

"Rich playboy?"

"I don't know, see what you can find out about both of them. And get hold of a picture of Franklin Steele, will you, and send it along? And the son, if you can. How are you and my dogs getting along?"

"They think I was put on the earth to take them to the beach. You should see the looks I get if a day passes and we don't go."

"Poor you. But I'll make it up to you when I get back. Meanwhile, you be careful with Franklin Steele and the son." I hung up and tried the roommates again, didn't get them, paid for my meal, and left.

I passed the occult shop again and on impulse went inside and bought a new pack of Tarot cards, a recently created feminist deck that had been sold-out on the West Coast wherever I'd tried to buy it. But the book that went with it was sold-out in New York, too. Opposite the wall of shelves crammed with occultia a long counter that ran the length of the other wall was piled high with heaps of various dried substances (eye of newt, toad ears, deadly nightshade?). On shelves behind the counter were a lot of little glass bottles with neatly typed labels, and I asked the man, a thin, very dark black man — Haitian, I thought from his accent — what they contained.

"Enemy powder," he answered rather laconically; perhaps he'd sized me up as unlikely to buy anything more. "Love potions, sex binding. You have lover you wish bind more tightly?"

"Well, not at present. What does the enemy dust do?"

"Sprinkle across path, harm come him most certain, very bad, very soon." He smiled and nodded his head with enthusiasm. "Very bad, yes, harm very bad. You wish? If not bad harm, thirty-day guarantee, money back. But money not asked, never."

I pictured myself hot on the trail of the real killer of Chloe Warren and Deborah Marten, getting close, throwing enemy dust across their path, and . . . but of course, I hadn't the faintest idea which of the several people who might have done it should have dust thrown across their path. I might throw it at the wrong one, something terrible would happen to them, and then how would I feel?

"Better not, I guess," I answered. "It's tempting, though."

"Tarot reading in back room."

"How long does it take?"

"Two hours. Very high lady, very good." He nodded, biting his lower lip and grimacing and squinting his eyes together to say with his face: very high. I decided I wanted to get on uptown to my cousin's apartment before meeting Muffy, so I settled for a business card to make sure I could find the place again if I wanted to. Then I paid for the Tarot cards and decided to get some enemy dust after all. I also bought a bottle for Muffy; working at a place like *Time* she was sure to need some.

As I drove uptown to the apartment, I wondered what I would find there. My Cousin George is rather like Toad of Toad Hall, from *The Wind in the Willows*. He has Enthusiasms, each one replacing the last as if it had never been, and his apartment generally reflects them. Rowing on the river, replaced by traveling with friends in the canary-colored cart, replaced by the mesmerizing new motorcar, had in my cousin's case manifested themselves as George the *cinema verité* filmmaker (two short but good documentaries and a fully equipped editing room remained); George the

Himalayan hiker in search of the abominable snowman (bright handmade rugs from Nepal bore witness to that one); and currently, George the Spartan health practitioner and New Age explorer. He'd told me all about the charms of his most recent new life when he'd last been out West, so I was not unduly dismayed to see that, other than the rugs, there was hardly any furniture in his apartment. There was a sturdy looking head-stand rack, though, and a bar hanging from the ceiling on ropes. The bedroom was entirely empty except for a thin cotton pad on the floor.

I unpacked and took a shower, then lay down for a half-hour nap on the pad, which was surprisingly comfortable. A cup of strong China Black tea found stuck at the back of a shelf behind a variety of herb teas revived me sufficiently to dress, pack an overnight bag for Poughkeepsie, and then walk the few blocks to the restaurant where I was meeting Muffy.

As we waited for dinner, Muffy and I went over my list of suspects. She favored the Princeton professor.

"If a person's trying to fight corporate greed, why then, they're insane by definition. Right? And murderers *are* insane, right? Insanely one-subject-minded, getting what they want at any cost—"

"Rather like corporations—"

"But corporations quite often don't have to shoot people to get their way — they've bribed everyone important and got all the laws fixed up in their favor. But who's your pick?"

"Well . . . Franklin Steele is the obvious one. He'd benefit the most. But in terms of an intuitive toss of the dart at the board and relying on zen to get the bull's eye, I just don't know. Maybe this Ed Corliss; he sounds like a nasty sort."

"Ah, but do nasty sorts commit murders? They get all that nastiness out in their little daily acts and probably haven't got left the impetus that's needed, don't you think?"

"Some of them do," I said, remembering my first case. "Celia's murder was nasty enough. Although it was all covered over with smiles and sugar, come to think of it."

"You see! I'll bet this professor is just as nice as pie, long-suffering and the type who'll do anything for you. Wonder why he decided he had to get the money now, after waiting all these years?"

"We don't know that he did," I reminded her. "And Mr. Rudleigh said he hadn't heard from him in years. Maybe he's dead."

"You'll find out he's alive, all right," Muffy said with the certainty of a wise old-timer.

She'd been working at *Time* for ten years, after all, and I'd only been a private detective for one. "You wait. I'll bet it's him, all right."

"Could be. The trouble is, it could be any of them. Ex-husband, ex-wife, Pudgie herself, the professor, the California relatives, the man in charge at the convalescent hospital, someone I don't even know about yet . . . or Peter Warren."

"Peter? Why Peter, for heaven's sake? Did you go out with him the other night in Poughkeepsie? What'd you think of him? And why's *he* on the list?"

I told her briefly what Stony had said about Chloe Warren writing him before she died and about the missing promissory note.

"Well, but that was all so long ago. Anyway, what'd you think of him when you went out with him? Before he got on the list?"

"Well," I said, "I liked him. More than I expected to — maybe more than I wanted to. I mean, why couldn't I have become attracted to some nice biologist busy saving the jungles of South America from extinction, or something, instead of this Republican businessman?"

"Well, he's smart, at least, so maybe he isn't really the worst sort of Republican. Have you talked about it?"

"Oh . . . no. I've been avoiding politics. And economics and basic human rights and Central America and etcetera — perhaps he has too. Of course, 'Republican' is just a metaphor, but I was afraid we'd get into some senseless argument and ruin the nice time we were having; I had enough of that back in San Francisco to last the rest of my life."

"Well, he's a ladies' man anyway, or so I've heard. So the prospects for anything long-term probably aren't great, even if you got straightened out the San Francisco thing. Don't say I didn't warn you. Of course, he *is* awfully appealing, isn't he?"

"I suppose a ladies' man would have to be," I agreed gloomily, not wanting to talk about it anymore. "But what did you think of re-unions?"

We exchanged impressions on who'd seemed the happiest, most successful, most miserable, and so forth, and our observations seemed to jibe quite well. We had both been a little horrified to observe that the rich house-wives out in the suburbs had seemed more serene, if not actually happier, than the women with the heavy-duty jobs. On the other hand, the smoothness of their lives, in some cases, seemed somewhat marred by feelings that their lives were a cop-out on the kinds of values and more radical views they'd held in college and which they still, several had said, held in their hearts. Also surprising had been the number of single mothers — themselves as surprised about it as anyone.

This brought us naturally to the subject of relationships *versus* careers, which was not finally resolvable, though we both of course believed it shouldn't have to be *versus*. But all too often was.

It was after eleven by the time I left the city, and when I got back to Poughkeepsie the streets leading to the college were dark and deserted. All the good people were in bed, apparently, and the bad ones, too.

FIFTEEN

First thing next morning I called the jail, and after a short wait Pudgie came on the line, breathless and sounding excited.

"Sorry I didn't call yesterday — I wasn't certain what was going to happen — but I'm getting out in a few minutes. Hayden's brought the money and it's all cleared. The bail was reduced to a hundred thousand, which meant we had to raise ten, which wasn't nearly as bad as we expected. Do you want to see us?"

"Yes, and hooray that you're getting out! Can you come over to Alumnae House, and then we can go to the convalescent hospital? Have you had breakfast?"

"Have you ever been in jail? Breakfast was hours ago."

We arranged to meet in the pub and I was just finishing my third cup of coffee when they arrived, Hayden smiling and happy, and Pudgie, though pale and tired, looking almost euphoric. As we drove over to the hospital, with Hayden and Pudgie in the front seat holding hands, I asked Pudgie several questions I'd thought of after listening to the tape of our talk in jail.

"You said you and your aunt usually went to the Vassar bookstore after you visited Sally. Did you know that the student who was killed, Deborah Marten, worked there? Do you remember her, ever talk to her there? Or remember your aunt ever talking to her?"

"The police asked that, too. But I don't remember her. Not at all. Of course the one picture they had that — the one from the Freshman Directory — wasn't much good, and the others" — she shuddered, then continued in a low voice — "were after she was dead."

"Pretty horrible, I know; I saw her. But I'll have a good picture soon, from her family; I'll ask you again then."

"All right."

"You told me that when you went back to pick up your aunt at the hospital, Dr. Horton was on the floor and that Mrs. Warren and he were talking. Do you know what they were talking about, did you overhear anything, or did your aunt say anything later?"

"No — I don't know. Let me think." She

sat quietly, frowning. "Just the usual, I guess. I didn't hear anything — they stopped talking when I came up. It was right after that, as we were walking over to Sally, that we had the — what the police call the 'violent argument.' About whether to walk back or get a cab. I told her it looked *sure* to rain any minute, and Aunt Chloe said" — Pudgie smiled briefly — "that I could do as I pleased but that *she* was walking as usual. I tried to talk her into a cab but I should've known better — there was never any changing her mind once she'd made it up. She could be awfully exasperating and very stubborn and I believe I said so. That was the famous argument."

"Horton must have overheard, then?"

"Oh, I'd think so — he was right behind us. I was trying to keep my voice down, but Chloe, typically, wasn't. He'd have to have heard us."

"Do you think he could have known ahead of time that you'd probably walk back? I mean, would he have known you usually did that, from your other visits there?"

She thought about it for a minute. "I don't know. It was no secret. I'd say probably we'd discussed it in front of him other times, when the weather wasn't good. But I don't remember anything specifically."

"Was he still there when you left that day? On that floor?"

"No, that I do remember because Chloe asked the head nurse for him after we saw Sally. She had something else she wanted to tell him, and the nurse said he'd gone down earlier."

"Good. That leaves him knowing you'd be on the path and with plenty of time to get there before you. Was your aunt's manner toward him any different than usual?"

"Not that I noticed. But why are you so interested in him?"

I told her about the possibility of there being something wrong at the hospital that Chloe had found out about. Then we pulled in and Hayden dropped us off at the largest of the big white buildings and drove away. Pudgie and I were going to walk back and meet him at Alumnae House later. We entered and walked through a plush lobby into a rather dingy, dirty elevator with doors at both ends. Pudgie pushed the button for the third floor, and as the doors rumbled shut I asked, "Did your aunt say anything to you about suspecting something wrong about this place? Something having to do with the sister of an old friend who was here, Emily Strong?"

"No, I don't think I've ever heard that

name. Is she a patient here?"

"I think so. Did your aunt mention she was planning to see Dr. Horton for a special interview? Do you know if she *did* see him, other than up there on the third floor?"

"Sorry, I don't know. She didn't say anything about it."

The elevator doors opened and we walked past a nurse's station, which was empty, and turned down a dreary, windowless hall.

Sally Steele was sitting in a line of wheelchairs at the far end, her face the only young one in a row of aged. She was very thin; she didn't eat unless she was fed, Pudgie said. She had long shining blond hair and the Alice-in-Wonderland effect was emphasized by a hair ribbon of pale blue satin and a full-sleeved, old-fashioned challis robe with small purple and blue flowers on a cream background. Her eyes were dark and empty.

There were eight or nine people in that section of the hall, and all but two were women. Some were staring at one dull beige wall and some at the other, depending on which side of the hall their wheelchairs were parked. As we approached, several of them reached out thin hands beseechingly. Thin, like Dachau victims. One of the men, the only one who still had hair, a lot of thick, white hair, held out a tiny paper cup. "Can I have a glass of water? Can I have a glass of water?"

I looked around and saw a water fountain, so I took the cup and got him some water.

"Thank you," he said, and drank it thirstily.

A woman sitting in the wheelchair across from him, with a red Kewpie-doll bow in her perfectly coiffed white hair that matched her cherry-red bathrobe, began a monologue that she kept up the entire time we were there. She had rosy cheeks and round black eyes and looked terribly sweet and grandmotherly. She spoke, at first, in a quiet monotone.

"God damn you, god damn you, god damn you, I hate you, god damn you, I hate you, I hate you all." The voice was, indeed, filled to the brim with venom and hatred.

As I walked over to where Pudgie was talking to Sally, the old woman went on more inventively.

"I hate you, I despise you! I loathe you, I hate you!"

Pudgie had brought a couple of straight-back chairs from farther down the hall and put them in front of Sally's wheelchair. She sat down on one and said, "Sally, this is my friend Maggie."

She just kept looking blankly at the blank wall. I sat down.

"Maggie went to Vassar, too, Sally. She, uh, we, wanted, we were nearby and wanted to see how you were doing."

"Pudgie thought she would talk to the people who run this place," I added, "and be sure you're getting good care." The false cheerfulness of our voices was repulsive.

Sally continued staring at the wall, but she took Pudgie's hand, clutching it, and didn't let go.

In the next wheelchair an unkempt-looking woman with scraggly yellow-white hair was hanging onto a faded cloth doll as though it were a lifeline, giggling quietly. The woman in the cherry robe, who'd been muttering all this time about how she hated and despised everybody, got louder.

"Where's my room? Some fool woman's in my room! Am I going to sleep here on the *floor* tonight? Won't somebody help me? I loathe this place! I detest this place! I despise this place! If I could just sit on the *edge* of the bed then I could be comfortable. They won't let you do anything at all!" An overweight nurse walked down the hall and went on past, ignoring her. She continued, "Aren't there a lot of fat women here, fat, F-A-T, fat."

Pudgie asked Sally desperately, "Is there anything you want, anything I can get for you,

195

anything I can tell them to do for you?" But Sally merely continued to stare at the wall. Pudgie looked at me and shrugged slightly as if to say, Hopeless.

"Does Sally ever talk?" I asked.

"She never has when I've been here. The nurses say she says things sometimes."

"I wish I could go away," said the cherry-robed woman.

The white-haired man across from her said, "Huh?"

"I wish I could go away," she repeated.

"Now be nice," he said.

"I don't like it here anymore," she said, now to him and not just the wall. "If they would just let me sit on the *edge* of my bed I'd be perfectly all right, I'd be . . . I don't like it here."

"I don't either," the man said, "to tell you the truth."

The other man, who was shriveled and up-right only because he was strapped to his wheelchair, suddenly raised his head and screamed, "Help! I need a doctor! I need a doctor! I need a doctor! Help! Help!" He went on like that, but nobody paid any attention and he stopped after a while and his head sank back down until his chin was resting on his chest again.

There were several nurses standing around down at the other end of the hall who couldn't have helped hearing, but they just kept chatting with each other, not even glancing our way. I thought of the little boy who cried wolf, and then thought there were certain advantages to dying young — at least you wouldn't wind up in a place like this.

"Do you, are you getting everything you need, Sally?" Pudgie asked again. "Ah . . . I'm going to tell them to order your special massage every day instead of every other. . . ." Her voice petered out weakly, and in the silence the voice of Ms. Cherry Robe seemed loud and shrill.

"Why don't they come turn down the beds, or at least put the tables out or do *something?* Are they all *dead?*"

This woke up the man across the hall who'd been dozing. He held out his cup again and looked at me imploringly. "Give us some water, water, a glass of water!"

I took the cup to the fountain. Maybe he wasn't supposed to have any, but so what? Bad for his health? He drank the water right down and smiled very sweetly.

Pudgie stood up, ready to leave. Sally still hung onto her hand with both of hers and, as Pudgie made motions to go, clutched harder and turned her head and looked up at her. The look said as plain as words, Don't leave me here! Oh, don't leave me here!

Pudgie extracted her hand as gracefully as she could and said brightly, "I'll be back, Sally, don't fret. And I'll tell them about the massage, and if there's anything you think of that you want, if you tell the nurse to tell me, I'll see you get it."

As we were walking off, the old lady in the cherry robe was saying, in a sort of whimper now, "Please, somebody help me, I need you so much, nobody comes, nobody comes, nobody comes . . ."

SIXTEEN

As we walked down the hall and the old voice faded away, Pudgie said, "Isn't it *awful?* I *hate* coming here. I just came before because Aunt Chloe made me, and now I'm in charge of the poor child and I'll have to *keep* coming. There might be," she added with a touch of gallows humor I'd not have expected from her, "at least one good thing about being found guilty — I'd never have to come here again!"

"I see what you mean." I smiled weakly. "Maybe if you'll just point out the staff, though, before you turn yourself back in. The ones you remember who were here that day and who might've heard you talking about walking back. And then introduce me to the administrator. Why is everyone so *un*happy here? Do you think they have to be? Or is it partly the place?"

"You — I — oh, *both* probably, but I can't help thinking they could do a lot better than they do. All they care about is keeping these poor people alive to get the money for them as long as they possibly can . . . but . . . Chloe looked at a number of other places, I went with her, and we didn't see any that were better. Do you know, when Sally first came here — but there's the head nurse. She would certainly have heard us that day, talking about walking back. She's the one with the curly gray hair and the thick eyeglasses."

"I'd better talk to the administrator first; now, if possible. But you were saying . . . Sally shared a room?"

"Oh, right. I just couldn't believe it — she had to wait for a private room. They were redecorating this floor, so everyone was all crammed together. And the other woman in her room had been in a coma for fifteen years, her nurse told me. She had a private nurse. And do you know what they do to her? They have a *pacemaker* put in every couple of years, she has heart trouble apparently, but the pacemaker keeps it going so they can keep her alive. Her brain's gone, she's a hundred and two, there's nothing left to come out of a coma to, which they're sure she won't anyway. But they get a hundred thousand dollars a year from her estate and so they keep putting in these pacemakers. Can you imagine? She was always moaning, too, you could tell she was suffering, at whatever level she was alive. They call it life support. I can think of something else to call it."

"A sort of . . . terrible crop." I shuddered. "How much do they get for Sally?"

"The base cost is about a hundred dollars a day, but that's only the beginning. They have ingenious charges for everything you can think of, and of course you feel so guilty having the person here in the first place, you pay up."

"If your aunt had so much money, why didn't she keep Sally with a nurse at home, then?"

"Well, insurance won't cover anything like that, that's why most of these people have to be here. But in Sally's case, of course, money wasn't a problem. But the doctors all push the nursing home, too, telling you the person needs twenty-four-hour access to doctor's care. Although I imagine ninety percent of the doctor visits are totally unnecessary — or aimed at keeping the patient alive beyond what is in any way appropriate — except for the making of money by the hospital. But the doctors practically tell you you *can't* have them at home, and then, of course, there's a lot of mumbo-jumbo about better care, which you're dying to believe. But, really, people just completely deteriorate once they're stuck in here. It's a horrible trap, really, these poor people are all in a trap, and so are their families. Some don't have anyone, it's just some lawyers somewhere. . . ."

The elevator opened and we stepped in.

"The administrator's on the first floor. He's just the manager; it's owned by a corporation, the Total Care Corporation."

"Total Care to part you from your last cent. Here we are. Which way?"

"Left, down at the end."

The floor here, in contrast to the linoleum-covered hallway upstairs where the patients were, was covered with a thick, velvety maroon carpet. The walls were painted a delicate blue, and oil paintings in heavy gold frames with little lights beneath them as if they were museum pieces were hung at regular intervals. They were of subjects like golden-leaved trees by clear-running rocky streams, green meadows with cows munching peacefully against a background of distant purple mountains, a snowy grandmother's house with a sleigh filled with a happy family. Our feet moved soundlessly, the world enclosed by the deep carpet and the blue walls feeling as unreal as the ones in the gold frames.

An anteroom at the end of the hall contained

ample plush seating and a rather pretty, rather young, receptionist. Pudgie smiled and said she wanted to see Dr. Horton.

The somewhat pretty face instantly shaped itself into a deep sympathetic look. "You have a dear one you wish to discuss bringing here?"

"No," said Pudgie shortly, "I have a dear one I wish to discuss who is already here. Sally Steele. I am Mrs. Brown; I thought you knew me."

"Oh, of course, Mrs. Brown," the girl murmured, looking secretly interested. "It's been a terribly hectic day, and I just wasn't thinking, I guess. I'm sure Dr. Horton can fit you in somehow — I know you come from out of town." Looking nervously over her shoulder — not sure if she'd been forgiven — she went through a door with DR. JAMES C. HORTON printed on it in small gold letters and came out again a few moments later with a pleased smile.

"You can go right in, Mrs. Brown."

Dr. Horton had already risen from a massive pale wood desk covered with neat stacks of papers, and he walked around it to meet us as we came in. He was a washed-out blond of about thirty-five, good-looking in a cold, Nordic sort of way, of medium height and slightly stocky, dressed in a conservative dark-blue suit.

"My dear Mrs. Brown," he began, holding out his hand and then taking the hand she offered in both of his, as if in wordless sympathy. "I am so deeply sorry about Mrs. Warren. Deeply, *deeply* sorry. But I know it was always a source of relief to her, that she could leave Sally in such good hands as yours, when her time came."

He didn't turn a hair, and if I hadn't known for sure otherwise, I'd have sworn Chloe Warren had died peacefully in her bed.

"Yes, well, I've unfortunately been charged with her murder," Pudgie responded. "This is Mrs. Maggie Elliott, who is a private detective working to help clear me."

"Deeply sorry," he murmured to Pudgie, and "delighted" to me as he shook my hand. I only rated the one-hand clasp; the one I got was clammy, and I noticed that there were beads of sweat on the noble brow. "Now what can I do for you ladies?" He smiled a benign and expectant smile. For the first time and in a flash, I fully understood the phrase "front office man." He was there to woo and soothe the people who could hand over the cash, and his particular act, I thought, was made up of about one-third sympathetic and financially disinterested funeral parlor man, one-third earnest young corporate executive on the way

204

up (which he very possibly was), and one-third, say, Duke of Windsor. The duke would have never noticed social faux pas, such as the mention of murder, but would have glided right over it, as Dr. Horton had.

"I thought," I said, "that since I wanted to ask a few questions of your staff who were present when Mrs. Warren and Mrs. Brown were here last, it would be a good idea to meet you first." I smiled as warmly as I could, which wasn't very. One thing I wanted to know was whether he'd heard Pudgie and Chloe Warren discussing walking back, but of course if he had, and had then rushed out to lay in wait with a gun, he wasn't going to tell me. I asked anyway.

"Mrs. Brown mentioned that you met with Mrs. Warren in your office that day, and that you were also talking with her on Sally's floor when she came back to pick her up."

He looked as if he was wondering whether he could deny it, decided he couldn't, smiled his friendly, open, cash-gathering smile, and said, "That's right, we did talk. Do you know, I had forgotten."

The smile stayed as I asked, "What did she want to see you about?"

He hesitated, then said, "Nothing special, she simply liked to meet with me from time to time, that's all. Many of our patients' loved ones do, of course."

"She hadn't asked for a meeting to discuss anything at all other than Sally?"

"Why, no," he said smoothly, "nothing else at all."

So he was lying. Good. "Afterward, then, when Mrs. Brown came back to pick up her aunt — you realize, don't you, that Mrs. Brown is in something of a mess? So, if you could cast your mind back to that afternoon, the third floor . . ."

"Anything we can do to help Mrs. Brown, we want to do, of course." He paused. "I have cast my mind back. And you wish?"

"You were standing at the desk and Mrs. Warren came over to you?"

"That is correct."

"What did she want?"

"Ah. Just the usual . . . more reassurance, I think. That we were in a constant state of vigilance to do everything that can be done for the poor niece. You have met her?"

I realized I'd been hearing a slight accent for some time without being conscious of it. "Yes, I met her."

"A sad case. With these old ones it is less sad; still sad, of course, but with the very young . . . What can you do?" He shrugged.

"Do I hear a slight accent, Dr. Horton?"

"I hope it is slight, yes." He smiled. "I am — I come to this country from Switzerland."

"I wasn't sure I was hearing it, it's so slight. But I'm sorry I interrupted. We were on the third floor and Mrs. Warren was asking you about Sally's care?"

He drew his brows together as if making an effort to remember. Then he shook his head from side to side several times. "I do not remember exactly, just the general gist. It was our usual conversation — she asks always if there are any particular problems or any signs of improvement; I say, but in the embroidered manner, you understand, no, to both. She goes to sit with the niece. The patients are in the hallway during the day, as we do not like them to stay in bed all day — it is not good for them and the doctors prohibit it."

"And then Mrs. Brown arrived and they walked away to see Sally? What were they talking about?"

He wrinkled his fine brow again and rubbed a manicured hand across his well-coiffed blond head. There was a long silence. Finally, he said, "No. I am sorry. I simply cannot remember. I wasn't paying attention, I was looking over some charts."

"Then what happened?"

"Happened? Nothing."

"I mean, did you stay up on the third floor and see them leave, or what?"

"No, I came back down here, to my office, shortly after the conversation with Mrs. Warren. I told the girl to hold the calls and I spent an hour or two getting through some important paperwork. Then I called the girl in for some dictation and then it was closing time. She left, I left."

Though his memory of the earlier part of the visit was hazy, the time covered by his alibi came out in vibrant, living color, I noticed. There were tall glass-paned French doors at the back of the office; I could see through to a lawn and, beyond it, a parking lot.

"I suppose you wouldn't have noticed who was in the front part of the building when you left? I assume you probably go out by your own door here, when you leave?"

"Usually I do, yes. It is the direct way to the parking lot, as you can see."

SEVENTEEN

After assuring us again that he desired to do his utmost to help Mrs. Brown in any way possible (naturally, as she was now the one in charge of handing over the cash for Sally), Horton took us back upstairs and instructed the head nurse to do her utmost, as well.

The nurse, fiftyish, twenty muscular pounds overweight, and gimlet-eyed behind the thick lenses of her glasses, was taciturn, however. Yes, she had overheard Pudgie and her aunt arguing about whether or not to walk back. Yes, she had worked at the hospital for several years, but she didn't know if they usually walked back or not, hadn't the slightest idea and, her manner indicated, cared less.

It was the nurse, then, who'd told the police about the "argument" between Chloe and Pudgie. She'd certainly not told me much, and I wondered why the difference. She probably just liked policemen: she looked like she would have made a good one herself if the force had been open to women in her younger days and she hadn't been forced instead into the more tender profession. Or perhaps she was accomplice to Horton in the crime, and the report of the disagreement was just another small piece of the frame.

I thanked her for the help she hadn't given, and Pudgie and I left the building. We crossed the road and entered the campus through two tall iron posts with a matching gate that looked as if it was never closed. The undergrowth on both sides of the path was impenetrable, unless you happened to have a machete along. Pudgie showed me where the man with the gun had first appeared and shot her aunt, and the tree where she herself had been tied. The steady, heavy rain of the last week had washed away even the police footprints, and there'd been no others except Pudgie's anyway, since it had begun to rain hard only after the murderer had fled. I hadn't really expected to learn anything new from the walk, and I didn't.

Pudgie and I parted at Alumnae House, where she went off to find Hayden and I got directions for the police station. It turned out to be in the center of downtown Poughkeepsie, and I had to park a couple of blocks away and walk back. The building looked like a bunker, windowless brown stone crouching low with a narrow door. Inside, a uniformed cop stood behind the usual counter fronted with wire-mesh glass, which rose to the ceiling. I said I'd like to see the person in charge of the Chloe Warren murder; he picked up a phone and mumbled into it, told me Lieutenant Bradley would see me first door on the left, and pushed the buzzer to let me in.

From behind a battered-looking brown desk the tall man who'd taken us to look at Deborah Marten's body stared up at me with an expression that looked as if he had a bad taste in his mouth. He had thick brown hair on the longish side, for a cop, a big nose and bony face, cold blue eyes, and a wide black-and-yellow-striped tie that made me think of a wasp.

"Oh, it's you," he said, relaxing the bad-taste look but only slightly, "the one who told me about the girl not showing up for work. We got her identified fast that way, so thanks. What can I do for you? I'm Lieutenant Bradley."

"I'm Maggie Elliott, and perhaps you can't do anything for me, but I'm a licensed private detective in California, and Pudgie Brown has asked me to find evidence, if I can, that someone else murdered her aunt."

"Pudgie, huh? We have her down as Helen.

Why you, all the way from California?"

"Mainly because I happened to be at the college myself for a reunion, I imagine. I saw her at the jail Monday and agreed to work for her — which means, of course, that I'm assuming she didn't murder either her aunt or Deborah Marten."

"In her place I might do the same. Hire someone. Though that could also be dangerous, in her case. What do you do when you dig up more evidence against her?"

"If I did, I'd hand it over to you, naturally. But I don't expect that."

"Well, the evidence is only circumstantial so far, but it's pretty good. And unlike you, I happen to think she did it. Probably by herself — her husband was in Philadelphia with a camera crew and an eighty-year-old dame they were videotaping, so he's out and he'd be the most likely. By the way, you might want to look over the laws in this state regulating the activities of private detectives, because I don't tolerate infringements by private dicks even when they're pretty and have big green eyes. Now, how can I help you?"

He could have started by not talking about my looks in a business conversation, but if I'd said so, nothing would have pleased him more. Still, I longed to comment on his not pretty, small, bloodshot blue eyes, but instead said, "As I'm sure you realize, there are several other people with good motives."

"Like these?" He pulled open a drawer and took out a piece of paper from which he read, "Edward Corliss, eight hundred thousand; Dr. Paul Lombardi, ten million; Claire Stone, twenty grand; Carter Steele, twenty-five; Franklin Steele, ten."

"Like those," I agreed. "And Corinne Brown, who is pretty bitter about her stolen husband."

"Huh. If I had a murder for every stolen husband, I'd have a lot bigger budget."

"Like also Dr. Horton at the convalescent hospital. According to Claire Stone, Mrs. Warren thought something funny was going on there and made a special appointment with him about it right before she was killed. He could have known that they usually walked back to the college after seeing Sally. He was supposedly in his office with calls held at the time, and there's a back door there he could have used without being seen."

"Opportunity, sure, probably forty percent of the population of Poughkeepsie had the opportunity, but so what? Motive?"

"If he was up to something illegal and Mrs. Warren found out and threatened to expose him, it might have been worth his while to kill her."

"Sounds like a good book." He lit a cigar and blew the smoke in my direction.

"Do you know of anything against him? Or the place?"

"Pure as the driven. Besides, we're short-handed and under-staffed and nobody is paying us to send the few guys we do have on wild goose chases."

"Did you happen to check on alibis for any of the others? From that list you read me, before you got sufficiently happy with the case against Pudgie Brown to arrest her?"

"We did a little preliminary work there," he admitted. "The big winner after Mrs. Brown, the Lombardi guy, was around Princeton that day, not airtight, but he would've had a hard time getting here, committing the murders, and getting back in the time he's not covered. Could've been done. Corliss is supposed to've been at the Yale Club in New York all day and says he has witnesses. San Francisco checked the Steele guy, the one who'll get most of the money if Mrs. Brown is convicted. He was cutting out a stomach cancer that day, no way he could've been here. The son was at a party that ran on through the Monday and Tuesday with a friend who says so. The old lady's secretary is vouched for by the cook, the gardener, and the maids. No. The one with the motive, the opportunity, and some good hard evidence, that's Mrs. Brown."

"The fingerprints on the gun — there could be many explanations for that, especially since she was knocked out—"

"Yeah, she says. Easy enough to ram her own head up against that tree or hit herself with the gun for that matter. It's only her word for this spook coming along and shooting the old lady, and her word's not selling a lot of shares these days. Then there's the rings, also with her fingerprints on them, hid up there in the room where she was staying for the reunion."

"Do you really think she's that stupid?"

"Listen. I'm quite aware that this Mrs. Brown is a graduate of your fancy college up there—"

"My fancy college—"

"—and therefore, of *course* I know the lady is by definition not *stupid*—"

"That wasn't what I—"

"—*but* while *she's* not stupid, she may very well think other people *are*. A bunch of hick Poughkeepsie police, for instance, she might expect to be stupid enough for her to get away with hiding the stuff in her room until she could find someplace better."

"She had plenty of time," I said in a purposely low voice, though I was longing to yell back, "to put that jewelry lots of other places before you searched that room."

"Not with never knowing when we'd show up and question her, she didn't. I think she expected us to buy that story about the 'townie' and put our attention there, not on her. But it didn't happen that way, so she never felt safe to shift the stuff. She didn't take it away from the room that none of those others, the Princeton guy and so on, would know she'd been assigned to for the weekend. Nah, I think she got scared and funked moving the rings when she saw we weren't real enthusiastic about her townie-hoodlum story and kept showing up to question her. She should have thrown 'em in the lake with the gun — too greedy, maybe. Or the rings had sentimental value even if the aunt didn't."

"Why *did* you look in the lake, anyway, five days after the murder? Was there a special reason?"

He looked across at me, puffing on his cigar and deciding whether or not to answer. Then he shrugged and said, "You got it. Anonymous call to the station, female, said she'd been on campus on Monday and seen a figure in a long black gown or something, pretty far away from where she was, throw something into the lake; after she got to thinking about it a few days she thought it might be the murderer and called us. Didn't want to get involved any further and wouldn't give her name."

"Anonymous isn't worth much, don't you think? Aren't you going to look for possibilities other than Pudgie Brown as the murderer? The convalescent hospital guy, for instance?"

"Not unless you bring me something that would make me change my mind. And remember what I said about the laws of this state and infringements by private eyes."

I got up. "I will. And I'm charmed to have met you, Lieutenant."

"Likewise." He half smiled, but bit it off before it could get to be anything much.

As I ran back to my car through the rain, I sang an old song recorded by Arlo Guthrie:

> *I know the po-lice*
> *Cause you trou-ble*
> *They cause trou-ble*
> *Ev-ry*
> *Where . . .*

> *But when you die*
> *And go to heav-en*
> *You won't find*
> *No p'lice-men*
> *There . . .*

It was the only one of the verses I could remember, but that was all right, it was the one I wanted, and so I just kept repeating it as I drove back to the college. Of course, down at the station Lieutenant Bradley might well have been singing his own version:

> *I know private ey-eyes*
> *Cause you trouble*
> *They cause trouble*
> *Ev-ry*
> *Where . . .*

EIGHTEEN

Back at Alumnae House I hung my rained-on clothes around my tiny room and took a long, hot bath. Afterward, I went downstairs, put my wet shoes in front of the fire that had been lighted again in honor of the coolness that had come with the rain, and then settled myself at the pay phone.

The phone on the Minnesota end rang and rang and then, just as I was about to hang up, Herbie answered.

"Abortion? Yes, I knew about that because the police asked me. That's the only reason I knew, though; Deborah didn't tell me. I didn't like to say anything in front of her mother, so I wrote you about it."

"Could the child have been yours?"

"That's what the police asked, too. *Could* have been. From when I flew East last summer. But we only — we didn't have — she wasn't into sex then. Or at least not with me. We only made love one time. When I came

219

East, I mean. To tell you the truth, I'd been hoping for a long time she'd get pregnant; I thought then she might agree to go ahead and get married. She was always real careful though, always used her, uh, diaphragm."

"What's your feeling? That she was pregnant by you, or someone else?"

"I don't know. I've thought about it a lot. I guess, what I think is, it seems unlikely. That it was me. I didn't know if you knew about it, so I wrote you about it when I sent those letters you wanted, and the pictures. I guess you should get them pretty soon."

I thanked Herbie for his help and then hung up and tried Deborah's New York roommates again. I was so used to not getting an answer there that I was surprised when someone picked up the phone at the other end and said hello.

"My name is Maggie Elliott," I began, "and I'm a private detective working—"

"Oh, yes," a rather drawly female voice interrupted, "Mrs. Marten told us you'd be calling. Did you want to come and see us?"

"That's right. I'm in Poughkeepsie now but will be in town tomorrow."

"We should all be home by six, I think, tomorrow. No one else is home now, but I'll ask and call you back, if you like."

I gave her the number; she agreed to call back collect and hung up. Then I called Harry, our secretary, but got the answering machine, and then I called my partner O'Reagan in Nevada. We went over my suspects list and then discussed my plans for the convalescent hospital.

"Why this Horton guy?"

"He was around, had the opportunity, and it looks like he was up to something the old lady found out about. Also he's one Mr. Very Smooth Article. The police lieutenant I talked to, Bradley, didn't think much of the idea, but then his imagination is clearly stunted as well as warped."

"Glad to hear you've lost none of your little prejudices; you just wouldn't be you anymore if you suddenly developed a tolerance for policemen. Had you thought of getting Farley to check Horton's record? And you should be able to dig up financial information on the place. Don't you know some money moguls who could help?"

"I do know someone, as a matter of fact; I'll ask him. How're you and the Native Americans getting along?"

"Slow, but it's coming. Should wrap sooner than I thought if Lady Luck keeps smiling on me. A few more days, maybe."

221

"Good. Then you can fly East and bail me out of the Poughkeepsie jail if she's not smiling on me when I hit the convalescent hospital."

"You need to work on your self-confidence, kid. Got your keys with you? Camera?"

"No, I'll get Harry to send them. You have my New York number, right?"

He said he did and we hung up. I tried Pudgie's number in New York but got no answer, then dialed San Francisco information, which led me to Hank Farley; I gave him what I knew on James C. Horton. C. for what? A name that Deborah Marten called him, matching his initials with the *C. H.* written next to the poem about the bitter word?

Once again I thought of calling Richard, and once again I didn't do it.

By then I was starving, but didn't feel like a slow, formal dinner, so I went into the Pub, a bar and hamburger sort of place on the other side of the dining room. The booths were all taken, filled with students or recent graduates, so I sat at one of the small tables and ordered a hamburger and a Vassar Devil. The last was rich chocolate cake covered with vanilla ice cream and marshmallow sauce topped by a very heavy chocolate sauce. I'd eaten several hundred of them while at college, and since I was fairly thin at the moment could contemplate such a course of action with pleasure rather than guilt.

The same old-fashioned murals covered the walls that had been there in my day, soft pastel scenes painted by a student in the late 1930s, I think, or maybe it was the early forties. They showed students holding up falling sets at a play, which made me think of Deborah Marten; sleepy-looking girls studying late at night, with decorative trails of smoke wafting from their ever-present cigarettes. The one of a girl in a long pink evening dress holding hands with her Ivy League date and running toward the dance at Student's made me think of that senior prom Pudgie had described, and Corinne's theft of Hayden Brown, which was to be reversed so many years later. . . . *Could* that be what all this was about? Hayden must have been devastatingly good-looking then, that dark, wicked sort of handsome that's usually so appealing to women, judging from what he looked like now and he must be at least fifty . . .

The other people in the Pub, all couples, provided a soft, murmuring background of conversation interspersed with bouts of laughter that made me feel lonely. And so I found myself thinking again of the broken relationship back in San Francisco, of O'Reagan, of

Peter Warren — of "going off somewhere" with one or the other of them . . . somewhere . . . living happily together as some of my classmates seemed to be managing to do, as some of Pudgie's classmates seemed to have managed. Usually, I realized that trying to imitate the pattern of other people's lives, no matter how good they looked from the outside, would never, never rescue me from the dilemmas of my own; still, it would have been nice to have a loving companion on a winter's eve . . . or a summer's night. I was forgetting, for the moment, some of the discomforts that occurred when the companion turned up *every* eve and wasn't really quite the right companion, but just taken in because the right one was nowhere in sight. Was *that* the truth about my being with Richard? And wouldn't a Republican businessman be even worse, after all that charm wore off? And why did I want to let myself get involved with a man with the kind of reputation with women that Peter had, after the misery of Richard and Ilsa? Because there was no one else in sight?

Ah, well. I finished my Vassar Devil and paid the bill. As I started into the dining room on my way to the lobby, I saw, of all people, the convalescent hospital slick, Horton. He was at a table having dinner and talking animatedly with an elderly lady, one of the ones who'd been sitting on the couch in front of the fire the other night talking about the sun in a picture frame. Horton was listening to her now, as attentively as if she were telling him what his future would hold. Neither of them noticed me as I backed up into the Pub and exited through the outside doors. When I walked past the front desk, the woman there called out that I had some telephone messages.

One confirmed the appointment with Deborah Marten's roommates; one was from Alice Langley Worthington; one from Harry; one from Peter Warren, with a number to call in Chicago. And one was from Richard. How had he known where to call me? The office, I supposed; I hadn't said much there about what was going on between us, but . . . I called Harry first.

He repeated the alibi for Franklin Steele that I'd heard from Lieutenant Bradley, then went on to the son. "Carter Steele is still back East, due here next week. I don't know about any alibi, but he's staying with a friend in Princeton — it's a town as well as a college, I guess. They have a big reunion blast this coming weekend at the university; he's staying for that. Address is 4415 Plum Tree Lane, very rich people named Chilton who travel a lot. The son, Louis, is the kid's friend."

"What's the group he runs with like?"

"My informant — a classmate of theirs out here — says they're rumored to be into a lot of recreational drugs. All seem to have plenty of money. My friend said the kid and this guy Louis are very tight; they're in some singing group together, something called the Nassoons, and also something called the Triangle Club, which is apparently some kind of drama group but very hot shot."

"Yes. They're in Triangle Club? That's unusual for sophomores."

"Yeah, they're both in it, but the friend's a junior."

"Ah. Anything else?"

"That's it. How'd I do, chief?"

"You did good. Thanks. How're the dogs?"

"I'm losing weight fast with all the running on the beach — which would've been all right if I'd been fat. You probably won't know me when you get back, but they're looking great."

"My first night back I'll take you to Mama's at Washington Park and you can order everything on the menu."

"Ah, when, when? I just hope you're not too late."

"I'll try and hurry the case along. Seriously, *are* you minding taking care of them, Harry?"

"No, no, I like them. Really. I'm fine, they're fine — don't worry."

"All right. But know I'm really grateful to you for taking them in. Now, there was something — oh, yes. Send me my big key ring and my cameras, will you? To the New York address."

Next I called Alice.

"Maggie? *Just* on my way out and Bill is glaring at me from the door like a — like a rhinoceros. Have you ever been to Africa? But I saw Ed Corliss and have some information — all *right*, darling! Are you in town? I'm *coming*, dearest!"

"I will be. Can you meet me at my apartment, noon? you have the address?"

"Yes, I'll be there. Luckily I have almost a photographic memory — *yes*, darling — twelve o'clock—"

The phone clattered into the cradle and was replaced by a dial tone, and I imagined Alice being dragged off bodily by the rhinoceros. I dropped in another two dimes and called the Chicago number.

"I was thinking it would be nice if you were here with me," Peter said, "and then I thought a phone call would be better than nothing. How's the case? Found out anything interesting?"

"Mmm . . . a suspect eliminated today, I think, and some interesting financial discrepancies to check out."

"Like what? Can I help on that?"

"Actually, you might be able to. I need a good financial run-down on that convalescent hospital and its owners, and any information you can get on the manager, a Dr. James C. Horton. Is that the kind of information you could get?"

"Sure. I'll say I'm looking into the possibility of buying the place, diversifying. Are you in a hurry for it?"

"I wouldn't call it life or death, but it would be helpful to have it as soon as possible. That's pretty wishy-washy, isn't it? Change that to yes, I'm in a hurry."

"I'll start first thing tomorrow; I should get something back, basic information at least, pretty quick. H-o-r-t-o-n?"

"Right, and thanks. And I'm afraid I'll have to skip dinner tomorrow; I have an appointment at six. Could I meet you at the play? Where is it?"

"Forty-fifth, Broadway and Seventh, eight o'clock — I'll wait out front. We can eat afterward."

Through the glass door of the booth I saw Horton and the elderly lady come out into the lobby, and I turned my head to the wall so he wouldn't see me.

"Uh, okay," I said, peering around to see Horton give what I hoped was a parting handshake prior to disappearing from my line of sight in the direction of the front door. "I have to go now, there's an old lady here I want to grill. See you tomorrow night, then? *Ciao, amico*."

"I didn't know you spoke Italian. How about we spend a few days there? Fly over, say, Thursday, or Wednesday night after *Peer Gynt?*"

"I could always use a few days in Florence, sure."

"Too crowded now. How about somewhere way down on the Adriatic maybe, or Sicily."

"Are you serious? I have work to do. Unless you could pronto — I mean, *subito* — develop a floppy disc that would do all my routine detecting; then I could take a few days off."

"I'll get those poor young geniuses I have down in the basement of my company working on it right away. If I'm ruthless enough, then maybe by the weekend."

"Great; *buona notte*."

"*Con amore, principessa*."

I hung up the phone thinking of really good cappuccino and brioche at a tiny table on the cobbled square across from Brunelleschi's orphanage, and not hurrying to start the day, of pale turquoise Mediterranean water glowing like light itself above pure white sand, of the pink and silver-gray silk of the Adriatic at the end of the day. Perhaps I wasn't as against computers and rich businessmen as I'd always thought I was. Italy — and Peter? I did not call Richard.

NINETEEN

As I emerged from the phone booth the woman who'd been having dinner with Horton walked past, coffee cup in hand, and sat down on the couch in front of the fire. Horton was nowhere in sight and, I hoped, had gone home, or wherever he went after buttering up rich elderly ladies.

I walked back to the Pub, got hot chocolate, and then came and sat down in the big chair between the couch and the fire. I figured he must surely be gone — though why I wanted so earnestly to avoid him I wasn't sure, other than wanting to become as vague in his mind as possible, which wouldn't happen in a million years if he *had* murdered Chloe Warren and Deborah, and if he hadn't, I was simply wasting my time anyway.

"How I love these summer evening fires when it's cold and rainy out," I murmured, smiling tentatively, to the woman on the couch.

"I do, too." She smiled back and looked quite amenable to further conversation. "Are you staying here?"

"For a few days — I was up for my fifteenth reunion, and then had some other business so I stayed on."

"I was here for a reunion also — it was my sixty-fifth," she said proudly.

"You were a classmate of Chloe Warren, then. What a terrible thing that was."

"Terrible. Yes, of course. Although, you know, it was a quick, clean ending. Had you thought of that?"

"I had, actually. I wondered if a more elderly person would, though. I wondered how her classmates saw it. . . ."

"Well, some of us didn't, of course. See it as a release, that is. But my sister is in a nursing home — she became, oh, senile and all the rest of it, very agitated and in fact sometimes violent and I couldn't have her with me any longer. I just couldn't do it. She is five years younger than I am, too, it just goes to show you never know how things will turn out, do you? I had to put her in a home and . . . well." She sighed deeply. "I think most older people are aware of the blessing of a quick death — but I *know* anyone who has a relative in a nursing home is."

"The man you had dinner with tonight, he's the director of the convalescent hospital, isn't he? Is he a relative?"

She looked surprised. "No, I have no relatives now, except Sister. Do you know Dr. Horton? He is rather hoping, I'm afraid" —/ she smiled a small, conspiratorial smile — "that, having no relatives other than poor Bettina, I'll leave my money there. I told him I plan to leave it to the college — a chair for the English department; I have always been so fond of Shakespeare. But he seems hopeful of changing my mind and so . . . of course he likes me to think it's for the pleasure of my company, but *I* am not senile, thank heavens. No, my sorrow is for the person who's become stuck between life and death, like poor Bettina. But my money will go for use by the living. Now Chloe may have been saved some terrible, long illness, for all we know."

"Do you know any of the other patients at the hospital? Do you know someone named Emily Strong?"

"Why, Emily was a classmate of ours, of Chloe's and mine! Did you know her? It was because of poor Emily that Chloe knew of the place, and it was through Chloe that I put Bettina there. Now there's a good example: when poor Emily died, we were both so relieved. So glad for her. Poor Emily had no family, just some attorneys back in Wyoming in charge of the estate. Chloe and I tried to have some private help hired for her — really, the staff in those places is *not* adequate, though I don't see why when they charge so much. Many of us hire extra help, just a few hours in the morning, you know, and a couple of hours at dinner makes such a difference. When Emily was alive, those Wyoming lawyers just wouldn't part with an extra cent — you would've thought it was *their* money, not hers! Probably making hay with it while they could. Well, as you might imagine, I am most reluctant to leave Bettina's finances in the hands of total strangers because of what I saw happen with Emily." She straightened in her seat and gave a delicate cough. "Yet I don't really quite trust Dr. Horton, either, I don't know why. Perhaps we'll be lucky and Bettina will be released before I am."

I was beginning to get a couple of ideas. I said, "You know, we've been talking all this time and I don't know your name. Mine is Maggie Elliott."

"How do you do, dear, I am Hortense McAffee. Call me Hortense, and I will call you Maggie, may I? I must say that is one of the new fashions I find I quite like. But then

I have never been one for formality; I was often criticized for that, in fact, in my youth."

"Hortense, then." I smiled. "You know, I wonder . . . do you know Chloe Warren's niece, Pudgie Brown?"

"We have met once or twice, yes."

"Since she has to look after her cousin Sally Steele's interests at the hospital, perhaps once this business of her aunt's murder is cleared up, you might ask her if she would be the trustee for your sister, should the need arise. She's very capable. Would you like me to ask her about it?"

"Oh, my word! Could you? I would not want to impose . . . but if you did just mention it and see what she says, why, I would be most grateful."

"I'll be happy to. If you'll just give me your address and phone."

She took a small pad and a gold pen from a newish black patent-leather handbag, scribbled on the pad, and gave me the paper. I glanced down and saw that she lived in Wappinger's Falls, which was quite near Poughkeepsie.

"When are you going home?" I asked.

"Tomorrow, dear, after breakfast. I stayed over to see Bettina and Dr. Horton."

"Could you tell me a bit more about your

friend Emily Strong? Was she from Poughkeepsie? When did she die?"

"About two years ago now, almost three. She was from Wyoming, originally, but stayed in Poughkeepsie after college and obtained quite a good job with Dell Publishing. Never went back to Wyoming, although I believe the family money remained there, administered by those stingy lawyers."

"What did she die of?"

"Heart, they said. Heart. That took my dear husband also, a heart attack. It was quite sudden and unexpected, just like Emily's. We had one child, a son, but he was killed in Spain. The International Brigade," she added quietly, "though I suppose you're much too young to know anything about that."

"The International Brigade? I wasn't born then, but of course I've read a lot about it, the people who were in it."

We sat quietly then, looking at the fire. She was thinking of her son, no doubt, and I was thinking of the famous brigade that'd fought in Spain. For the survivors, it turned out to be the high point of their lives, but so many were killed . . . I finally pulled my attention back to the present.

"When," I asked, "does your private person go in to help your sister?"

"What, dear? The person helping Bettina?"
I nodded.

"She is there for two hours in the morning, getting her to the bathroom, you know, and then seeing that she gets lunch — Bettina has to be fed, or she doesn't eat. Then she comes back about five-thirty and gets her up again for dinner."

"And you didn't hire her through the hospital? She works for you, not for them?"

"Yes, that's right. Quite a few of the patients have private help arranged that way." She yawned, patting her lips delicately with a tiny, wrinkled, ring-covered hand. "Perhaps I shall see you in the morning? I think I will retire now."

"I'll probably see you at breakfast. It's been very pleasant, talking with you."

"Thank you, dear. I've enjoyed it as well."

After she went upstairs, I sat by the fire a while longer and thought over the plan that I'd been forming as we'd talked. I didn't see anything wrong with it; if it still looked good after I slept on it, I'd approach Mrs. Hortense McAffee about her part tomorrow.

In the narrow but comfortable bed, I found the sound of the rain falling through the leaves and tapping against my window very soothing, and all my plans and schemes and strategies

dimmed and then disappeared, as my aware-
ness narrowed to the soft, gray sound of the
rain falling on the green summer lawns of
Vassar.

TWENTY

I was in the dining room eating breakfast and writing down a dream about some carved jade beads made in the Garden of Eden when Hortense McAffee came in and sat with her back to me at the other end of the room. I decided to let her have her breakfast in peace before making my request. At the next table a girl was saying, in a voice that still retained traces of the deep South, "You can sleep late, lie in a white bed, and I'll come back after job hunting and fix dinner."

"How delightful," said the handsomer of the two boys with her, a redhead. "I can stay bedridden for days."

The other boy, thin and rather scraggly looking, poked at his plate and complained, "It's a runny omelette, how disgusting! I hope you'll cook better than this when you get married, Charlotte."

Had the women's movement, I wondered, never been?

"But I don't understand about this apartment, Charlotte," the redhead continued. "I thought you were going to go through it and take all the stuff your sister didn't want."

"That's right, you *don't* understand," she agreed. "The apartment and my sister are in California."

"I'd hate having to scrimp and save, go to thrift stores," the boy with the runny omelette put in. "I got most of my stuff out of my grandmother's attic. Don't you have any grandmothers?"

"They don't have attics anymore," the girl replied glumly.

Through the tall French windows I could see a bit of sunlight breaking through the gray sky and turning a small grassy plot beyond the terrace to brilliant emerald, with the thick tangle of bushes and trees behind it remaining quite dark. They reminded me of the tangle of bushes behind Sunset Lake, and perhaps of the general tangle of my unsolved case. I put away my notebook, picked up my coffee, and went over to Hortense.

"Could I join you for a few minutes? Have you finished your breakfast?"

"Please do sit down, Maggie. Did you sleep well, dear?"

"Like a . . . rock, thanks. What about you?"

"Very peacefully, thank you. With the rain falling down so. Would you like more coffee?"

"I'm fine, thanks. I was hoping I'd see you this morning. I have a favor to ask of you."

"Yes?" She looked a little taken aback, as if she weren't used to having favors asked of her before she'd finished her morning coffee.

"Yes. Are you aware that Pudgie Brown has been charged with her aunt's murder? I am working for her — I'm a private detective in California—"

"Why, how interesting! I have never met a private detective before! How interesting! It's so wonderful what you girls do nowadays, just like Hercule Poirot!"

"Perhaps," I said noncommittally. "But Pudgie has hired me to find evidence that will clear her — which means, basically, evidence that someone else murdered her aunt."

"Oh! How will you do that? Won't it be terribly difficult? Everyone lies, I should think, and then where are you? And you wish *my* help? I don't quite see . . . but I'll be very glad if I can . . . how can *I* help you?"

"Well, the fact is, I'd like to look around that convalescent hospital a bit, at a time when Dr. Horton isn't there." No need to tell her I was planning to break into his office, if necessary. "And I got to thinking about the woman you hire to help with your sister."

"Mrs. Jameson? You want her to do something for you at the hospital?"

"Well, no. I was wondering if perhaps I could go in with her one evening."

"Why, I don't know . . . it doesn't seem . . . why would you want to do that?"

"It would give me a reason to be inside, so I could look around, you see, without anyone noticing."

"Well, I suppose it might be all right . . ."

"Would you be willing to arrange it?"

"I suppose I could. But why do you want to go there at all?"

"I have to look into all the possibilities, Hortense. And Mrs. Warren's secretary told me that Chloe Warren thought there was something not quite right about the place, something that involved your friend Emily Strong. Have you any idea what that could have been?"

"Why, no . . ." She frowned and then coughed. "No, what could it be? She died about three years ago. I went to visit Bettina and stopped off to see Emily, as I always did — I remember it quite clearly because she had just died — and there were several people there fussing over the body."

"Did you actually see her after she died, see her face?"

"Oh, yes. It was, let me think, in the fall. October or November, almost three years ago now. But why would that help you in your investigation for the Warren girl?"

"If there was something, perhaps illegal, that Mrs. Warren found out, she may have been murdered to keep her quiet about it. Sounds melodramatic, I know, but after all, *someone* murdered her and then planted the evidence on Pudgie, and this lead seems as likely as any."

"Oh! Do you suspect Dr. *Horton* then?"

"Or someone else at the hospital. So I want to look around the place a bit."

"And when do you want to go there? Right away?"

"No, the rest of this week I'll be talking to the various people who inherited money from Mrs. Warren. It would have to be next week — Tuesday or Wednesday."

"Either would be all right, I suppose . . . Mrs. Jameson's day off is Friday. Let me think. I can tell her — what can I tell her?"

"It would be better if she didn't know the truth. Tell her you're thinking of hiring someone for her day off; if she offers to do it herself, say you feel everyone should have at least one day free. Say you want to send me in with her to learn the routine. Then, later, you can tell her that you decided not to hire me after all."

"All right. I'm quite a good liar; I've always rather prided myself on my lying, though I prefer to think of it as tact." She smiled and nodded. "Tuesday or Wednesday, then. I'll speak to Mrs. Jameson and she will be expecting you. At five-thirty."

"I should have a name, how about . . . Merle . . . uh, not Haggard — Merle Johnson."

The small pad and the gold pencil were brought forth once more, and Hortense carefully wrote down my new name and "Tuesday or Wednesday," which I read upside down.

"I'll telephone you in a day or so, then. When I know which day. And you should have my number in New York."

It was duly recorded in her old-fashioned hand, and we parted company both quite pleased with ourselves.

TWENTY-ONE

I got into New York with no time to spare, stopped at an Italian delicatessen downstairs from my cousin's apartment and bought some things for lunch, then hurried upstairs.

Relieved not to find Alice waiting on the doorstep, I put water on to boil and laid out the food on the small glass table by the windows. I had opened one of them and was looking down the twenty-three stories onto the tops of tiny toy trees marching north across Central Park when several firm knocks announced Alice.

"Oh, good, I'm simply starving," she said as soon as I opened the door, and headed for the food. "I wondered what you'd have on such short notice, you just came in this morning, didn't you? But this looks all right. I thought it might be tins from the absent owner's cupboard. Not much furniture," she added, looking around. "Was he repossessed or something?"

I explained George's current belief that life without furniture is healthier, while Alice, standing, helped herself to a large slice of prosciutto and poured some wine. "I've been at the hospital all morning" — a couple of gulps of wine followed the ham — "trying to put some order into those volunteers, which always leaves me weak with frustration and hunger and exasperation." Two brioches, buttered, disappeared next. "But, of course, with Bill's position at the hospital I simply have to do it, and they do all say I am so good at running the volunteers." This last was muffled by a mouthful of tortellini.

"I'm sure you are," I murmured, not insincerely. "Would you like coffee, or do you want to stick with wine?"

"Coffee. After all, we do have work to do." She smiled a pleased-with-herself sort of smile. We sat down on the mat with our coffee and she began.

"Luckily, I did more than you asked me to — it's just the way I am, extremely thorough. Do more, get more, as I'm constantly telling my volunteers. But to business. Ed Corliss claims he was at the Yale Club all that Monday, in the library. Doing research for that novel he's supposedly been writing for fifteen years. Ha! Just another ne'er-do-well, I've always thought. I'm hard to fool, where character is concerned." She took a few enthusiastic sips of coffee. "Not bad coffee."

"Thanks. And?"

"And he was *not* at the Yale Club library all Monday. He definitely lied to me, which I took care to find out about, and so of course I did find out." The end of Alice's long nose twitched slightly with excitement or pleasure, and her brown eyes gleamed with triumph.

"Good work. How did you find this out?"

"I sent my brother over there. Yale '66. He questioned the servants and one of them said he remembered that Ed had been in the Sunday before and the Tuesday after the murder, but not on Monday. Do you think that means he did it?"

"Possibly," I said cautiously. "But he could be lying for some other reason. Or he could just be mistaken, too. Is he a vague type, or a well-organized sort of person?"

"Hmm. Little of both, I'd say. But he didn't just get his days mixed up. He was lying."

"What makes you so certain?"

"Because we were talking specifically about the murder. I said what *I'd* been doing at the time it happened, vouched for by two local girls I had cleaning the house — our house in Maine." She poured more coffee into her cup and drank some.

"And then?"

"And *then* I asked Ed what *he* had been doing at the crucial time. He could hardly refuse to tell me, after I'd said where I'd been, without looking funny, I thought. I worked it all out beforehand and I must say it worked perfectly, just as I expected."

"What did he say, exactly?"

"He said — he laughed and said that as a matter of fact he had an alibi too, not that he needed one, since he'd heard that serious evidence against his ex-wife — that's what he called her, 'my ex-wife' — had been found and she'd been charged. Then he started talking about some exhibit or other at the Modern, de Chirico, I think."

"So how did you find out about the Yale Club?"

"Asked him, of course. When he finally paused in talking about the exhibit, I just broke right in and asked him. If he had an alibi, what was it? I must say he looked *quite* irritated when I asked him point-blank like that. Tried to hide it, of course. But I'm hard to fool and *never* sidetracked when I'm set on something. My husband says — but never mind that. Anyway, that was when Ed said he'd been at the Yale Club."

"And did he volunteer the details, or did you have to drag them out?"

"I dragged them out, all right! He was *so* annoyed, sitting there smiling and trying not to *look* annoyed — oh, it was quite an amusing afternoon. For me, of course; not for him. I pretended to be terribly interested in what he was doing at the Yale Club, so he told me the rest of it — that he'd been in the library doing a little writing and a little research, as he put it, on his novel. Novel! I'll bet it was a little. I was going to ask him how many pages he had actually written, but decided I shouldn't antagonize him any further, in case you want me to do any more work on him."

"Mmmm — I think I better talk to him next. But what you've done is terrifically helpful, Alice. Who did your brother talk to at the Yale Club? And how could he be so sure about the day?"

"Because — the fellow's name is Jones, I don't know his first name, anyway they all call him Jones. And Jones remembers that on Tuesday evening when he served Ed at the bar, Ed was very chatty with him, which was unusual; he said usually Ed's not at all friendly. My brother is, as it happens, chatty, so he was an excellent choice for talking to the help — they all like him. Funny how different people in the same family can be, isn't it? Anyway, the waiter thought it was odd at the time, Ed being so talkative. And one of the things Ed said was how nice it was to have the club library to do the research he needed, but after three days in a row he was looking forward to getting back to his own office at home. Jones said he didn't say anything, but he thought at the time it was funny because he'd had occasion to be in and out of the library several timers the day before and was sure Ed Corliss hadn't been there."

"Did Jones remember what time he had gone in there?"

"Yes, as a matter of fact. I had John, my brother, call him back to find out." She picked up her purple purse and took out a small but formidably thick leather notebook, turned to the proper page, and read. "He was in about twelve o'clock, again about one-thirty, and again at three."

"Perfect." I smiled. "But how do we know Corliss wasn't just in the men's room or something?"

"Because, the reason the waiter went in — he doesn't, normally — was because there were several urgent phone calls for one of the members, and each time he looked not only in the alcoves of the library, where a person can't be seen from the door, but also in the men's room, the bar, and so forth. The man he was looking for wasn't in any of those places — and neither was Ed Corliss."

"That sounds pretty solid, all right. Wonder why he lied?"

"You don't want me to have another talk with him and see if I can find out?"

"No, I really think I have to talk to him now. He lives in Stamford? Is he at home often, do you know?"

"He's usually there weekdays, I think, supposedly working on his book. Don't know what he really does. Reads, perhaps. Writes an occasional article for the local paper." She sniffed and tossed her head, which left her literally looking down her nose.

"Why is everyone so sure the book is make-believe? That's what Pudgie said, too."

"Well, he's supposedly been working on it for about twenty years now. Even *War and Peace* didn't take that long."

"There's Proust . . ."

"But it came out, parts of it were published every few years. I'm a literature major, you won't catch me out on that subject! Anyway, Karen Sorenson wandered into his office once at a party, looking for the bathroom. She said. Of course, she's always been very curious, almost as curious as I am, and she's a terrible gossip, which is quite different from me, of course. And she said that she *happened* to notice the famous novel in a bottom drawer, which she said was open, and the paper was all yellow and what's more it was only thirty-eight pages. And it was the same one, all right — *Remembered Anger,* which is the title he always refers to when he's talking about it. And that's how we all *know* the book-writing business is utter nonsense."

"I see. He sounds rather . . . pitiful."

"You wouldn't think so if you met him. Terribly sure of himself. Acts like the King of Siam. Sneers. Very superior. I never knew why Pudgie married him. When will you go? I'll give you the address." She flipped through the thick notebook again and wrote it down. "No, better make you a map, too; it's out of the way."

I poured myself more coffee and tried to think of the best way to approach Ed Corliss, who had no reason to want to talk to me and quite possibly every reason not to. Alice handed me her hand-drawn map, which, with typical thoroughness, included the roads to take from New York out to Stamford and Dar-ien. A pleasant breeze was blowing in through the windows, the kind that usually meant rain.

252

And it had been so nice to see the sun this morning, driving into New York.

I sighed, and Alice said, "Well, if I can't work anymore on Ed Corliss, is there anything else I can do? I have a suggestion, in fact."

"What is it?"

"I'm going out to San Francisco Sunday — Bill has an annual medical meeting and I always go. We happen to know Franklin Steele — is he a suspect? He and Bill knew each other at Princeton and they're both surgeons, so we run into each other quite regularly at these seminars and things. We usually have dinner with him, in fact. Of course, he's a friend of ours, but Pudgie is a much *better* friend, so I'm quite willing to sacrifice Franklin if necessary. I can easily find out about his alibi, I'm sure. Did Chloe Warren leave him any money? I'd always heard it mostly went to Pudgie, but of course you never know for certain until the person's finally dead. People tend to be so *emotional* about how they leave their money when really it's just a practical matter; after all it's blood that counts, isn't it. *Genes*, actually. *Does* he stand to gain anything by the death?"

"As a matter of fact, if Pudgie should be convicted, he gets most of it."

"Well, then he's a respectable suspect, isn't

he?" She smiled happily. "I'll see what I can find out."

"All right. But I had someone from my office check, and apparently he has an airtight alibi for all day Monday—"

"He could be lying, like Ed Corliss. I'll—"

"I don't think so; both my employee and the Poughkeepsie police say he was in surgery all day. I suppose he could have hired someone to do the murder, though. What sort of person is he?"

"Well, you know how surgeons are. Think they know everything and think they're God and that everyone else should do just whatever they want and instantly. Of course, I don't let Bill get away with that, but Franklin's been divorced for years. I'll see what I can find out."

TWENTY-TWO

After Alice left I took a bath, changed into clothes that would see me through the evening, and took a cab down to the Museum of Modern Art, where I'd arranged at the reunion to meet a friend. Rachel was sitting at a table downstairs in the garden, having a beer and jotting her thoughts, or jotting something, into a blue-and-white notebook. The threatened rain was still only threatening, and it was pleasantly cool in the middle of the soft city-green trees and the white stone sculptures. She put away her notebook and, smiling, asked, "Ready for de Chirico?"

"No hurry, it's so pleasant. It's been a long time since I was last here. I love San Francisco, but I do miss the museums in New York."

"Don't you have museums out there?" she asked in mock-horror, having lived her entire life in New York City, where there are as many large art-stuffed buildings open to the public as most people could ever wish for.

"Nothing like here. The main one has a grand collection of Oriental ceramics; another has a lot of rather faded old tapestries and some Rodins — well, that's not fair, it has some good post-Impressionists, too. But they're so out of the way you almost have to make a day of it; you can't just pop in to look at some particular thing. And the special exhibits draw so many people you can't see a thing except the packs of the people in front of you."

"Here, too. Not like the good old days, with only three or four of us in a room. But this one's been here for a while and shouldn't be bad now."

As we walked upstairs she asked how my investigation was progressing, adding, "I'd hate to have to find out things from people instead of books. Of course, they lie in books, too, but usually the truth's down somewhere and if you just patiently cross-check long enough you'll find it."

We entered the first room of the exhibit and were confronted with a typical de Chirico street scene of ominous emptiness, a faraway clock, a tiny figure walking into the distance. I peered at the title, which read "The Melancholy of Departure."

"He had the right word, all right," I said.

"Melancholy it certainly is. But something more . . ."

"Something very terrible and imminent — look at that one, for instance." She waved toward a picture on a far wall and we walked over. It was the one that had always been my favorite, and I'd forgotten all about it, "The Mystery and Melancholy of a Street." The small silhouette of a young girl pushed a hoop along an empty street amidst towering, ominous buildings, while the huge shadow of an anonymous figure menaced her from behind. Deborah Marten and her raspberry hoop, with the shadow of the murderer approaching. . . .

"I went to see my client in the Poughkeepsie jail on Monday, after everyone had left. You should see that place. It reminds me of these paintings — the present is cold and empty and the future will be worse."

"Is she still there? Of course I've read about it in the *Times* everyday. Do you have a plan of investigation, or what?"

"I wish I did. She's out on bail. I'll try to talk to everyone who might have a motive, and have a look around the convalescent hospital where they'd been before the murder. A series of stabs in the dark is more like it, I'm afraid."

"Well, but that's probably always the way,

257

in the beginning," Rachel said soothingly. "No doubt something useful will drop to the floor behind the arras if you stab enough of them."

"That's what my partner said, too. Good old Polonius. It's great advice, but at the moment it seems a little intangible."

"You sound like me at the beginning of a book. I know what the subject is, and I know what research I have to get through to write it, but I can't really believe that any of it will lead anywhere much. Perhaps we should have just married and moved to the suburbs, like some of our more serene-looking classmates."

"Some of us did get married," I reminded her, "twice, in some cases."

Twice-divorced, Rachel smiled and said, "So we did, I'd forgotten. But I never tried the suburbs part, being supported by someone else and all that. Still, it's probably too difficult a way to get money. Or would be for me."

The rest of the exhibit was anticlimactic, with nothing affecting me the way the girl pushing the hoop had, though I did like the head-and-shoulders portrait of Guillaume Apollinaire: a sensual mouth, straight nose, and large, dark sunglasses, with fossils and a shadow looming in the background. It wasn't a bad image for my unknown murderer, and it fit pretty well with the idea I'd formed of Edward Corliss and his false alibi.

Regretfully refusing an offer of dinner at her apartment, I left Rachel standing at the crosstown bus stop and walked over to Sixth Avenue to find a cab. It took a while, being rush hour, and then we crawled miserably up Broadway the fifty-odd blocks to 106th Street. The driver was silent the whole way and I used the quiet to review what I wanted to ask Deborah Marten's roommates. I finally got out and walked the last two blocks, past stands of vegetables, cheap hardware, and clothes set out on the sidewalk to lure the needy, the greedy, and the bored into the stores behind them.

The buildings in the area around Columbia had never been fancy, and time hadn't changed them much — fifteen stories or so of nondescript stone in varying shades of beige. I came to the right awning, entered a small lobby containing two stunted plants and a rose-colored couch, and went up in an elevator that was more like the ancient thing at Vassar than the fancier ones I'd grown accustomed to in New York.

It was a few minutes past six when I rang the buzzer by the plain brown door. It opened almost immediately, and a small, neat, rather antiseptic-looking blond girl unsmilingly invited me in. She turned, and I followed her through a dark hall filled with empty cardboard boxes to a small living room at the end that was still lit by the late afternoon sun coming in through the one large window.

Two couches and two large chairs were crammed into the space, and on one couch sat a plump girl with short brown hair, straight and well cut, a bony face, and a sallow complexion. She was dressed in the sort of suit you wear to your first job in New York, if it's a job involving business and commerce rather than the arts. A tall boy with a teddy-bear plumpness and blond hair falling over a broad forehead slouched in one of the chairs and got up reluctantly as I came in.

The girl I was following turned to me and said, "I'm Marian; this is Susan and that's Henry, Mrs. Elliott."

"I prefer Maggie. Hello." I smiled, and Henry smiled; the one called Susan said in a prim, upper-class Boston-accented voice, "How do you do?"

Marian indicated the empty chair, which I took; she offered tea and when I declined, thinking that fussing with it would use up half the time I had to spend with them, she sat down on the couch beside Susan.

"Mrs. Marten told you I'm a private detective working for Pudgie Brown, trying to find out who killed Deborah and old Mrs. Warren?"

Marian and Susan nodded.

I took the Edna St. Vincent Millay book I'd bought on the way to the museum and opened it to the poem about the bitter word. "Deborah had this book in her room at college; she'd marked a number of places in the introduction and also a poem."

Henry, reading the title from where he sat, said, "She was crazy about that Vincent Millay, all right."

"Saw herself," Susan contributed, "as being, you know, not another incarnation" — she looked mildly pained at the thought — "but, well, very much like her. A lot in common with her, I mean."

"And she was diligent," Marian said dryly, "in taking any likeness and playing it up."

Henry objected. "Marian, that's unfair, don't you think?"

Marian shrugged her shoulders. "How can we help you?" Her voice was low and languid, and its tone said clearly that she didn't expect they could help in any way but they were obligated to be polite.

I turned to the poem and read it, ending with the marked-up *Why do I remember you/As a singing bird?* Do you have any idea why she specifically marked this line? Who it referred to, what experience?"

"Well, presumably her abortion," Henry said. "I mean, whoever it was who got her pregnant."

"Do you know who that was?"

They all shook their heads. Susan said, "I do know it wasn't the boyfriend from home. Does that help? But she didn't say who it was, just who it wasn't."

"One of the ways in which she modeled herself so assiduously after Vincent Millay," Marian added, "was in keeping herself to herself. I mean, she liked to be mysterious."

"How do you mean — could you give me an example?"

Marian thought, then shrugged. "Nothing in particular. Just an air she had."

"Back to the abortion, then. Haven't any of you any idea who she was seeing that could have got her pregnant?"

"It was someone she met last summer," Henry said. "Someone she just saw a few times — she went overboard, he didn't."

"When was this? Where?"

"Some guy she met while she was at the theater workshop in New Jersey last summer."

"Someone also working there?"

"No — someone she just happened to meet by chance. Or that's what she said. In a store or something, wait — that's in the poem, some showing of some old house or something, you know, the historic-tour bit."

"Do you know where? Any hints? Or when?"

"Don't know when. It would have been in August, I guess, judging by when she had the abortion."

"That would be right," Susan agreed. "She had it in early November and said she was about three months. There's a doctor in Poughkeepsie who does them. I was afraid she was going to ask to borrow money when she told me about it. I would have had to refuse, of course; it's never good practice to lend money on a personal basis. But she had enough money, as it turned out, from her summer job."

"You know that the mystery man didn't help pay, then?"

"That's right," Henry said. "She'd only seen him a few times and then he dumped her — that's the sad tale she told me. Asked me if I'd ever been in love, that sort of thing, one day at the Pub."

"Any hints at all," I asked again, "about

who the person might be? Any sort of physical description?"

The two girls shook their heads, but Henry said, "Nothing specific, but I gather he was something of a stud — very good-looking. She said he was a real ladies' man and she should have known better, said he was a professional heartbreaker, something like that. But nothing like 'blond, dark, short and squat, or tall with a limp,' or anything like that." Ladies' man? Just the phrase Muffy'd used for Peter. . . .

"But you must realize, Mrs. — Maggie," Marian said, "that Deborah liked to romance, to make things up. Anyway, the guy was only visiting or passing through, I believe, there in New Jersey."

"Did you ever hear her mention the name Peter Warren?"

They all thought for a moment and then shook their heads no.

"What about a man named Horton? James, or maybe a name beginning with the letter C."

That name also struck no chords with any of them.

"Did she ever date an older man? Ever see her with anyone like that or hear her say anything about dating an older man? He'd be in his mid-thirties, blond. Or maybe tall, with light brown hair and pale green eyes." No answer. I asked Henry, "Do you have any impression at all about the age of the man who got her pregnant?"

"Nope, 'fraid not."

"If you had to guess, what would you guess?"

"Well, I don't know — I never thought about it and she didn't say . . . I guess he could have been older. Maybe you'd be more likely to meet someone older, at a place like that, on a historical-house tour."

"What about you, Susan? Did you get any idea about the man's age?"

"No."

"And if you guessed?"

"I'm sorry, but a guess would be meaningless; I would have nothing to base it on."

Nothing but intuition, I thought. Oh, well. "Marian?"

"No impression at all, sorry."

"Okay. What about this past year — did she have a boyfriend?"

"No," Marian answered. "I thought maybe she'd lost interest. In men, I mean. In sex. Because of the abortion. She was awfully depressed, after."

"But are you sure there was no one recently? She had sex shortly before she died."

"She did!" Henry exclaimed. "Huh! And she turned me down just that week, said she wasn't having sex with anyone, how do you like that."

"*I* didn't know that, Henry," Marian said coldly.

Was that perhaps the explanation for Marian's rather obvious animosity toward Deborah? "Who do any of you know with the initials *C.H.*?"

They all looked at me blankly and could think of no one that they or Deborah knew with those intitials.

"All right. How about Mrs. Chloe Warren? Do any of you think Deborah might have known her?"

"The old lady who was murdered?" Susan asked. "How would Deborah know *her?*"

"That's what I'd like to know, if she did. One possibility — Mrs. Warren had a great niece at the convalescent hospital behind the campus and she hired extra help to come in and look after her sometimes. Pretty good money. Any possibility Deborah ever did that job, even temporarily?"

Henry was now looking absently at a *Time* magazine he'd picked up from the table beside him. Marian gave him an irritated look and said, "No, I'm sure she didn't; she had all she could manage with that bookstore job. She had a hard time finding time for that because she spent so much time with theater projects. I'm sure she never worked anywhere else. It doesn't pay very well, but at least it's convenient."

"Mrs. Warren came to the bookstore from time to time. Deborah never mentioned her, or anything special about an old lady who came there?"

Henry shook his head no, flipping through the magazine but not looking at it; Susan and Marian said No in unison.

"Were you three good friends of Deborah's, would you say?"

"Well . . ." Susan and Marian looked at each other. "Sort of," Susan said. "I mean, we were roommates all three years; we were assigned together to begin with and then just kept the arrangement. I think mainly because none of us had anything we wanted to do instead. We were used to each other; it was simpler to stay together. But we did have different interests. I'm economics, for instance; this summer I have a job with a stock-broker, which is what I intend to become. And Marian—"

"I'm pre-med, and so is Henry. I mean art's all right, but you can't make money at art, not until after you're dead, anyway, so what good is that? I've never had any interest in being a starving artist and I don't think that's just a cliché, either. I think that's usually what happens to artists. Deborah didn't seem to mind the idea, I don't know why. I told her she should be preparing herself for something practical, like the rest of us, but she wouldn't listen."

"Thought she'd be rich and famous soon, that's why," Henry said. "A lot of them think that. Some do, of course. And she *was* talented, everyone said so."

"Especially Deborah," Marian said.

If these were her friends, I wondered, what were her enemies like?

"Did you ever hear her mention a man named Lombardi? Paul Lombardi? He teaches at Princeton and is involved in something to do with seeds, corporate involvement with seeds."

"No," Henry said. "She mostly just talked about the theater, dance, that sort of stuff."

Susan added, "Patenting and ownership of seeds has become highly thought of as a corporate activity, I know that. It's considered an excellent yield and a very safe growth area because people will always need food." Her sallow face flushed slightly, animated by the thought of the growth and profit that could be wrung from people's continued need for food.

I ran through the final names on my list. "Ever hear her mention Edward Corliss? Corinne Brown? Franklin Steele? Or Carter Steele — he's a student at Princeton?"

"She never went down to Princeton that I know of," Marian answered. "I don't think she knew anybody there. She had that boyfriend back in Minnesota, you know, until this year. Never heard any of those names, either."

"Okay. Thanks for your time. I'll have pictures of all these people soon, and then I'll ask you to look at them and see if you've ever seen them before, especially with Deborah. Is there anything at all that struck you as odd, perhaps, that Deborah had said or done lately? Anything she seemed to be, oh, secretive about, anything like that?"

"She was too busy dancing," Susan concluded with just a hint of judgment in her voice. Unfavorable judgment: you can't make much money from dancing.

TWENTY-THREE

I left my inchworm taxi on Broadway and walked up Forty-fifth Street to the big *Peer Gynt* marquee, where a lot of people were standing about hoping for last minute cancellations. Peter turned and smiled as I came up behind him — exactly, I thought, as if he had eyes in the back of his head. He gripped me lightly by the shoulders and looked down at me as if he liked what he saw, then said, "Come on, it's starting," and hustled me inside. The overture was just starting, generating, even in the lobby, that special excitement that goes with Broadway, greasepaint, acting, theater. An usher appeared, but Peter waved him aside and led me to seats that were, predictably, front and center.

"You seem to know your way around here," I murmured as I settled back into the comfortable dark-green velvet.

"I'm one of the backers and get to use these seats from time to time. Part of the return on

270

my investment, you might say."

The music swelled and grabbed my attention then, a combination of simple country melodies and loud, crashing dissonances that were well suited to what I remembered of the play — which wasn't much, mostly just a memory that I'd once liked it very much. Even in faraway California, I'd heard about this production, an extravaganza several hours long, using terrific actors and sets in some way combined with film and elaborate sound effects that had succeeded in knocking the theater world flat-out as nothing had for years.

Peter put his arm around the back of my seat and I leaned into it as the lights dimmed and the curtains parted to reveal a wooded mountainside with a stream running through it, a young man, an old woman, a summer's day — a scene of everyday reality, evenly lit, and rather bland. The exchange between Peer Gynt and his frantic, nagging mother went on for a bit and then gradually the walls of the theater around us came to life with images of the make-believe story Peer was telling, growing stronger and more vivid as the "reality" on the stage paled and dimmed. Flashing color and darkness, lights and sounds, bounced from the walls, the ceiling, even the floors beneath us. The play was suddenly all around the audience, and we felt ourselves riding on the backs of reindeer across the high and windy ridge, then falling toward the surface of that glassy lake far below, as all about us the flickering light, the mountains speeding past, the rushing reindeer, the sound of their hooves pounding the hard snow, the howling winds from behind, beneath, on all sides, the wild cacophony of images and sounds pushed the audience into the middle of the imaginary scene the hero was describing. At the end of his story, the images and sounds surrounding us disappeared with startling abruptness as Peer snapped his fingers.

Through the five acts these switches continued, alternating between the reality rather flatly shown on the stage and the fantasy surrounding us throughout the whole theater. Swallowing us up as if we'd been eaten by alligators, the drama pushed ever more furiously to Peer's final cry to the heroine — now old and blind after waiting at her spinning wheel for the return of Peer, who'd been rattling all around the world having lavish adventures. Finally, he cried,

Mother and wife! You stainless woman!
Oh, hide me, hide me in your love!

then buried his head in her waiting lap. She murmured,

I will rock you to sleep and guard you!
Sleep and dream, my dearest boy!

The curtain fell and the lights came up. Gradually I became aware of the theater, Peter's arm around my shoulders, felt his eyes on me, and turned. He was smiling slightly, eyebrows raised.

"Wow. And thank you for bringing me." Then I sat there, finding it hard to return from the world of the play to the reality of the emptying theater. "I'd forgotten that ending, though. Although I guess you can see it coming for an act or two, or maybe five."

"Touching?"

"Are you kidding? All those years sitting there spinning and saving his soul with her patient waiting, but what about *her* soul?"

"She was good and didn't need saving, weren't you paying attention?"

"Sure, that's what *he* says — stainless woman. She'd be better off with some stains, though. Imagine sitting there spinning and reading your Bible for fifty years, then he arrives, gets his soul saved, and goes to sleep! Sickening."

"Well, of course if you look at it from *her* point of view, but Ibsen never dreamed anyone would want to do that. It's Peer's play; she's just a symbol."

"That's just what I mean, 'my dearest boy,' that's *just* what I mean. But it's a wonderful production and I did love all of it except that ending."

"Would you like to go backstage, or do you want to eat?"

I opted for food, because it was late and I hadn't had dinner. We caught a cab and Peter gave the driver an address in the East Seventies, then said, "I get tired of eating out sometimes; I've fixed dinner at my place. We'll be nice and quiet there, and I have your information on the convalescent hospital. We can go over it after dinner, if you like."

Hmmm, I thought, but what I said was, "That was fast — anything interesting?"

"Pretty much what you'd expect. For the hospital, nothing unusual in any way except that the profits are remarkably high. Could be something there. For Horton, a fifty-thousand-dollar salary that he seems to live well within, good credit, one checking and one savings account. Of course, it isn't an in-depth search. I know someone who could do a good one if you want to go further."

274

"I think I do. And I should probably get a financial rundown on several of the others, too."

"That's easy," he said, "just tell me who and I'll have a man I know take care of it; he can find out almost anything in the area of assets and who's hiding them — but here we are."

We got out in front of a brownstone, and a small elevator took us to the top floor. The apartment took up the whole floor, with a combined kitchen and living room at the back and a large skylight above. Peter pulled open dark green curtains, revealing a wall of glass and a small deck on the other side.

"I like it up here because of the light," he commented. "A painter had this place before me. Put on some music, why don't you" — he indicated a stereo in the corner — "while I get dinner. And here's that report." He declined my offer of help and went down to the kitchen end of the room.

I took Albinoni's *Adagio for Strings* from near the top of a pile of records on the table, put it on, and looked around. The room felt comfortable, lived in, peaceful. The colors were soft but not wishy-washy, and the whole place had a strong sense of space; there was enough furniture, but only just, nothing extra. The few pictures on the walls were paintings that I immediately liked, and I walked over to one and looked more closely. Good Lord. It was a Ben Shahn; there was also a Prendergast and what looked a lot like a Bonnard, though it wasn't signed. Some fine black-and-white sketches of nudes, male and female, completed the collection.

I went over to the couch and began to look through the report, but then Peter started bringing food to the table near the glass wall, so I got up and helped.

"Candles and all, I'm impressed," I said as we sat down. "When did you cook all this gorgeous food?"

"Threw it together before I met you at the theater, having heard" — he grinned — "that the fastest way to a woman's heart may be through her stomach." He served me and then himself.

"In the case of this woman, I think it's probably true."

The dinner was awfully good, scampi in garlic-and-sherry sauce, French bread, and a crisp salad with a marvelous dressing, but I found that, though I hadn't eaten since lunch, I wasn't very hungry, after all. There seemed to be butterflies in my stomach, interfering with my appetite. I made myself eat a fair amount anyway, not wanting to discourage a man who cooked so well from doing it again. When we had finished we sat out on the deck in long comfortable lounge chairs and Peter wrote down the names of the people I wanted a financial rundown on.

"What does he cost, roughly?"

"Don't worry about that; this will be my contribution to helping clear Pudgie."

"All right. But how much does he usually cost?"

"A thousand or so per report. Depends if the information's hidden, and how well. I can get the routine stuff first, through my office; that won't cost anything. Then he can do the digging on the ones you want more on. I should have the early stuff by the weekend. And something on Horton from the expert early next week, with luck." He looked over the list. "Who's this Lombardi guy at Princeton?"

"He's inheriting ten million dollars from the estate of Matthew Warren to start an institute — something Chloe tried to block but that will happen now. It has something to do with seeds, trying to keep the corporations from getting control of them."

"You'll be going out to see him?"

"Yes, Sunday."

"This weekend? Princeton reunions are this

weekend. I'd expected to be out of the country, but now I'm not leaving until Monday. Why don't you come to my reunion with me? I have friends we can stay with, and you can see this Lombardi fellow. And the Steele kid, if he's there."

"It's many a day since I've seen a P-rade." I smiled, remembering the Princeton name for the alumni parade. "When would you want to go?"

"Let's see — how about if I come and get you tomorrow, late afternoon?"

"I'll be in Darien and Stamford, and I don't know when I'll be finished. You go ahead and I'll take the train out Saturday morning."

"It'll be crowded."

"That's all right. Meet me at the college, not Princeton Junction. I seem to remember the potential for confusion there." I stirred my tea, which was spearmint and had nothing in it and didn't need stirring, and took the plunge.

"Stony, Mrs. Warren's secretary, said that Chloe Warren wrote you just before she died. Which was, she said, very unusual." I stirred my tea some more.

Peter looked surprised, then thoughtful. Finally, he said, "So I'm on your list too, huh? What's my motive, though? I didn't go see her before she died, by the way; she'd never been very nice to me and I was damned if I'd run right out the minute she crooked her little finger. I was busy, anyway, and then she was murdered. I suppose you want to know what she wanted with me?"

"Well . . . yes."

"Beats me," he said cheerfully. "The note just said it was important that I come. Didn't say important to whom. Or why. And the secretary was right, it was unusual. She'd never wanted to see me before. It said to come as soon as possible, but, as I say, I didn't. Of course, after she was killed, I was sorry I hadn't. I didn't kill her, either, by the way. Why should I?"

"A possible scenario, based on Stony's information, would go something like this: Chloe wrote a long postscript on the letter, saying that she'd been going through old papers and had found the ancient loan note given by your grandfather John to *his* father when John borrowed the money to start his business. As family rumor has it, your grandfather put his business up as security; the note was to be paid off within a certain time or the business was forfeit. But when John and Matthew's father died, the note was nowhere to be found and John claimed he'd paid the money back. But there was no evidence of payment. If Chloe had found the note it could have meant you'd lose your business to her and Pudgie. And at that point it was more than just the family business you'd inherited, it was a huge affair you'd developed yourself into a big-time money-maker. So, you decided to—"

"To shoot an eighty-six-year-old woman and blame it on Pudgie. Thanks a lot. And I suppose I strangled that poor student, too? Remind me to see if I can't help Stony get a new job. In Albania."

"It's not her fault," I said mildly.

He laughed abruptly. "Fair enough. I guess it would do for a motive at that. Except for one thing. If there *was* an old note on my company, and if Chloe *had* by some remote chance come across it, the statute of limitations would have run out on it long ago, making it worthless. I had all that checked when I started expanding the company: I'd heard that old family rumor myself. I have the legal report on it somewhere; I'll dig it out for you."

"Thank you. At least that would eliminate one name from my rather long list of possibles." I hesitated. "You know — as a woman, I want to trust you. And I do. But as a detective, I can't. Are you really angry with me?"

"No," he said, looking at me steadily. "No. I was, though, until I thought about it for a minute or two. You wouldn't make much of a detective, would you, if you pulled some of your punches."

He got up and leaned over me, took my chin in his hand, and tilted my head up so that we were looking directly into each other's eyes. "It's all right. I'm not all that thin-skinned, *principessa*. Have you thought any more about our Italian trip?"

"I think of little else" — I smiled — "but I'm waiting on that floppy disc to do my job for me while I'm gone. Any progress?"

"Mixed, so far. But they're working on it. Want anything from the kitchen?"

I shook my head, and he got up and went inside. He came out a few minutes later with another brandy and we dropped the subject of the murder and talked instead about ourselves. He was thirty-three years old, I found out, three years younger than I, so I asked him about his company and what he did there. He said he had a knack for getting the people together who could come up with new solutions to various problems in computer development. Then he lost me talking about something called gray memory boards but soon saw that he had and grinned.

"Sorry, I forget and get carried away. It's an addiction, really, like racing was. But what about you? Were you ever married?"

"I was; my husband was killed in a highway accident about eight years ago. I thought at the time that that was what drove me into drinking and pills, several years of it, but now I realize I'd probably have been an alcoholic anyway, sooner or later. I've come to think it's genetic, mostly.

"Anyway, about three years ago I finally dragged myself to an AA meeting, dried out, started getting my life back in order. Or" — I smiled grimly, thinking of all the unsettled business back in San Francisco — "relatively in order."

"Too much order is not life-sustaining, is what I say. Any children?"

"No. You?"

"One son. He lives here in the city with his mother, so I see him quite a bit; he stays here a good deal."

"How old?"

"Eight."

He didn't say any more, and after a while I got up and walked over to the railing at the edge of the deck. From the street the Upper East Side looks like block after block of solid buildings, but behind them are gardens lying back to back, creating in some blocks almost the feeling of being in the country. I looked up at the trees rustling gently in the wind, sniffed the air, which carried the scent of flowers growing in the gardens below, and thought about the man lying in the deck chair behind me: a fixer of too-tight shoes right there in a restaurant; provider of a good dinner prepared with neither grumbling nor arch helplessness; generous in helping his cousin. Not to mention awfully pleasant to look at and be with and talk to. . . . No wonder he had lots of girl-friends. If he did, he deserved them. But it was late and tomorrow would be busy. I should go home. *I should go home.* I said, half-turning my head, "It's been a lovely evening. Thank you for the very wonderful dinner, and for *Peer Gynt.*"

"That sounds just like a leaving speech," he said, getting up and walking up behind me. He put his arms around my waist and pulled me back against him, saying softly, his lips just brushing my ear, "Don't go. Stay here with me tonight, Maggie. I want you to."

I leaned back into his warm body, thinking about it as I looked up at a sky dotted with pale city stars and a thin, sickle moon. But hadn't I already decided, really, by the time

I'd come up here with him, maybe even before that?

"All right," I said, "I want me to, too." I turned in his arms to meet his lips coming down on mine.

TWENTY-FOUR

I woke with the thread of a memory about wild horses in Wyoming, and Indians, but though I lay very still and tried to coax them back, they wouldn't come. Then I suddenly remembered I wasn't home (wherever that was, these days), wasn't in Poughkeepsie, wasn't at Cousin George's apartment. I quickly opened my eyes, but I knew by then I was alone; the bed beside me was empty though disheveled. Memories of the previous evening came back to me, then, and I lay there for a while and considered them. Peter's apartment was utterly quiet except for the birds singing out back and the occasional sound of honking horns from the street. Finally, I stretched and sat up lazily, saw the note lying on Peter's pillow, and read the spiky scrawl.

Hadn't the heart to wake you though it was extremely tempting, but I'll see you at the Princeton station tomorrow — take the first train after nine, if you can. This key will lock the front door,

*coffee's on the stove, and bacon and eggs in re-
frige. XXX P.*

I found what I needed in the unfamiliar
kitchen, cooked the bacon, scrambled the
eggs, toasted and buttered bread left over from
the night before, put it all on a tray with coffee,
and went out to the deck. The air still had
that wonderful, cool, summer-morning feel to
it; I was hungry and the food was delicious
— my appetite had come back, and then some.
As I ate I tried to focus my thoughts on the
case and on the day ahead, though thoughts
of Peter slipped in from time to time. But.
Molly had convinced Hayden's ex-wife Corinne to see me at one o'clock, and Cinnie had
managed an appointment with Ed Corliss at
three. And there were things to do before I
saw them, so I'd better move. I quickly
washed my dishes and started to leave a note
but couldn't decide on what to say, so in the
end I merely made the bed, collected my
purse, took a last long look at the Bonnard,
and locked the door behind me.

At Cousin George's I showered and
changed, stuck Herbie's photograph of Deborah Marten into my purse, and took a cab
over to Park and Eighty-fourth. A doorman
in dove-gray announced me and let me into
the lobby, which had a good Oriental, soft,

flowery couches, and large, flowered Chinese vases that went well with the couches. The well-polished wood elevator opened onto a small vestibule with two doors; Hayden opened the one on the right and led me down a long hallway to a huge living room with big square windows looking down on a garden. The room was furnished with slip-covered chairs in yellow and dark green, a couple of long couches covered in pastel stripes, and lots of small paintings and prints on the putty-colored walls. A large, long-haired gray cat was curled in a ball on one of the chairs, and he stretched and gave me a mistrustful look as we came in, then settled down and went back to sleep. Pudgie came in with coffee and cups on a wicker tray. Her euphoria of two days before had dissipated, and she looked weary and worn, with dark circles under her hazel eyes and a dried-up look about her skin. Hayden looked darkly handsome, as usual.

I filled them in on what I'd found out so far and what I had planned for the next week or so, then told them about the financial reports that Peter would be getting from his expert.

"*Dear* Peter," Pudgie said, "that's really sweet of him—"

"We'll have to pay him back, of course,"

Hayden interrupted, "but it's damned nice of him. I'll call him this afternoon."

"That's a good idea, dear," Pudgie said.

I showed them my newly acquired picture of Deborah Marten, and they both said they were sure they'd never seen her.

"That reminds me," Pudgie said, and she went over to a small desk, picked up a manila envelope, and brought it back, taking out several pictures. "I found a fairly good picture of Corinne, with the children, that Hayden had stuck away; and I managed to dig up this one of Edward and me — I thought I'd thrown them all away. And here's the one of Aunt Chloe I promised you."

"Great," I said, looking at them and then putting them in my purse. "I'd like to go through your aunt's papers, too. Were you planning to do that anytime soon?"

"I don't know. Why don't I just tell Stony it's all right and then you can do it on your own whenever you want, wouldn't that be better?"

I agreed that it would; we talked a bit more about the various suspects, and I left shortly after that. Since I still had an hour or so before I needed to leave for my appointment with Corinne, I walked over to Eightieth and Fifth and went into the Metropolitan Museum to have a quick look at a few of my old favorites:

288

El Greco's *View of Toledo*, some velvet-suited boys by Goya, and Degas's nearly life-size copper statue of a young ballerina, complete with silk tutu and a faded ribbon in her verdigris hair. Standing at an invisible boundary, straining forward with exquisite joy toward puberty, toward dance, toward the unknown and magical future, that statue always simply melts me.

There were posters up all over the place advertising a special exhibit on Eighteenth-Century Woman that had been donated by a cosmetics company, and since I still had a few minutes I walked downstairs to take a look. Eighteenth-century woman was illustrated by endless mannequins in elaborate silk and satin and velvet gowns, fans, flowers, and hats; a black child mannequin dressed in pink and powder-blue silk held a gold, flowered parasol over one of them. The constriction and rigidity of those women's lives was something I couldn't even imagine, and I found it repulsive to look at a display of a bunch of human clothes-hangers. Of course, the majority of the women who had lived in the eighteenth century had looked nothing at all like this . . . but it was time to go. I took a cab to the garage, where I picked up my rented car and, consulting Alice's excellent map, headed for Darien, Connecticut.

The street Corinne lived on was wide and the houses were large and old, with gracious lawns, stately trees, and elegant gardens. There wasn't a person in sight except for an old black man seated on a shiny tractor mower going back and forth over the yard next to Corinne's, though it didn't look as though it really needed it. Corinne's needed it a lot more, and the paint on her house wasn't as fresh as that on the houses around it, either, though you couldn't quite call it shabby. Not yet, but headed that way. An indefinable feeling of neglect and sadness hung about the place.

I walked up shallow steps to a wide, old-fashioned wood-planked porch and rang the bell. I stook there watching the man next door mow the lawn, then rang again, keeping my finger on the bell a little longer. After a few moments I heard shuffling feet approach and the door was opened by a listless-looking woman who'd obviously once been beautiful — the bones of her face were fine and she still had large, clear aquamarine eyes and a short, straight nose. But her mouth had turned down at the corners, the frown lines above and between her brows were deep, her dyed brown hair was limp and thin and showing gray at the roots, and she was about twenty pounds underweight. Her whole persona shouted misery. I introduced myself and she nodded, opened the door, and walked off, shuffling down a wide hallway to a small dark room at the back. I followed her, and she nodded her head again, this time toward the couch, and I sat down. Then she walked over to a bar next to the television set, which was on with the volume turned low, and asked, "Gin, vodka, or Scotch?"

"Nothing, thanks. Unless you have just some tonic water or ginger ale or something?"

She rummaged around in a shelf underneath the bar and finally pulled out a bottle of tonic. She filled a glass for me, added ice, and handed it over, then poured herself some gin over a tiny amount of ice, took a healthy slug, and sat down in the chair that faced the television. She swiveled it slightly so that she was almost, but not quite, facing me, and drank more of her gin.

"Molly said you wanted to talk to me about that old woman's murder. I can't imagine why."

"You know that Pudgie was charged with the murder?"

A small smile, quickly suppressed, crossed her face and she said, "Yes."

"Well," I lied, "some new evidence has

turned up and they may release her. But the new evidence doesn't point to anyone in particular and if the murder isn't cleared up, then everyone who has any sort of motive" — I paused to let her know that this was a group in which she had a paid-up membership — "everyone involved will be left with a certain . . . stigma. So I'm still working on the case, looking for evidence that will pinpoint the murderer — and clear the rest of you."

"She did it, if you ask me."

"Any particular reason?"

She laughed harshly. "She's quite capable of it, I'd say."

"You mean, because she took your husband?"

She inhaled sharply and then took another swallow of gin. "You could say that. Left me with nothing. Nothing! My looks gone . . . Who would want me now, the way I look? And I used to be beautiful! Beautiful — here, look, I'll show you."

She got up clumsily from her chair, weaved across the room, pulled open the drawer of a big mahogany chest, and grabbed a handful of photographs. I realized she was quite drunk. She handed me the photographs, which were dog-eared and limp from handling, and I saw they were all of her and she was right: she had been beautiful. They were society pictures, mostly: Corinne at parties, Corinne elegantly dressed on horseback, Corinne playing tennis or at least holding a racquet, Corinne lying by the sides of various swimming pools.

"How beautiful you were."

"And then he didn't want me anymore, after I was no *longer* beautiful. After I got *old*." Her mouth twisted bitterly.

I didn't see how this quite explained her husband's desertion, since Pudgie was as old as she was, but I naturally didn't say so.

"Left me with nothing, nothing, nothing," she was muttering now, "nothing, nothing, nothing."

"The house? Your children?"

"Empty. The children despise me. What's the point of it all, d'ya think? Mary, wha's your name? Wha's the goddamn *point?*"

"Do you mean," I added evenly, "the point of living?"

"Tha's right, I'd be so much better off dead. Abandoned and dead. Raise children, live in a marriage until the children go 'way and don't want you, *he* sure as hell doesn't want you — as soon as I get up the nerve I'm going to kill myself."

"I used to want to kill myself, too," I said

quietly. "Often and for a long time, but I don't anymore."

"Oh yeah, how come? Why don't you want to kill yourself anymore, Marty?"

"I stopped drinking. Going to AA was the crucial thing, I'd say."

She looked for a moment like she'd been slapped, then pulled herself up out of her chair and went to the bar and refilled her glass.

"What'd you want to talk to me about, anyway?"

"I was wondering what you were doing a week ago Monday."

"Same thing I'm always doing, sitting here and watching television. Do you think I'd want to *go* anywhere, looking the way I look now? Wearing these rags? No money for clothes now, oh, no, no money for old Corinne *now* . . ."

"Were you here by yourself — a week ago Monday?"

"Of course I was, I'm *always* by myself, always by myself . . ." A few tears brimmed at the edges of her aquamarine eyes and rolled down her shrunken cheeks.

"Aren't your children ever here?"

"College. Never come home, not if they can help it. They used to love me when they were little, but not anymore. Nobody loves me.

Nobody, nobody, nobody." The tears were coming down faster, and I got up and handed her a Kleenex from the chest of drawers.

"Thanks. Sorry to cry on you like this." She blew her nose vigorously and made an attempt to pull herself together, smoothing back the lank hair that half covered her face.

"Take three deep breaths," I suggested.

She did, three deep, shuddering breaths, and then lit a cigarette.

"Do you," I asked, "have a maid?"

"Maid? My parents had *maids*, a cook, gardeners. Can't have those things anymore, don't have enough money."

"Well, but don't you have someone who comes in and cleans every now and then?" The house didn't look dirty, which it should have if it had only Corinne to clean it.

"Oh, sure. Pearl. Pearl comes, sometimes, moves the dust around. You know Pearl?"

"I'm not sure, do you have her address?"

"No — she lives somewhere over in darky town. I wouldn't want to go over there; anyway, I never go anywhere now. Pearl has a car; she comes here."

"When does she come, Corinne?"

"Pearl comes Wednesdays, Mondays, sometimes — you know her? You need a good cleaning girl? I mean she's not too good really, but at least she comes, you can count on Pearl. Do you know Pearl?"

"I'd like to, do you have her phone number?"

"Sure . . . somewhere." She looked blearily around the room, got up, and stumbled to the bar, where she poured herself more gin. There was a phone on a small table near the door and I found an address book underneath it. Pearl was under the Cs — for cleaning? I wrote down the number and then dialed it. A woman answered and said she was Pearl; I said I was calling for Corinne, who couldn't remember and needed to know if Pearl had cleaned for her the week before on Monday.

"Sure enough," she said. "Just like I always do, Mondays and Thursdays these pas' few weeks. You that AA lady?"

"Not the one you mean. Could I have your address? I'd like to come by later and ask you about that Monday. What about Corinne? Where'd she go that day?"

"She didn't go nowhere, she was there anyway till I left, four o'clock. Why do you want to know all this?"

"You sure she was home all day?"

"I surely am. Why you—"

"I'll come by there later, then, and explain, if that's all right?"

"I guess." She gave me directions, and I thanked her and hung up.

Just after I put the phone down, it rang; I picked it up and said hello. A woman asked for Corinne and I took the cordless phone over to her. She mumbled a lot of nos, and a not tonight, and then hung up.

"Wants me to go to an AA meeting," she said slurrily, "but I don't want to go to any old AA meeting, I wanna stay right here. Can't make me go, can she? Wanna drink?"

"No, thanks. I'll leave you my phone number; if you ever change your mind about the AA meeting, give me a call and we can go together. It's much nicer, I've found, living without wanting to die."

"*You* look all right," she said grumpily. "No reason *you* should want to die, you're not old and ugly and abandoned and don't have anybody and nobody loves you and your children hate you and your husband left you and took everything away, all the love, to go off with that fat cow miss prim and proper pudgie pudding face. I hope she does get hanged; I hope she gets the chair, and won't it just serve her right, that rotten fucking bitch . . ."

Her voice got louder and louder and followed me down the hall and out the door; I could still hear her yelling as I drove away, but the words were no longer distinguishable.

I found Pearl's house without any trouble, and she let me in to a neat living room with lots of light pouring in through windows on three sides, a relief after the darkness and gloom at Corinne's. She was a tall, big-boned, cocoa-colored woman in her thirties who said she'd swear to Corinne having been home all day that Monday, and from what I could gather, though she worried about Corinne's health and her drinking, she was not particularly friendly with her nor likely to give her a false alibi. Pressed for details, she thought a UPS delivery man might have shown up about midday, and that Corinne had signed for the package. Which pretty conclusively took Corinne off my list of suspects if it checked out.

I stopped at the UPS office on my way out of town and left a message for the guy who delivered to Corinne's area to call me collect at the end of the day. Then I consulted Alice's map again and found the back road that led from Darien to Stamford.

TWENTY-FIVE

Edward Corliss's house was on a country-seeming road with the houses on either side buried behind trees and bushes, with just the occasional graveled driveway disappearing between them the only sign that you were in a suburb and not the wild woods. I turned in at the mailbox with the number I was looking for, wound my way down the driveway, and then came rather suddenly upon the house, huge like Corinne's, but this one modern, a sprawling architect's dream of rich natural wood and lots and lots of glass. It had a small, well-kept lawn in front, but the main impression was of a giant treehouse surrounded by a multitude of green.

A fat black dog ran up to the car, barking, and by the time I reached the front door it was opening and the man standing there was saying, "Maggie Elliott? Not what I expected, I must admit; maybe this won't be so dreary after all. I'm Edward Corliss, come in."

That seemed to take care of the amenities, so I followed after him, this time to a large, light-filled room at the side with a very high ceiling and two glass walls that looked out on a large pond and more woods.

In the bright afternoon light, Ed Corliss looked older than the fifty I knew him to be; he was a tall, thin, rather stooped man with long dark hair streaked by silver, observant gray eyes, and just the hint of a bulge above the belt. He offered the inevitable drink, and while he got out ginger ale for me and sherry for himself, pouring them into spotless Baccarat crystal, I looked around the room. In spite of its size, the two-story ceiling, and all the light, it looked cluttered. The shelves lining the two non-glass walls were filled with what I suppose would be called *objets d'art*. There were lovely old Chinese-looking vases mixed in with metal and stone and ceramic and wood and fabric objects ranging in size from tiny to quite large. Bright abstract paintings were hung on the three doors, and each of the low tables scattered about the room carried its share of more art. Richly complex Oriental rugs lay scattered over the wall-to-wall carpet.

I was having a daydream in which Edward Corliss, hammer in hand and nails sticking out of his mouth, boarded up first one wall of glass and then the other, so he could put up more shelves and fill them with more objects, when he joined me at the other end of a long teal-blue couch sitting against the window. We turned sideways to talk, and I said, "I appreciate your seeing me; Cinnie said you were, understandably, not eager."

"Yes, well, but now that I see you I find it's quite all right, quite all right — charming young woman that you are."

I smiled a tight smile and didn't say anything.

The silence apparently made him uncomfortable; he soon said, "But what's it all about, anyway? As I understand it, the evidence against my poor ex-wife is quite conclusive. So they've hired you to try and find someone to take her place, eh? And I suppose" — he took a long sip of his drink and eyed me warily — "you rather naturally thought of me because of that surprisingly large amount of money Chloe has left me. Of course, I'll be delighted to help in any way I can, short of taking dear Pudgie's place at the gallows myself, but I'm afraid I am going to be something of a disappointment." He smiled happily. "Perhaps we can clear all this up, though, rather speedily, and then" — his smile deepened — "you might like to see the rest of the place. I've a rather famous jade collection, if I do say so, and some sculptures and paintings that might interest you. They're rarely on display . . . are you interested in art?"

"Yes, but not professionally," I said. "Professionally, I'm interested in you, right now."

"Ah, yes." He held up his crystal glass and turned it in the light, so that it refracted several large rainbows into the room. "Ah, yes. The alibi?"

"The alibi," I agreed.

"As I said, I'm afraid I'm going to have to disappoint you there. Poor Chloe was murdered on Monday last, was she not? As it happens, I was in the library at the Yale Club for three straight days. You see, I'm writing a novel — one of those huge, long, sprawling novels, I'm afraid — and there was quite a bit of research I needed to do there. When I get to browsing I tend to lose all sense of time. Anyway, I was at the Yale Club library all day long for those three days — Sunday, Monday, and Tuesday. I'm sure several people will remember seeing me; I got to chatting with an old codger, now that I think of it, what day was it? Yes! It was on Monday. Don't remember the old fellow's name, but I could find it if necessary. And oh, several others, regulars, and I imagine the bartender will remember me, too."

"Yes, well, the fact is, Mr. Corliss—"

"Do, dear lady, call me Edward. Would you like more ginger ale, or are you sure you wouldn't like something stronger, a little white wine, perhaps?"

"No, thanks, I'm fine. And about your alibi — the fact is, Edward, I don't think it's going to work."

About to take a sip of sherry, he paused slightly, then took the delicate sip. "I beg your pardon. What do you mean? It's not something that's intended to *work*, it simply *is*."

"I'm afraid not. There are at least two employees who have already made sworn depositions that you weren't around on Monday. On Tuesday, yes, and on Sunday — but not Monday."

"How would they know?" he asked pettishly. "The stupid — the employees don't come into the library. So it's quite irrelevant whether they remember my being there or not."

"Perhaps usually they don't go in there, but that Monday there were urgent telephone calls for someone all through the day, a death in the family, ironically enough, and so a couple of the employees were going into all the rooms, including the library and the men's room, every hour or so to see if the man had come in. And they remember quite well that the man never did show up — and that you weren't there, either."

"I see," he said slowly, taking a sip of sherry. "Which, I suppose, were the case against Pudgie not so good, and were she not already arrested and charged, might make a suspect of me." He shrugged. "But if the police are satisfied with Pudgie, dear lady, then the question of my alibi or lack of one doesn't really matter, as I see it."

"Yes, well, you see, there's some new evidence and the charges may be dropped. But unless it's discovered who did kill Mrs. Warren, there will always be the stigma of suspicion on everyone concerned — including you, of course. That's why I'm still working on the case. At this point, I'm just trying to eliminate as many as possible from my—"

"What is this new evidence, anyway?"

"I'm afraid I'm not at liberty to say," I said priggishly. "But I am trying to eliminate as many as I can from the list of suspects so that I can go to the police with just a few names, even, perhaps, just one name, that can't be eliminated. If I do a good enough job, then they'll no doubt be able to hound down the suspect or suspects from there. So, it really would be to your advantage if you could be eliminated now, by me, without all the difficulties that a really thorough police investigation would bring. And of course they might tend to be more suspicious of you because you did lie about your alibi."

"Anybody would," he said crossly, "if they didn't have one." He sighed, got up, and headed for the bar. As he was pouring, he remembered me and asked again if I didn't want something more; I merely shook my head. He came back and sat down, having made up his mind what to say.

"All right, then. I admit I did just tack Monday onto the Sunday that I *was* at the club, and then went again on Tuesday after I heard about the murder. As it happens, I had no idea that dear Chloe was leaving me that enormous sum of money, but I did know that she was leaving me a little something and so it seemed . . . wisest. That was before poor old Pudge was charged, of course. . . ." He turned the glass in his hand, making more rainbows.

"You're saying you have no alibi at all for the whole day?"

"Well, in a word — yes. Yes, I have no

alibi. I was here at home, working on the book a bit, doing some cataloging on one of my collections, oh, and photographing the white jade pieces for the Chinese man at Harvard. The Chinese art man."

"And you didn't leave the house all day and no one else was here, no maid or anything?"

"That's correct, I'm afraid."

"No deliveries?"

He shook his head.

"No phone calls?"

"I had the phone on the machine all day. I often do that," he added hastily, as if he felt I didn't believe him. "I loathe petty telephone conversations; I prefer to have people screened first, by the machine. That way I never have to talk to anyone I don't want to talk to."

"Were you outside at all? I can just see the edge of a house way over there. Maybe someone saw you and would remember."

"That's just the corner of an upper story; you can't actually see over here from there. Anyway, I didn't leave the house all day."

Now if I could just find someone who *had* seen him out . . . "You didn't go to your mailbox, didn't take your car out and run to the store, didn't see anyone, didn't talk to anyone?"

"That's about it, yes."

"Well, I guess I can't cross you off the list then."

"Well, but I really do think Pudgie may have lost her head and done it, you know. Not really a very stable woman, though she acts the part well enough."

"For instance?"

"Oh . . . nothing I would care to go into, but I did live with her for over twenty years and let me tell you, she is *not* what she seems, believe me."

"It would help me to believe you if you could be more specific."

"Having that affair, for instance. This will probably surprise you, but it was not the first! I'm sorry to say this, but I believe she is what used to be called a nymphomaniac — I don't know the clinical term for it these days. She tried to bed down with everything in pants when we were married, believe me. Of course I tried to keep it quiet, play it down; I could see that underneath she was a sick woman, a very sick woman, very unsure of herself." He was speaking rapidly now and little specks of saliva were coming out of the corners of his mouth. "It probably has something to do with the tragedy of her parents drowning, then having to live with an elderly aunt and uncle where feelings were totally repressed." He shook his head sadly and patted at his mouth with a handkerchief. "Of course her behavior totally ruined our marriage long ago, but still, I knew she needed looking after . . . her strange moods . . . that temper that so rarely shows but when it does . . ." He shuddered. "I stuck it out as long as I could — I happen to believe in the sanctity of the marriage vows. But finally I just couldn't take it any longer, I told her I wouldn't put up with it any longer, I couldn't live with her any longer. Then she took up with that fellow Hayden. Don't know how he puts up with it all — he's not a patient man. Poor Corinne — have you seen her?"

"Yes."

"They'd pretty much run through Corinne's money, what wasn't in trust, she and Hayden — she had quite a bit, when they married. And he's been desperate for money for that silly little video business of his, so I suppose he knew Pudge would soon have Chloe's money. Come to think of it, Hayden's a pretty good suspect himself, isn't he? Or they might have been in it together — they needed money desperately, I happen to know, and, as I said, poor old Pudge is not the sane, stable woman she appears to be, not by a long chalk."

"Hayden has an alibi, actually. One that

holds up, I mean."

"Oh. Well, then the smart money is on my ex-wife, I'm sorry to say. But I suppose since she's your client, you must look elsewhere, mustn't you? Would you care to look at my rather extraordinary collections of Chinese jade and twentieth-century sculpture now?"

He did have some lovely, astonishing, and amusing pieces, sometimes all three, and I murmured appreciatively as I followed from shelf to shelf and table to table and room to room, but the main thought in my head was where he'd found the money to buy it all. Almost every other object he'd describe with the disclaimer that he'd got an amazing buy, considering its value — but an amazing buy on, say, a tenth-century something-or-other dynasty vase is still a great deal of money. No wonder he and Pudgie had run through her inheritance; the surprising thing was that it had lasted as long as it had. I was extremely curious about what he was doing these days to earn the money to purchase more amazing bargains, because he was clearly a collector of the addicted variety, not at all the type to let a little something like running out of money stop him. How he had solved this problem was, perhaps, something Peter could find out; if not, it would be worth putting the expert to work on it. Because in terms of which suspect would be most happy to see Pudgie spend the rest of her life in prison, Ed Corliss looked like the best bet.

TWENTY-SIX

The new Pennsylvania Station is a mighty sad sight to anyone who remembers the old one. Built in 1906 and torn down in 1966, the original station was the kind of place where ornate Victorian iron gates led to journeys synonymous with adventure, mystery, and romance. Even if you did only end up in Chicago, at least in setting off there were those moments when you could feel in your bones the very archetype of journeying: the station sent you off into a world where all things were still possible and where something unexpected and delightful was even then inching around the very next corner.

From the new Pennsylvania Station, one goes on business trips.

Saturday morning found me in that boring circular space beneath the low bland ceiling, finding the right ramp for the Princeton train with no time to spare, and buying my ticket on the train. It was so crowded I had to stand, along with a lot of others who got out with me at the small station of Princeton Junction; we hurried across and got on the tiny, toylike train that waited to take us the remaining distance to Princeton. Then everybody on the train got off, festive and laughing and talking loudly. Peter was standing on the platform and frowning when he didn't see me among the first to get off, then did see me and smiled happily. He put an arm around me with a brief hug, took my small canvas case and said, softly, "Hey, California girl. I was afraid you'd missed the train." Then he grinned and added, "And I'm not taking your suitcase because I think you're weak and fragile, I'm taking it because *I'm* weak and fragile and need the exercise, all right? Sitting at a desk all week being a mogul."

"All right." I laughed. "You can have the suitcase." I felt a little nervous but also happy to see him again, and held his arm lightly as we walked toward the campus, which was beautiful and green. It occurred to me that what I remembered best about Princeton was Orange Blossoms — the kind that come in a highball glass and consist of gin with a little ice and orange juice. My weekends at Princeton had seemed full of Orange Blossoms, and I remembered too the loud, loud music of every kind — rock, blues, country, but especially Dixieland — blaring from the clubs on Prospect Street. And hung over Sunday mornings drinking Bloody Marys. Princeton has always seemed to me to have strong intimations of the Deep South, unlike Yale or Harvard, and one of those is a kind of romanticized dedication to the ideal of the gentleman drunk. I mentioned this thought to Peter, who denied it hotly and then, after a moment, said, "Perhaps you're right, though."

Prospect Street was lined with people waiting for the alumni parade, always called the P-rade. Peter hailed people he knew but continued walking briskly until we arrived at a faded pink brick mansion with white columns that I remembered was Cottage Club — the one, I recalled, with stronger ties to the Deep South, in terms of its members and their girlfriends, than any of the others. Scott Fitzgerald's club. We joined a waiting group and were handed Styrofoam cups containing, sure enough, Orange Blossoms, and Peter introduced me to six or seven people whose names I immediately forgot. Then he and the other men went off to take their places in that long, amazing fertility rite, the P-rade. It soon wound past us led by two very old men in Princeton-colored wide-striped black-and-orange jackets, ties to match, and white pants — the only surviving members present of the class of 1915. They were loudly cheered, a band blared "Roll Out the Barrel," and the two old men were followed by a parade of others: alumni with their children and grand-children and sometimes their wives. The ex-Princetonians had produced quite an enormous number of children, which, it seemed to me, had always been the main point of the P-rade. I suddenly wondered why Peter didn't have his son with him.

When the last scion had departed, Peter and his friends came back and we had drinks and reunion talk in their club. An early nineteenth-century Princeton president had once described the university as "the finest country club in America," and uniformed black men serving drinks gave the feeling that not much time had passed since. Peter was having a fine time talking to old friends he hadn't seen, in some cases, since graduation, but he kept an arm loosely around my shoul-ders, always introduced me, and I felt in-cluded and even rather cherished. It was a nice feeling, but after an hour or so I found a phone and dialed the number where Carter Steele was supposed to be staying. He answered right away and agreed to meet me in his rooms as soon as I could get myself over there, since he had to go out later.

Peter walked me over, and I asked him what, if anything, he knew about this cousin of his.

"Not much, actually. But he's not my cousin, you know; he's Chloe's relative and I was related to her only by marriage. I do know he was being considered for Cottage this year, went through bicker, and then didn't get in after all. I don't know why. Probably was pretty disappointed, because he didn't try for anything else. And clubs are important because you eat there, all your social life is there. He could still join something next fall, though; there's a late bicker then."

"Cottage and Ivy used to be the most . . . exclusive, prestigious. Are they still?"

"Well — probably. They've kept to the old ways the most — members are still served dinner by servants; no women. Most of the other clubs let in a few women when the university did."

"How generous and tolerant of them."

Holder Hall is a large fieldstone building that matches much of the earlier Princeton campus. Upstairs, a slim dark-eyed blond youth of infinite appeal opened the door and offered sherry. He and Peter talked a bit about family, about old Mrs. Warren's murder and Pudgie's arrest, and then Peter left and I repeated my line about eliminating as many suspects as possible from the list.

"You're only marginally on the list, Carter — because of the twenty-five thousand dollars she left you and the fact that your father would inherit most of the money if Pudgie were convicted. But the twenty-five thousand's not really a motive, since it's to finish school with and she would have paid that anyway, if she'd lived. If you can account for where you were at the time of the murder, then I can cross you off."

"My alibi, you mean. Sure, you should be able to cross me off, I think. What about my father?"

"Ironclad; apparently he was in surgery all day."

"Thank God. I wanted to ask him about it, but he's a funny guy in some ways, and I decided I better not. But if Pudgie were cleared, my father would be a hot suspect, I can see that. If he didn't have an alibi, I mean. I've been following the case avidly, I must admit — I read a lot of murder mysteries, and a group of us here are working on a thriller screenplay now. And here's this crime right in the family! Do you actually think Pudgie

Brown didn't do it? Who do you think did, if she didn't?"

"I haven't got that far, unfortunately. But do you have an alibi for that time?"

"I was at a party the weekend before — out at my friend Louis Stinson's. That's here in Princeton; I'd been staying there until last night. I have to stay here now because I'm working at the reunions. Anyway, the decadent truth is we just kept the party going through Monday, Louis and I, and Tuesday as well." He forced his mouth into a rueful grin.

"And someone can vouch for your being there all day Monday?"

"Sure, Louis can. I told the police that — I don't know if they checked with him or not. But Louis can. My date had to leave Sunday night; Louis's did too. So he and I just fooled around the place that day, and the next. Laid back, drank a little, smoked a little, swam in their pool, listened to music. Sort of catching our breath after the end of the term and before the summer started. Louis is going to Europe, but I'll be working in San Francisco."

"Doing what?"

"Some hospital job my father arranged for me at U.C. — that's the hospital at the University of California. I don't know exactly what

I'll be doing, but it'll keep me off the streets, I guess. I'm flying back tomorrow. But I'd really like to know more about your investigation — I'm very interested in crime. And it could be a big help with my script, too. How a real detective goes about it, you know, any gory details. Any chance of your letting me in on any of that?"

"I don't really have any gory details so far . . . if you were sticking around I'd be glad to talk to you about it after I found out a bit more myself, but since you won't be here . . ."

"What's that policeman like? Bradley, isn't that his name? I saw him on the news a couple of times. Have you talked to him? Is he any good?"

"I talked to him but not — there wasn't a real meeting of minds, let's say. He's a terrible chauvinist for one thing, but not stupid. I think he's probably pretty good at his job. But I have a picture to show you."

I took Deborah Marten's picture out of my purse and handed it to him. He looked at it with interest but not, apparently, any special recognition. "That student who was murdered, isn't it? They had a different picture in the papers, but that's who this is, right?"

"Yes. Have you ever seen her before? Did

you know her, by any chance? You're only a year behind her in school."

"No," he said slowly, "I'm pretty sure I've never seen her. I was at Vassar a couple of weekends this spring, seeing a girl I know from California, Barbara Browning, but I don't think I ever saw this girl. I'm sure if I'd met her, if she'd been a friend of Barbara's or anything, I'd remember her. I pretty much have a photographic memory. Nope, sorry." He returned the photograph. "Never saw her."

"Do you mind if I take your picture?" I asked, taking my camera out of my purse, a Polaroid that Harry had sent me from the West Coast.

"My picture? Well — I guess not. But why?"

"I need one of everyone on the list. I suppose I don't really need one of you, if your alibi checks out, but I like to be thorough and I do have one of everyone else, so . . . if you wouldn't mind?"

"Oh, that's okay then."

I snapped the picture and then the camera developed it, a good clear one in which he did not show up as gorgeous as he was in the flesh, partly because his extraordinary good looks depended on the contrast between his dark eyes and deep sun tan and silky yellow hair, but the image was still quite recognizable. In the background was a big white dove, part of a poster for next Saturday's anti-nuclear march hanging on the wall behind Carter.

"Too bad you have to go back and miss the march Saturday," I said, nodding at the poster. "I'm going. Everyone says it will be gigantic."

Carter glanced around and said, "Oh, yeah, I'm sorry I won't be able to make it. But there'll be something going on out there, too, I think."

I stood up. "Well, thanks. I guess that about covers it. I'll just need to talk to your friend Louis and get his confirmation of where you were that day."

Carter arranged for his friend to come by Cottage a little later that afternoon; I thanked him again, and left. I found my way back to the club without any difficulty and joined Peter for more visiting with friends. Louis turned up about half an hour later and confirmed that he'd been with Carter all day on Monday, June fourth. He was very tall, several inches over six feet, thin, with a high-bridged Roman nose and soft dark hair that he kept brushing back out of his eyes. He looked somewhat like an alert sparrow, and I liked him.

"We slept late that day," he continued, "until about one — we'd been up most of the night, talking and drinking. In fact, it was actually getting light out when we went to bed. But Carter woke me up a little after one. We went for a swim, I remember, then had breakfast and more or less started in again. Kept going until Wednesday morning — my parents are in Europe, so we had the place to ourselves. Then we decided to wrap it up and take care of business again. But he was asleep at my house all morning Monday," Louis repeated, "and with me, awake, from one o'clock on, so that should be all right, shouldn't it?"

"How do you know it was one o'clock when you woke up?"

"Oh, I always look at my watch first thing, get the worst over with. I remember I thought, that morning, it wasn't so bad, considering how late we'd gone to bed. Does that cover it, the times you wanted to know about?"

"Was there anyone else there, servants or anyone?"

"No, there's a maid and a sort of yard man, but they're off Mondays and Tuesdays. They have to work the weekends, when my parents are home."

I thanked him for coming and he left. If he was telling the truth, I was left with Horton, Ed Corliss, and Paul Lombardi as the real possibles, with perhaps a slot for Franklin Steele if he'd hired someone to commit the murder for him. But how the hell would I ever find out something like that? Did surgeons run into hired-gun types very often? Presumably hit men get cancer as often as anyone else. I'd see what Alice came back with and then maybe ask O'Reagan, if he wrapped up his Reno case, to get to work on Steele Senior while I concentrated on the three East Coast suspects. And perhaps I should ask him to see what more he could dig up on the kid. After all, friend Louis might just be a very good liar; they might be in it together, a sort of contemporary Leopold and Loeb. But would a boy commit two murders so that a father who was still under fifty, and as likely as not to live another twenty years, could inherit? And what would be in it for a friend who was already rich, had everything? Kicks? Back to Leopold and Loeb. I reminded myself to take a look at the legal papers concerning the old promissory note that Peter had promised to get for me. I would have to keep reminding myself, however, because it was difficult to think of him as a suspect now.

After more reunion talk for Peter, combined with a few more drinks (mine plain orange juice, which I was getting awfully tired of), we went off to his twelfth reunion dinner, which wasn't very big because it was an off year. We sat with the couple we were staying with, whose names were Marshall and Ellie and who were friendly and funny, Ellie possessing a kooky sort of humor that was well complemented by her straight-looking husband. Marshall taught seventeenth-century English literature to undergraduates and Ellie, a retired actress, spent her days raising their three children, who were away at their grandparents' for the weekend. I liked them both and we all laughed a lot, which helped me forget about the murder case for a while.

The rest of the evening went much as I remembered from past visits to Princeton when I'd come down for the big spring house parties weekends or graduation and reunions: huge canvas tents were set up in the courtyards between buildings, with the tenth, twentieth, and twenty-fifth reunions being the boomingest, as really good Dixieland poured out of the twenty-fifth's, a great country-and-western band swung at the twentieth's, and sixties' rock shook the tenth's. We made the rounds and danced, and Peter drank a good deal and saw old friends and I ran into a few myself. I saw Carter Steele at the tenth reunion, working behind the bar; I gave him a wave and then got carried away with the great music, dancing with Peter and others for a long time, happily flinging myself around like a rather floppy orangutan perhaps. After a while I had to stop to catch my breath, and at that point a voice from behind, loud enough to be heard above the thumping, throbbing music, cried, "Maggie, oh great! Darling, this is that private detective I told you about."

I turned, and Alice Langley Worthington introduced me to her husband, a roundish man in rimless spectacles who was an inch or two shorter than her and going bald. Peter came back with drinks and he and Alice's husband chatted a bit about reunions; Alice said they were going back to New York that night because they had to leave for the coast the next day. I wished her good hunting.

Then Peter and I went over to the twenty-fifth's party and listened to "St. James Infirmary" and a few other perfect timeless pieces of that marvelous stuff that had originated with kidnapped black-skinned people carried away to a strange country and forced to do all the manual labor by the white-skinned people in charge there. After that we went to the thirtieth reunion and danced slowly, cheek to cheek as they used to call it, body to body, to soft, dreamy fifties music played by a Lester Lanin type of band. Finally, at the end of their version of "Slow Boat to China," we all turned as one and headed for the door. A long, slow kiss outside the tent in the darkness and another when we got to the car followed, and then we managed to keep our hands off each other long enough to drive back to where we were staying. Luckily our hosts were nowhere in sight, and we went straight upstairs, Peter undoing the long zipper at the back of my dress by the time we'd reached the top. Once in our room the clothes fell in a heap as if by magic, and we had fast, intense, almost violent sex.

Afterward, Peter smoked and we talked desultorily of ourselves; then we made love again, more slowly, and building to an intensity that was even greater. Then we lay silent, holding each other, Peter's chin on my head, my head on his chest, listening to his heart beating close beneath me as if it were my own. How good it was to feel such . . . wholeness . . . such total silky contentment; it had been a long time. My thoughts drifted back to Richard; the sex between us had never been quite right somehow, and in the past months had virtually ceased altogether. How glad I was to be out of that situation, and how much I liked being with Peter, though of course only temporarily — perhaps *because* temporarily? Still, my heart had a nasty way of getting involved when I slept with someone. I'd have to watch it.

TWENTY-SEVEN

Ellie woke us up Sunday morning by knocking on the bedroom door and yelling that breakfast was ready; regretfully, we dressed and hurried downstairs. The three others were, understandably, heavily into Bloody Marys along with the bacon and eggs. When we had finally all finished, Peter and I helped wash up and then sat outside in comfortable old-fashioned lawn chairs.

He had brought along the preliminary financial reports on all the current suspects, and also gave me an impeccably legal-looking document from a firm called Smith, Smith, and Hardy, in New York, which was the legal opinion on the old promissory note. Then he went off to talk to Marshall, and I began to look at the research on the old note. Dated six years earlier, it first recapped the hypothetical situation of such a note existing and being found years later, then cited a number of court cases, and finally concluded that no present demand based on such a note would be in any way valid — both because the statute of limitations would have run out long before, and because of the impossibility of proving or disproving the authenticity of the note since all the parties to it were so long dead. It was what I had expected from what Peter told me, but I breathed a sigh of relief anyway. I decided, though, that I should ask Mr. Rudleigh to have the report checked to be certain it was genuine, knowing that where Peter was concerned I needed to bend over backward to be — well, I couldn't be objective, but I could at least be thorough.

The financial reports, stripped of jargon, boiled down to this:

Ed Corliss was close to broke and had been for some time. He'd been desperately trying to borrow money based on his expectations of Mrs. Warren — which he'd described as amounting to "about a million dollars." So his statement that he hadn't known Mrs. Warren was leaving him so much was another lie. An understandable one, of course. He had not succeeded in borrowing much, and had been selling off parts of his art collection over the past six months; he had already taken a second mortgage on his house.

Corinne Brown was okay financially, with

a smallish trust fund whose principal she couldn't touch. It was enough to pay the bills and keep her in gin, but not much more. But the UPS guy had confirmed that she'd been at home and signed for a package at noon on the day of the murders, so she was definitely out as a suspect. Not that she'd looked in any condition to plan, much less execute, this particular murder and frame in the first place. I read on.

Franklin Steele had zilch credit rating, but the report said details were not yet in because of his living on the West Coast; more information coming in a few days. The report had a footnote, though, to the effect that son Carter was always hard up for money, spent a lot, ran with very wealthy classmates but managed to keep up somehow. Chloe had sent a small allowance, which his father augmented periodically.

Paul Lombardi made fairly good money as a tenured professor and appeared to live within his income. But that was meaningless, of course, if he'd become fanatic enough about his institute to murder for it.

In-depth information on James Horton and Total Care was still to come.

I thought about it all for a while, but the data had been pretty much what I'd expected and certainly didn't help eliminate anyone. When Peter wandered back to see how I was doing, I asked him to get the expert to work on Ed Corliss and Franklin Steele as well. Then it was nearly time for my appointment with the professor, so we said our good-byes and thank-yous to Ellie and Marshall, packed our few belongings, and drove over to the university. Peter directed me to the main science building and went off to his club; I went upstairs to office 408 and Paul Lombardi.

He was working at a desk but got up when I knocked on the open door and greeted me with a smile and a strong handshake. He was tall, well over six feet, a little overweight, with thick red-brown hair that was longish and lightly streaked with gray. He had amused-looking light brown eyes and was handsome in a rough-and-tumble sort of way that probably caused at least half his young female students to fall in love with him. I'd have picked him for some sort of athletic person, or the outdoorsy type, anyway, instead of a college professor. I knew he was fifty-one years old, Harvard educated, and considered to be something of a maverick in his field. He came right to the point.

"I imagine you're interested in what sort of alibi I have for the time Mrs. Warren was murdered, aren't you? I would be, in your place. Ten million smackers and my lifelong dream of the institute come true at last, after being stonewalled by that determined old — ah, lady for ten long years. Sit down."

I did and he resumed his place behind the desk, which was in front of a crowded row of potted plants; light was shining on them through the window behind, giving a pleasant, informal air to the area where we sat. I repeated my story about new evidence and my plan to clear not only Pudgie but the other innocents of any lingering suspicion.

"I'd like that." He nodded. "I don't really give a damn personally, but something like that could be used to hurt the institute. How can I help you?"

"Well, first, what exactly *is* the institute? And why did Matthew Warren give you money for it?"

"Ah." He smiled. "That's what I like, a new person to turn on to germ plasma. As to Matthew — ever hear of the potato famine in Ireland?"

"Sure, vaguely. I know a lot of people starved to death because of it."

"Right. One in eight, from the time the blight hit in 1846 until it ran its course three years later. And another two out of eight emigrated to keep from starving, which, as it turned out, was my very good fortune. Because one of those emigrants was Matthew Warren's grandmother. She lived through the worst of the famine before coming over, and she told him stories when he was a child about people in her family, her friends, her neighbors, all starving to death. Stories so horrible he never forgot them. Hence his interest in my work on preserving and extending the varieties of seeds being planted."

"I don't quite see . . ."

"That's because I haven't got to the part about why the famine happened. It started with Sir Walter Raleigh bringing the potato plant back from the New World in 1588. It grew so well in Ireland it soon became the staple food. But Raleigh brought back only one strain of the plant — although there were several — and the one he brought had no resistance to the blight disease. Now if he'd brought several varieties, some of them would have had immunity and all those people wouldn't have starved to death, or been forced to leave their homes and emigrate. Almost a third of the country's population. You with me, so far? Want some coffee?"

"You're not putting me to sleep. Go on."

"Okay. Now the same thing could easily

happen in a number of places in the world today, very much including the good old U.S.A. — mostly because the multinational corporations have gotten into the act. They've wangled it now so that they can *patent* seeds, and they push just a few varieties for worldwide distribution and suppress the others. There's a list in Europe, for example, which makes it *illegal* now to sell over two hundred varieties of seeds that once were commonly grown there. In America, in Europe, and increasingly all over the world, the major crops are very uniform genetically — and therefore very vulnerable to widespread attack by disease. Not only that, the corporations buying up the seed companies and doing the patenting are the big chemical companies — so they can start their pesticide treatment at the seed stage now. And that's an especially nice little gimmick: once seeds have been treated with the chemicals for a few generations, they lose their natural immunities. And then, of course, there will be no choice but to buy the necessary chemical treatments from the corporations pushing the poison pesticides and fungicides."

"Rotten," I agreed. "But where does the institute come into all this?"

"We believe the tremendous variety of the genetic pool of plants that's come down to us through the millenia is a resource belonging to the human race, and we'll do everything we can to stop it from being stolen and destroyed by a few transitory, super-greedy humans. We'll publicize the situation with good information about what's going on, information as slick and graphic and compelling as the handouts the corporations use to push their stuff. Money for so-called lobbying, we'll do some of that, although of course, when it comes to the enormous amount of money it takes to bribe governments, we can't compete with the multinationals there. But we will establish private germ-plasma banks. Some governments have a few, but they're too politically vulnerable to really provide much safeguard."

"What is germ plasma?"

He beamed at me and went on. "The stuff in the seed that determines the personality of the plant. With our plasma banks, breeders will be able to come to us for the raw materials to broaden the genetic base of their plants. The corporations are working very hard now to establish patenting for themselves in those very areas where the majority of seed varieties came from in the first place — that's an area near the equator, running from Peru through Russia and on to Malaysia. We'd have been fighting them ten years ago, when it would have been a lot easier, had it not been for Mrs. Warren. Does that mean I finally ran out of patience and murdered her? Not on your life, though I admit I've done a good deal of teeth gnashing and grinding. I'll even admit that I have looked forward over the years to her demise." He grinned. "So whatever your questions, fire away."

"Well, the best would be if you had a hard and fast alibi for the time of the murder on Monday, June fourth."

"I don't. I worked in my lab from eight to nine A.M., with six graduate students. Then I'm afraid there's no one to vouch for me until about four P.M., when I went back to the lab for a bit. In between I spent the day in the woods collecting some local plant specimens. It was a nasty day, and I didn't see a soul."

"So you could have made it over to Poughkeepsie and back, though it would have been tight."

"Could have," he agreed equable, "but didn't."

"Did you by any chance know the student who was killed, Deborah Marten?"

"No, and I didn't murder *her*, either. Of course I don't remember everyone I've ever met and I meet a lot of students, but from the name, from the picture in the papers, I don't remember ever seeing her."

Had he known her, and was he hedging so that if someone had seen them together he could say he hadn't realized it was the same girl? I took Deborah's picture out and handed it to him

"Interesting face," he commented. "An artist, I'll bet. But I don't remember ever seeing it. Was she an artist of some kind?"

"A dancer; extraordinarily good, apparently."

"Too bad."

"Yes. Do you mind if I take your picture?"

He grinned sardonically and didn't ask why, merely said, "Shoot," and I did; it was a pretty good picture.

We talked a little more about his institute, and then he walked me over to Cottage, telling me that he enjoyed teaching but wouldn't have much time for it now that the Matthew Warren Institute was about to come into being. He left me at the door with a friendly backward wave and strode off in the direction of town.

Well, here was the biologist saving the jungles, more or less. Too bad I didn't feel the strong attraction to him that I did to Peter the Republican. I resolved to stop calling him that for the time being. I'd been wanting to work on being less narrow-minded and judgmental, hadn't I? A Republican would be as good a place to start as any.

On the way back to New York, Peter took me to three local airports, where I showed the pictures of Paul Lombardi and Carter Steele to the staff and anyone else hanging around. No one remembered seeing either of them before, and no small-plane flight plans had been filed for Poughkeepsie or anywhere nearby on the date in question. Earlier in the week I'd checked the commercial airlines and found that there had been no combination of flights available that could have got either suspect from Princeton to Poughkepsie within the allotted time.

We hadn't eaten breakfast, so we stopped at a barbecue place on a back road near the last airport, even though the erotic charge that had been gradually building between us since early morning was by then very strong. As we hurried through our food, I told Peter something about germ plasma and the seed professor; meanwhile the charge just beneath the surface grew stronger. We drove back to New York in near silence, touching lightly from time to time, and when we got to Fifty-seventh Street Peter miraculously found a parking place and came upstairs with me, shutting the door firmly behind him.

"And now . . ." he said, walking over and pulling me to him, running his hands down my back and across my hips. "You know, I like these silk clothes you wear, Maggie, so . . . soft" — I leaned into him and we kissed, short, smiling, exploring kisses — "only . . . all day . . . I've been wanting to get you some place . . . where I could just rip them off you. . . ."

"What's wrong," I murmured, "with right here?"

But he didn't rip them off, he took them off slowly, undoing each of the tiny pearl buttons in front, sliding the thin straps of the slip from my shoulders, holding my breasts, kissing them, drawing the stiff nipples into his mouth. I reached for his belt but he said softly, "No, let me do it all . . . this time . . ." and pulled me gently down onto the bright Nepalese rug. "Just lie there . . . just lie there . . . God, I love to look at you . . . touch you . . ."

I watched him take his own clothes off; then he laid down beside me, his body warm and smooth and perfect against mine, and when he entered me we moved together very slowly until I couldn't stand it any longer and I cried out, and came. He became still for a bit, then began moving inside me again, slowly, slowly.

338

I moved in rhythm with him, against him, toward him, away, toward, and soon I gasped and came again, and so did he.

TWENTY-EIGHT

Peter left early Monday morning and I went back to sleep. I woke up again around noon and took myself and my photograph collection out to the theater in Provincetown, New Jersey, where Deborah Marten had worked the previous summer and had been due to work again this one. A young, hopeful, famous-someday-star let me in, a skinny red-headed girl with freckles and enormous mascaraed green eyes, and took me backstage, where Deborah's old boss Bromley Longworth was working on this summer's batch of sets.

"Thousand miles behind, as usual," he commented. "How d'ya like it?" He tilted up the large flat he was painting, which appeared to be a sort of enlarged free-wheeling interpretation of Picasso's *Woman in a Mirror* — bright multicolored bits of jagged shapes that resolved themselves into a woman's head and torso facing itself, if you looked long enough.

"Picasso, sort of?" I ventured.

340

"Very good!" He looked pleased. "See, John! I told ya it's perfectly recognizable. Hey — not so much blue over there! Harvey! I said not so much *blue*, goddammit!"

Bromley Longworth then went on with his painting, having forgotten me. I watched for a few minutes and then said, "I'd like you to look at some photographs, Mr. Longworth, if you would. What I want to know is, Did you ever see any of these people, or see Deborah Marten with any of them?"

I handed over the pictures of all the suspects, including one of Peter; he took them and riffled through them.

"Call me Bromley — Mr. Longworth I don't recognize myself. Hmm. No. Never saw any of these people before, not that I remember, not with Deborah or anywhere else. She was a pretty good kid. Too bad what happened. She talked to me about a boyfriend from her hometown, once, can't remember his name. He was here a few days last summer. But I don't know of anyone else. Don't know when she would've had time, anyway, this place is one of those work-around-the-clock deals. Harvey! C'mere and see if you can do any better with these pictures!"

Harvey relinquished the dripping blue brush and came over, but didn't recognize any of them either.

"There was somebody for a while," he said. "You know how people act when they're in love." He was a solid, chunky kid with a pale, ingenuous face, who looked about ten years old.

"Did you ever see him, the guy she was in love with? Know anything about him?"

"Sorry — never saw him. She went around and couldn't stop smiling for about a week. After that she looked terrible for a while. But she didn't say anything about it, just, in the beginning, that she'd met a man she liked. Later, when I asked, she said it was all over."

"Young guy, or older?"

"Don't know. She really didn't say anything about him. Sorry."

He went back to the overly blue flat, and I asked Bromley, "Is there anybody else here who knew Deborah, who might have seen her with this guy, or with one of these other people?"

"Not right now, the rest of the kids are new this summer. There's a girl, Shirley — she and Deborah used to hang together a lot; she's off camping somewhere, but she'll be back in a couple of days. Want me to ask her?"

"Thanks, yes. I'll have to mail you copies of all the photographs. Ask her to call me, will you? Whether she knows anything or not."

I got the address, gave him my phone number, and left, quite disappointed. I'd had a strong feeling I was going to track down that elusive lover at last, and thereby single out the one person on my list of suspects whom Deborah Marten had known. But perhaps I still would, when that dratted girl came back from camping.

Back in New York I left the snapshots off at a photographer friend's to be copied, then went for a walk in Central Park while I waited for them. I kept expecting to run into someone I'd known when I lived in New York, and even had a moment when I realized I half expected to see David, my husband who'd been dead these eight years, come around the next corner. We'd often met for lunch in the park, and it suddenly seemed odd, now, to be there without him. I felt his presence, a friendly one that wished me well; then I felt it recede and go far away again, and I became aware of a tattered old black woman walking ahead of me muttering in a loud continuous singsong: "Jus' doan put me in no wrong, jus' doan put me in no right, jus' doan put me in no wrong, jus' doan put me in no right . . ."

I imagined her going on and on that way

into infinity, jus' doan put me in no wrong, stumbling along among the stars, jus' doan put me in no right . . . but our paths diverged at Sixty-fifth Street, where I left the park and picked up my pictures. I mailed a batch off to Bromley at the theater, bought hot dogs and a coke from a street vendor, and ate hurriedly, sitting on a bench on Central Park West. I love New York street hot dogs, they are the best in all the world — but what is it that makes them so?

When I'd finished three of them, I took a bus up Broadway to a 106th Street and showed the photographs to Deborah Marten's ex-roommates, but drew more blanks. "No," they each said, "no, never; no."

I picked up some sushi-to-go at a Japanese place a couple of blocks away, then took a cab back to my borrowed apartment. Peter was flying to London on business but had promised to stop by on his way to the airport and drop off the expert's report on Horton and Total Care.

He got there just after I did. We kissed lightly, and I said, "Come sit down — you look tired."

"Not getting enough sleep lately for some reason. But this trip will give me a chance to catch up." He grinned.

"My fault, you're saying. All right. I'll make amends. If you take your shirt off and lie down on this pad over here, I'll work on your back a bit, which should free up some energy. Lie on your stomach."

He did, and I ran my hands lightly over his smooth, finely muscled back, then began pushing on the pressure points above his shoulder blades.

"Ouch!" he yelped.

"I know, but stop gritting your teeth and just breathe into the pain, it'll get better in a minute . . . that's right, deep breaths, stay on the edge of the pain until it's gone, keep breathing . . ."

I finished up with light, feathery strokes across his back and got up. "Just lie there a bit and relax; get up when you're ready."

"Mmmmm, thanks. That report . . . in my jacket . . ."

I got it out and asked if he'd read it.

"Nope. Didn't have time." He got up slowly and stretched, looking at his watch. "I'll be back next Sunday night sometime. Will you spend the day with me Monday? I want to go out to my shack in the country and I'd like to take you with me."

"Shack in the country?"

"Connecticut — a cabin I built, with some

friends. We all went in together on an old farm and helped each other build the cabins a few summers ago. It's surprisingly remote, and very beautiful. I think you'd like it. We could stay over Monday night, maybe, come back Tuesday."

"All right. If nothing urgent happens on the case, I'd love to."

"Great. Then how about spending next Sunday night at my place? I'll be back late, I don't know what time, but if you go on over after whatever you're doing that evening, then we'll have Monday morning to . . . get an early start, or have a long, slow breakfast, or whatever. Or I could come here, I guess, if you'd rather. It would be nice, when I get back to town, to know you were there . . . or here."

He smiled his wide, attractive smile, and I thought for a minute and then said, "Your place, then; the music selection's better, not to mention the bed and the cooking."

He laughed and held me lightly, gave me a good-bye kiss that wasn't much in itself but held some promise for the future, and went off to catch his plane. I felt restless after he left but finally got myself to put aside thoughts of the weekend just past, and of the days to come in remote Connecticut. I went into the kitchen and put several of the sushi on a plate, then sat on a cushion and began to read the report on the hospital and Horton.

It was written in good, clear English, no jargon, and said that Horton was still a Swiss national, and that he was a surgeon trained there but licensed to practice in New York. In Switzerland he had developed what was thought to be a particularly effective version of the lobotomy, because it eradicated most past memory, and therefore the agitation and anxieties that went with the memories.

The report noted that for several years, however, he had not practiced his profession but had derived his income, instead, from his administrative position at the hospital. The expert's digging had uncovered the fact, apparently well hidden, that Horton was not a mere manager of the hospital but, along with three sisters, the whole corporation. They also owned three other hospitals — in Florida — with one of the sisters in charge at each. Compared to other institutions of that sort, the profits at all four hospitals were enormously high. Whatever it was he was up to, then, it was all looking perfectly legal, the taxes paid and no fuss. He probably hated paying those taxes.

The expert next addressed the question of

where the big profits, or Horton's share of them, were going. He wasn't spending it on high living, it seemed, instead putting about half directly into a couple of Swiss bank accounts. The rest was going into short-term investments that could be liquidated quickly. "In no case," the report went on, "would the turnaround take more than two days. And in most cases a few hours would be enough." A final tidbit was particularly interesting: on June third, Horton had issued orders to begin liquidation of those holdings that would take more than a few hours to turn into cash, then canceled the order on June fourth — the day Chloe Warren was murdered.

The pieces, I thought happily, were falling into place. The motive, the opportunity. The initials *C.H.* that fit the poem. And living right there in Poughkeepsie where he could have met Deborah Marten in any of a dozen ways.

The rest of the day came and went without much to show for itself except for a trip to a thrift store to buy my costume for the convalescent hospital. Then I wandered restlessly around the apartment, feeling there were lots of things I should be doing but unable to put my finger on what they were, and unable to settle down to anything. I climbed up on

George's wooden rack and did a shoulder stand for a while, then remembered the Tarot cards I'd bought at the occult shop. I got down and laid out a reading, using only the major arcana and choosing the High Priestess to represent myself. I mentally asked about the murder case, and turned over the first card, the obstacle. It was the Emperor, which represents reason and order. A funny sort of obstacle: What did it mean? In the slot for the past, I turned up the Devil, which has to do with wrong seeing, with being taken in by false surfaces. It presumably referred to me: Was I looking at this case incorrectly in some way, maybe too much from the standpoint of reason? The card for the immediate future was next, and it came up as the Tower, a naked black woman holding two bolts of lightning. In traditional decks two tiny figures fall headlong, terrified, from a lightning-struck high tower, and the card represents illumination, the kind where you suddenly see the truth after previous false beliefs are suddenly overthrown. The process is painful. Well, at least whatever I was seeing wrongly would now get corrected, suddenly and dramatically, and in a way that was nothing to look forward to. I wished they'd had the book that went with this deck; maybe the interpretations in it would have been more positive than the ones I was applying from other decks.

I turned over the final, outcome card: Temperance. A masked woman dancing before a fiery sea. In older decks, an angel stands with one foot in a stream and one foot on land, pouring water onto a lion and fire over an eagle. This particular Temperance refers to tempering, as of metal by fire and water, rather than to abstinence, this card was not altogether encouraging, either.

So I might not have accomplished much, but tomorrow, I consoled myself, would be much better, being the day I'd arranged with Hortense McAffee to insinuate myself into the convalescent hospital. I went to sleep on this encouraging but also scary thought and dreamed of a post-Renaissance artist's painted room of stones and giants: Giulio Romano's walls were moving in on me, the heavy, crushing stones coming closer and closer as the space around me shrank.

TWENTY-NINE

I woke fairly early and wrote the dream down, then found myself again unable to settle down to anything. My canvas carryall was packed and ready to go to Poughkeepsie by ten o'clock, and so was I. I tried meditating but couldn't get into it, flipped up onto the shoulder stand again, and stayed there about ten minutes, but restlessly. Then the phone rang, and to my surprise it was Alice.

"Maggie? Do you have some time today? I'm just back from the coast — had to take the midnight flight last night because one of the children was sick, but of course she's *fine* now that I'm here, it's so aggravating. But luckily I did have Sunday night and all day yesterday to work on the Franklin Steele business, and I want to let you know what I found out. I have to be in meetings most of the day, but noon would work for me. Is that all right for you?"

I said that it was and, since her meetings

were at the Metropolitan Museum, agreed to meet her there. I arrived early and wandered through the Egyptian section, looking at murals that were full of animals: ducks and tigers, cats and falcons and pigs, fish and alligators, and some long-horned cows that would have felt at home in Texas. There were lots of boats and trees, and people who were always carrying something. Beneath the frescoes several mummies continued their long sleep while huge, smooth black-granite figures — a bird-winged woman, a wolf-headed man — brooded protectively above them. But the exhibit rooms were too crowded with talking people for the mood of those ancient beings, half human and still half animal, to envelop me, so I walked upstairs to look at the nineteenth-century displays.

Nothing really caught my eye until I got to the Redons, glowing with such an intensity of saturated colors they seemed to jump right out of their frames and almost knocked me over. Next to them everything else, even the Monets, even the Renoirs, looked pale and bland. I went back downstairs to meet Alice.

The dining room had an endless line waiting to get in, so we went outside and bought hot dogs from a street vendor and sat on one of the broad white steps, as many others were doing. On a gorgeous day, as this one was, it's one of the best eating spots in the city — as long as the pigeons miss you.

"Well, I've found out that Franklin can't be the murderer, Maggie," Alice began. "Although I also found out, through persistent questioning of our mutual acquaintance, that he's dreadfully on the rocks, financially. So as far as *that* goes, he'd have an excellent motive."

"Why is he in so much trouble financially? He's a surgeon; do all his patients die or something?"

"No, no, he has a big income, but he's terribly, terribly extravagant — country houses, boats, fancy cars, an airplane — *women*. And he pays enormous alimony to two ex-wives. He always *was* foolish about money, but apparently, lately he's got much worse, spending everything he can get his hands on. According to what people say, he's about to lose everything. But, as I said, we'll have to cross him off the list as the murderer."

"Because of his alibi, you mean?"

"No, no, I mean it's totally unlikely, even that he would have hired someone. The fact is" — she paused, unsmiling, round-eyed, and serious — "the fact is, he has cancer and hasn't much longer to live. And he's known about it since well before the murders. Months ago. He isn't telling people, but he mentioned it to us because Bill is an old friend and, more important, his specialty is the kind of cancer Franklin has. He probably hoped Bill would know of some new cure, but unfortunately all he could do was to confirm that there *is* no treatment and that another year and a half is about what Franklin can expect. He showed Bill all the tests — we were at his house for dinner. It was rather depressing. Anyway, under the circumstances, there wouldn't be much point in his murdering Chloe and getting Pudgie blamed for it. Because by the time Pudgie was convicted and he got the money, he'd be dead. Or so close to it that it wouldn't matter much. And it's not as though he was just denying it all, or anything like that. He knows he's dying; he's furious about it."

"The poor man," I said. "But you're right. He can be crossed off the list. And I doubt anyone but you could have found that out, Alice. As usual you've done a great job. Thanks."

"I thought I did, too," she agreed. "Now, who does that leave for suspects? What have you found out while I've been in California? What else can I investigate?"

"I'm not sure, at the moment. I'm going to

concentrate on Horton next, the manager of the convalescent hospital, then we'll see." Before she could ask more about my plans, I asked her for the time, and when she looked at her watch she realized she had to return to her meeting. I promised to call her in a day or two with her next assignment, and she reluctantly went back into the museum.

I still had that restless feeling and some time to kill, so I consulted my New York AA meeting directory and found a one o'clock meeting at a nearby church basement. When I got there the room was crowded, but there were still a few spaces open around the central table and I took one. The regular opening from the fifth chapter of the AA book was read and the secretary passed the hat, the usual formula extended with New Yorkese: "We have no dues or fees — but we need the money, cough up." We would never browbeat people about money like that in San Francisco!

I settled uncomfortably into the metal chair, already beginning to soak up that reassurance I almost always take away from a meeting, the feeling that everything is happening just as it should be and there's no use in my trying to force it into some other shape that I, with my limited viewpoint, think would be better. That much needed reminder: that I'm not in charge of running the universe as I had thought. A young girl with shining, shoulder-length blonde hair told a typical AA story:

"All the time, I kept thinking I could always join AA when I hit forty, or I could go into a mental hospital. . . ."

I thought of Corinne Brown, a few years past forty now . . . but AA is for those who want it, as they say, not for those who need it. The discussion got under way and an older member commented, "I like to indulge myself, think that I'm one of those who is sicker than others, but I know that's just pride."

Everyone laughed, even the haggard and ill-looking, and a man in his early thirties droned on for a while about lust and how he seemed to have just as much as when he'd been drinking, did other people have that problem? Another man said he had plenty of it again now that he'd stopped drinking, but didn't consider it a problem and neither did his wife. Then it was two o'clock and the meeting was over. I talked to a couple of people who'd said things I liked and then headed back to the apartment feeling better, and more or less ready for the evening ahead. I picked up my suitcase and was just going out the door when the phone rang.

"Is this Maggie Elliott? This is Shirley

Clarke, and Bromley said I should call you. . . ."

"Oh," I said, gathering my wits about me, most of my brain cells being already in Poughkeepsie at the hospital. "Bromley; yes, the theater. You're the girl who was friends with Deborah Marten."

"Yes. Bromley said if I knew anything about Deborah getting involved with someone last summer, I should call you."

"Right. *Do* you know something about him? That's good news, no one else does."

"Well, it isn't much, but I do know he was a blond—"

"How do you know, did you see him?" Good; Horton had blond hair. It was another piece in place. Maybe she'd even be able to identify him.

"No, I never saw him; Deborah just said something right after she met him, about his beautiful blond hair. When she was talking about how good-looking he was."

"Young, or older? I mean, her age more or less, or older?"

"I don't know. But he was a real ladies' man, she said. She said he had a nickname — 'Heartbreaker' — kind of ominous I thought at the time. Did *he* kill her, do you think? It's just so terrible, what happened to her."

"Yes. I mean, yes it's terrible what happened to her. I don't know if this guy was the one who killed her, but I'm working on it. I really appreciate your calling to tell me this. Is there anything else you can remember about him?"

"No, I'm sorry. It only lasted about a week, you know, and after, she didn't want to talk about it. She was really just *crazy* about him, though."

"You didn't recognize any of the photographs, I take it?"

"No, sorry."

"Well, thanks very much for calling me. You're the only person who's had any information on him at all."

She gave me her phone number and agreed to call again if she remembered anything else.

THIRTY

I got my rented car from the garage and two hours later was in Poughkeepsie. I checked into another seven-dollar room at Alumnae House and changed into the thrift-store clothes. Wearing one dumpy-looking too-large dress on top of another made me appear considerably heavier. I sprinkled some talcum powder onto my hair and massaged it partway in, which gave me a graying look, drew some pink lipstick beyond the edges of my own lips, which gave me a rather sloppy, sickly look, pulled my hair into a bun at the back, and placed some clear glass plastic-framed spectacles on my nose. I put my special key ring and the tiny camera for photographing documents into the shabby black purse from the thrift store, along with some money, a small flashlight, and several Hershey bars, and went downstairs to the cloakroom, where I looked at myself in the full-length mirror and decided I would do.

I arrived a few minutes early at the convalescent hospital, so I waited in one of the leather chairs in the lobby, holding a magazine in my lap. Soon footsteps approached and I looked up to see James C. Horton. He looked at me, and I quickly dropped my eyes to the magazine. While my heart pounded away and the bottom fell out of my stomach, he walked on past, apparently paying me no particular attention, and went on out the door. After a couple of minutes, I got up and cautiously looked out the window. Horton was just getting into a long black car and soon drove away. After several more minutes my heart slowed down to normal, and a woman with gray hair so thin her scalp showed pinkly through, mild blue eyes, and a tilted nose too small for the rest of her face came from the back, asked if I was Merle, and introduced herself as Charlotte Jameson. We took the elevator to the fourth floor, seeing no one, and at the nurse's station she introduced me to the small dark-skinned woman in charge as someone who might be coming in to work for Bettina Martin on her day off. The other woman nodded pleasantly and was clearly uninterested. I followed Charlotte down a couple of corridors, all empty, to a room where two patients lay comatose in their beds. The fourth floor was much quieter than Sally Steele's floor had been, the only sounds being the *clip-clop* of footsteps down the linoleum corridors. There was a pervasive smell of strong cleaning compound, and under that, of urine and something else.

"First I just lift her into this wheelchair, see," Charlotte said, doing it, "and tie her in; she's really hardly conscious anymore most of the time." She looked at the bed and went on. "Oh, good, not too bad tonight, just wet, *that's* a good girl." The good girl weighed perhaps seventy pounds, had yellow-white hair so wispy it made Charlotte's look abundant, milky blue eyes, and no teeth.

Charlotte showed me where the clean sheets were, where to take the old urine-soaked ones, and I helped her change the bed. The big racks with the floor's dinner trays arrived at the nurse's station, and Charlotte showed me how to prop poor Bettina up, holding on to her with one arm while she poked what looked like baby food into her mouth with the other. This was accompanied by a constant stream of talk at the old lady, who by now was awake, at least enough to swallow, though she clearly did not want to and spit out at least half of it, shaking her head and moaning. "*That's* a good girl, just a little more now honey, that's good."

The patient in the other bed was unconscious or asleep, with an IV bottle dripping into her; occasionally a white-uniformed attendant would come in to check it, but none of them paid me any attention. Finally, Charlotte got about half the food down Bettina's throat and turned her on her stomach, lifted up the blue cotton hospital nightgown, and gave her a lengthy alcohol rub. As she pushed and pulled at the flabby, wrinkled skin of the terribly thin old body, she went over the whole routine again for me and asked if I would be able to remember it all when I came in on Friday.

"Oh, yes, I'm sure I can. Is that it, then?"

"Yes, this is the last thing, except at the end I check the bed again and change it if it needs it." She felt down beneath the old lady's hips and said, "It's dry though, tonight. Doesn't always need changing again, only sometimes."

Before she was quite finished with the backrub, I said I had to be going but would talk with Mrs. McAffee about coming on Friday, and thanked her for showing me the ropes.

"Oh, that's all right, dear, I'm glad to think someone will be here on my day off. I've hated to think of her lying here hour after hour in a wet bed — and sometimes worse than wet,

I'm afraid. Remember to come in the back door; the front is locked at five-thirty and, anyway, they like the help to use the back." She smiled vaguely and started looking around for the top to the alcohol bottle, which I spotted and handed to her, then I thanked her again and left.

So far, so good, but now for the hard part. A short male attendant or nurse, wearing a white uniform like everybody else, was on the elevator when I got in but got off at the second floor. I got out on the first, where dim lights along the walls mingled with the summer twilight to give the place a sad, murky feeling. No one was around and the only sound was the elevator automatically heading back up. The pseudo museum-piece paintings all sat sedately in their frames as I walked quietly down the carpeted hall to Horton's office. The door was closed but not, I discovered, locked. I knocked softly and then very slowly pushed it open. There were no lights on in the room, but in the fading twilight I could see that it was empty, with the door to the inner sanctum closed. No light showed around its edges, either.

I carefully closed the door behind me, tiptoed over to the other one, and eased it open. There was a movement over to my right and

I froze, my heart pounding like a rock-and-roll drummer, a good fast one. I slowly turned toward the sound and saw the leaves of a magazine riffling slightly in the evening breeze blowing in from a partly open window. I slumped into a big chair in relief, took several deep breaths, and looked around. It was almost dark, but a bit of gray light still came through the tall French doors behind the desk, and from the one window; I'd have to wait a bit.

At last it was dark enough; I took some giant-sized plastic garbage bags and some thumbtacks out of my purse, unrolled and separated a few of the bags, and then tacked them over the doors and the window. Then I shone a small flashlight around the room, wondering where, if I were going to hide something here, would I hide it?

I went through the desk first, which contained a lot of blank letterhead stationery and envelopes, a half-empty bottle of Scotch, a paperback Louis L'Amour western, and the usual assortment of paper clips and ballpoint pens. Emily Strong, Emily Strong, what was Horton up to that Mrs. Warren had found out about?

Then I heard the door to the outer office open.

I crouched down behind the desk where I'd been standing, the rock-and-roll drummer at work again. The light in the outer room went on, there was some rustling about, then, after what seemed like a very long time, the light went off again and I heard the door close. A cleaning person? I sat there, crouched down, for a good five minutes but didn't hear anything else.

Then I did something I should have done to begin with: went over to the French doors and quietly turned back the bolt so that I could get out of there in a hurry if I had to. Still no sounds from the front office; I tiptoed across the room, opened the door a crack, and peered out. Seeing no one, I opened it wider and shined my flashlight around: no one.

I went back into Horton's office, closed the door, and had a look at the standing four-drawer filing cabinet, each drawer locked separately. I tried a few keys and soon found one that opened all the drawers. The bottom drawer was alphabetically filed under the general heading "Patients — Deceased," and I looked for Emily Strong's. No luck. The third drawer had "Patients — Current," and "Strong, Emily" was right there where she shouldn't have been, in perfect alphabetical order. I took her file over to the desk and looked through it. A first sheet gave the name and address of those financially responsible, a brief statement of condition, and the treatment being provided. There was also a rundown on the average monthly charges, which in this case were a little over six thousand dollars. The space at the bottom reading "Died" was blank. A notation on the "condition of patient" stated that Emily was "holding her own nicely" as of two weeks before.

I photographed the two pages and then, following the idea I'd had when I first heard about Emily Strong from Hortense McAffee, I methodically went through the rest of the Current Patient files looking for those who, like Emily Strong, were handled and paid for by lawyers rather than by individual relatives. I found twenty-seven of them, eleven from out of state, out of a total of about a hundred and sixty. I photographed those first pages and statements of condition, and was going to return the files to their drawer when I thought of something else.

I was getting nervous about taking so long, though, so I stood and listened for a minute or two, but still didn't hear a thing. Then I went through the two top file drawers until I found what I was looking for, a computer printout of monthly payments received in the past year. The legal firm of Bender, Bender and Funk of Bend, Wyoming, as of the previous month, was still paying their monthly six thousand for Emily Strong. I photographed the statement and went to put it back, figuring I could cross-check with the other twenty-seven names handled by lawyers in more relaxing surroundings. As I turned toward the file cabinet I happened to glance at the door, and froze.

It was opening, silently but not slowly, and Horton followed it into the room with a gun in his hand.

"So it *was* you. I thought so. Do you know, it was only a few minutes ago, as I was watching television, that I suddenly realized why that drab-looking woman in the lobby this evening looked so familiar. I am usually excellent with faces and it bothered me. The little detective friend of Mrs. Warren's niece. Yes. And what have you there — *don't move!* That's better. Now what is so interesting . . . ah, my patients' files. What is so interesting about them, though?" He picked up the computer printout and nodded. "And this very ordinary list of payments?"

"I just was looking through your files in hopes of finding something, I didn't know what," I tried. "I just got started, though."

He picked up the top file and glanced at it, but didn't look away from me long enough to do me any possible good — the gun remaining steadily pointed at my chest, too far to reach out and grab it, too close to hope to survive a shot from it if I tried to duck to one side. The gun itself wasn't big, but the bullets were .38 caliber.

"Emily Strong. Now how did you get on to that? Something from Chloe Warren's papers, I suppose." He sighed. "I had hoped I would hear no more of this. I get rid of that — how do you say, nosy? Yes — nosy old lady, that wretched, trouble-making Mrs. Warren, and now you. Well, well, well. And these others, Lucy Jenkins, Prudence Wills, Lawrence Smith . . . Emily Strong . . . all the same category, aren't they? Clever of you to figure it out." He smiled, but it was not a warm smile. "Lie down."

"Lie down?" Was he intending to rape me? If he tried that I'd have a better chance to get his gun—

"*Lie down! Now!* In one minute I shoot and if you think I mind shooting, you are much less smart than I think."

"Right here?" I asked. I glanced down at the floor and saw my tiny camera. I'd dropped it when he'd come through the door and Horton hadn't seen it yet because the desk was still between us. Maybe I could nudge it underneath with my foot . . .

"Walk around the desk," he commanded, "very slowly, that's right. Now, lie down here. On your stomach with your hands behind you or I put a very large hole into you." He lowered the gun slightly so that it was pointing at my stomach. So that when he shot, death would still be certain, but not instantaneous — and very agonizing. "A large, very painful hole in your intestine. Well? Do you lie down, or do I shoot? The choice is for you to make."

I laid down.

"Turn your head the other way."

I turned my head the other way. Now he was behind me and I couldn't see him but sensed that he was leaning toward me. I started to turn but something slammed into my head causing terrible pain and then I knew nothing further.

THIRTY-ONE

The pain was where my head should be, I thought groggily; they must've taken away my head somehow and put the pain there. It rolled over me in waves, endless as the sea, and I felt very sick, felt like vomiting, but knew if I moved at all, if I couldn't keep myself from throwing up, the pain would simply kill me. I concentrated on not moving, not throwing up, not moving, then the waves rolling up from my stomach could not be resisted any longer and, as the warm bitter taste filled my mouth and my body convulsed, a thousand sledgehammers crashed inside my head and put me out again.

Some people were standing over me, talking, but I couldn't make sense of it. I felt dizzy and my head hurt, but not, I realized thankfully, as badly as before. The people were all blurred.

"Intravenous . . ." they said, "feeding . . . operation . . ."

"Saturday . . ."

The words clicked into focus, but the people were still blurry. They were just white uniforms at first, then I saw that it was Horton, looking down at me with a slight smile, and next to him that hateful head nurse from the floor that girl was on. What girl? My brain seemed to fade in and out, seemed to work, then blink out. I tried to turn away from Horton's staring eyes, from the nurse's huge gray eyes magnified behind her thick glasses — and discovered I couldn't move. At all. I gave out a choked-sounding cry — was that me? — and strained at whatever was holding me. But I couldn't move, not at all.

"Do not distress yourself," Horton murmured, never taking his eyes off me. "You are strapped down. It is what we must do with our . . . violent patients. Rest, now. Just try to relax and rest." He turned to the nurse and said, "Saturday, yes, the operation will be Saturday."

"Unh, uhh, whuhh ahshun?" I pushed the sounds clumsily through thick stiff lips. "Whuh opayshun?"

But he didn't answer, just murmured something to the nurse I couldn't hear. She nodded, and they walked away.

What had they said, exactly? An operation.

371

When? Saturday. Saturday. But what was it now? I could see daylight out the windows, but which day? What *kind* of operation? And was he talking about an operation *for me?* What kind of operations did people get in places like this, very old people, senile people, violent people? And what had that report said, Peter's expert . . . *lobotomy.* Horton did lobotomies that took away your memory. *Was that going to be the operation?* Or had he said all that just to scare me? Well, he had certainly succeeded. But since he'd admitted he had killed Chloe Warren, what was I doing here strapped down waiting for some horrible operation? Why hadn't he already killed me? Did he plan to kill me during the operation, so that way my body'd be easier to get rid of?

None of it made any sense. And maybe he hadn't been talking about me at all, about an operation for me. It occurred to me that if I didn't get out of there before I knew for sure, I'd probably live to regret it — not for very long, perhaps, or maybe not in a way that I would want to continue living. . . .

I lay there immobilized and tried to think. The room was less blurry; the pain in my head had dulled to a steady ache; I didn't feel as dizzy and sick — but how could I get out of there? Hortense knew I'd come last night —

but was it last night? And, anyway, Hortense would be in Fisher's Island by now, walking on the beach and enjoying her summer cottage, not expecting to hear anything from me until she got back on . . . Sunday. Sunday came after Saturday; Sunday would be too late. O'Reagan knew of my plan, but he wasn't expecting to hear from me right away, either. By the time he got worried, even if he sent people to find me, even if he came himself, if Horton *had* been talking about an operation for me, O'Reagan would be too late.

A wave of pure terror washed over me, so strong I couldn't think at all. I just lay there and felt the horror and a great coldness rolling through me. But it subsided after a while, and I tried again to think about escaping before whatever they had planned for me could be done. The first step, obviously, was to get loose from the straps. And whatever I did I had to do tonight: tonight, because Horton and the bad nurse probably wouldn't be around then and I'd have a better chance with whomever they left behind. Tonight, because tomorrow might be Saturday. I had no idea how long I'd been here; it was Tuesday when I came but how long had I been out? Tomorrow might be Saturday, tomorrow might be their operation . . .

I lay there, drifting in and out of consciousness, thinking, or trying to in my lucid moments, all through the day. The bad nurse came and checked on me several times, even brought a bedpan once, and I needed to go so badly I used it right away, the brief interval that the strap over my hips was loosened of no other use to me. Horton came back twice, that I was aware of anyway, but there was no further conversation. As the room started getting dark and the wall lights came on, the bad nurse came one last time. She held a syringe and pushed the plunger until a drop or two came out the tip of the very short needle, then, as I shrank back in horror, she forced my lips apart with hands of steel and pricked the needle into my lower gum, then above, then on the other side, upper, lower. The numbness rushed into my tissues; I realized it must have been a huge dose because it affected me so much more quickly than it did at the dentist's. She took my blood pressure, murmuring something again about how the novocaine would keep me from talking to what she called the wrong people, then peeled the tape from my inner arm, removed the needle that had been feeding something into me from a large hanging bottle, and went away.

A little later another nurse came in and pried

my mouth open and poked some little yellow pills down my throat, massaging my neck until I involuntarily swallowed. Like a dog, I thought, just the way I give pills to my dogs. She went away and I concentrated very hard on how sick I felt, how nauseous, thought of anything I could to make me sicker, that dead horse carcass from *The Tin Drum* with all those slimy disgusting eels feeding off it, clinging to it as it was pulled from the water, clinging to the dead, rotting flesh . . . then the woman who couldn't stop eating eels — I threw up the pills, I could feel them, not dissolved yet, or only partly, floating there in the sour bile in my mouth. I turned my head and moved it as far to the side as I could, spit the stuff out of my mouth, and then put my head over the spot so no one would see it. I felt suddenly sleepy. The waves were of sleep now, and overpowering.

When I became conscious again it was full night. There was a faint light in the room from a lamp beside the bed; the darkness outside was absolute. I felt sleepy but now had a choice about going under, and I fought to stay awake, flexing my muscles, group by group, shoulders, arms, chest, stomach, buttocks, legs, feet, turned my head back and forth, fast, faster, grimaced and squinted my face muscles around as much as I could. My mouth was stiff and felt like cotton still, but when I ran my tongue along my gums I could faintly feel them.

I still didn't have a plan, though, and it was night. The night followed by Saturday? My heart pounded in my chest and I breathed deeply, slowly, trying to calm it, my poor heart: it was so frightened. As it pounded I wondered if I might have a heart attack, and the picture of the man on the bus flashed through my mind, the man in San Francisco who'd had the heart attack and died, right there on the bus. A big, strong-looking older woman had lifted him from behind and pounded on his chest, tried mouth-to-mouth, but he hadn't responded, he was dead. Heart attack? If I could fake one, might they take the straps off my chest? I looked around to see what I could use as a weapon.

By the time I finally heard steps in the hall, coming toward me, I had thought of nothing better. So I held my breath to make my face congest, started gasping, and was well into it by the time steps came into the room. Not the bad nurse, thank God, not Horton, but a slightly built, grim-faced Hispanic woman. She hurried to the bed.

"Pain," I gasped, "chest — pain — terrible

— help — help—"

She pushed her hand down on my chest, hard, and tried to reach underneath to lift me, but the restraints were in her way. She cursed, *chinga, chinga,* and released the strap holding the arm on her side of the bed and my chest, felt under me, and then lifted me slightly as she pounded on my chest. I moved my arm back and grabbed the metal table lamp and brought it crashing down on her head as hard as I could — this her reward for trying to save my life. She made a tiny whimpering sound, then slowly slid off the side of the bed and onto the floor. I hoped I hadn't killed her.

My heart was pounding again, but more with excitement than fear. I pushed back the covers and undid the straps on my other arm and across my hips. Then I leaned down and released my feet. The nurse might not be out for long; I'd have to hurry.

As I sat up, a wave of dizziness almost put me down again, but I weathered it and got weakly to my feet, holding on to the bed. I slowly, painfully, shoved the nurse underneath it with my foot — I'd have liked to put her on the bed but didn't have the strength — then realized I didn't have any clothes on. I went over to a closet by the bathroom and looked inside, but it was completely empty.

So I dragged the nurse out from under the bed again and finally managed to get her white uniform off. I put it on; it was a tight fit and too short, but it would have to do. At least I was able to close it up the front; it could have been worse. I put on her shoes too, which were too small, but I could walk in them with the laces untied. If no one saw me up close I might pass. I hobbled cautiously to the door and slowly put my head around the edge and looked out.

The hall was dimly lit and quite empty. In the distance I heard the elevator hum, then stop; I hoped to God it wasn't someone coming to look in on me. The room I'd been in was at the end of the corridor, and next to it was a door with a push bar and a red light above it. A white uniform came around the corner at the end of the hall, and I pushed down on the bar and half fell through the door, a wave of dizziness and sickness catching me so suddenly I almost groaned. I slid onto the floor by the top step, put my head between my legs, and the dizziness gradually passed. I heard footsteps in the corridor behind me and started sliding down the steps on my buttocks, scuttling, trying to be quiet. Where was I going?

Out. I had to get out. Even if I got to a phone and called someone, they'd find me before help could come, and that would be that. I took the too-tight shoes off but held on to them, got on my feet, my legs wobbly but working, and stumbled down the steps, heart thundering, body swaying in dizziness, head pounding now, too. After a nightmarish long minute when the floor landings seemed endless, I reached the one with the number one painted over the top of the door and paused.

At that moment a loud alarm bell went off and I heard steps and shouting from upstairs, coming down. I pushed through the exit door and found myself in an area of the first floor I didn't recognize, a long corridor with closed doors on both sides. I ran to the end and went through a door into a gigantic kitchen, empty and gleaming with stainless steel, the huge refrigerators humming. I suddenly realized the alarm had stopped, because I could hear the refrigerators. I could also hear footsteps in the corridor behind me. Frantic, I spotted a door in the far wall and ran over, opened it, and went through into a supply room. Good, was I getting myself trapped like a rat in some dingy corner? There were no doors inside, but in the far wall was a window. I heard voices now in the kitchen, coming closer. I rushed over and tried the window, tried and tried and tried. It wouldn't budge. Tears slid down my cheeks; I blinked them back and noticed the window was locked, undid the lock with frantic, bumbling fingers as the voices neared the door of the supply room, pushed with all my might — and the window flew up, silently. I undid the screen, swung out onto the window ledge and, with the door behind me pushing inward now, dropped to the ground below. Had they seen me?

At first the pounding in my head and the nausea were so bad I was blinded, but my vision cleared and I saw that I was behind some bushes and to the left was the back parking lot. Which meant that the road — and the back gate to Vassar — was that way, also. Men with flashlights were stalking the grounds to the right and left of me, and I heard, above, the voices that had followed me into the kitchen at the window now. I heaved myself up and ran.

I got to the edge of the highway before the shouting started — "*Alla, por alla!* There she is! There she is!" — and then I heard them pounding down the pavement behind me. I slipped through the back gate and raced down the path, branches whipping my bare legs, blackberry thorns catching the uniform or tearing skin whenever I weaved too far to one side, but I hardly felt them. I soon came out at the lake, the yelling men not far behind. I kept to the bushes as I skirted the open space of the Outdoor Theater and then I ran into the open, ran for my life, ran straight for the President's House. If anyone was home at Vassar now, she would be. I rang the bell, and rang, and rang, keeping my finger on it. Behind me in the Shakespeare Gardens I could see flashlights raking the bushes, the men holding them silent now. But they were coming closer fast. I wondered whether I should give up on the president and try somewhere else? But where? The college was closed up now, and I was so tired . . . so dizzy and so tired. I could see the white-jacketed men clearly now; one caught me with his flashlight beam and started toward me. The door opened.

I fell inside and slammed it behind me, frantically scrabbling for the lock, finding it, locking the door. "Is the back door locked?" I gasped.

"Yes," President Tomlinson said calmly, her tall, spare person seeming a bulwark of strength in its flowered cotton bathrobe. She went to the window and peered out. The bell rang.

"Don't let them—"

"Don't worry. Here, sit down."

She opened a small talk-through panel in the door but didn't unlock it, and said, "Yes?"

"Patient escaped, ma'am," a man's voice said. "Violent, I'm afraid — we saw her at your door. We'll take her now, before she does any harm. If you'd just open the door, we can take her back to where she'll be safe, and yourself, too."

He paused, waiting, and she turned and looked at me.

"They killed Chloe Warren," I said slurringly, the novocaine still numbing my tongue. "I'm a private detective, working for Pudgie Brown — you know about that?"

She nodded.

"Those people out there — trying to kill me — don't let them in."

Then I slid off the chair in a dead faint.

I woke in a bright, daylit room, with striped wallpaper and flowered chintz furniture and curtains. I had a strong need to go to the bathroom. I got up and saw that I was wearing a long flowered nightgown; then I remembered the president and the night before and felt gratitude and enormous relief. While I was in the bathroom there was a knock on the door, and when I came out, a small gray-haired woman was putting a tray beside my bed, a tray with wonderful smells wafting from the coffee and scrambled eggs and toast.

"Oh, good, you're up." She smiled. "How are you feeling? The police are here. Do you feel up to seeing them now?"

"Yes," I said, "but could you tell me — what day is it?"

"The fourteenth, I believe; yes, the fourteenth."

I tried but it was too much for my brain to untangle, so I asked again, "I mean, what day of the *week* is it?"

"Oh! Thursday. It's . . . Thursday." She smiled uncertainly and then went out, closing the door behind her.

Since I didn't have any clothes and the nightgown was a sheer one, I got back into bed and pulled up the sheet. I ate the eggs and was halfway through the coffee when there was a quick rap on the door and Lieutenant Bradley and a sidekick walked into the room, the lieutenant smiling grimly.

After a weak amenity or two I told him everything that had happened, or at least everything I could remember, from the time I had gone into the hospital to work for Hortense McAffee's sister to passing out in the president's tastefully furnished front hall. I stuck to the truth — except for saying the file cabinet drawers hadn't been locked.

"Dr. Horton seems to have left town," he commented, "or at least, we haven't been able to reach him. I don't imagine that nurse will be around either, but we'll get her eventually. Tell me again about those files you were looking at when he found you in his office."

"But what about the other nurse? The one I hit? She isn't . . . dead, is she?"

"Not that I know of," he said easily. "Nothing like that reported from the hospital. If she wasn't all right, we'd have heard by now. I think you can stop worrying about it. But what about those files?"

"They'll be gone now, if Horton is. But all right." I repeated as many of the names as I could remember, including Emily Strong's.

"What happened to the camera? He took it?"

The camera. The files would be gone, but the *camera* — "I pushed it under the desk with my foot. After he told me to walk around the desk and lie down. I forgot, I'm sorry. He may not have seen it."

"Okay." He stood up. "I guess you're supposed to stay put for a day or two, mild concussion, but you're lucky it was nothing worse." I nodded weakly. "The president told the doctor you might as well stay, since you were already here. I'll let you know if we find the camera. Or Horton, or the nurse."

"Do you know — he's Swiss? A Swiss citizen. I got a detailed financial report on him this week that said a lot of his money's stashed away in Swiss bank accounts. So I'd think he might go there."

"The report name names?"

"Some. If you want it, I took a room at Alumnae House before I went to the hospital. My purse is there and the report's in it. Room . . . I don't remember. But they'll know."

"Thanks. You want it back?"

"No. But what will happen now to Pudgie Brown?"

"I'm going to the D.A.'s office now. The charges against her will probably be dropped, but it may take a day or two to work it out."

"I'm glad. Thanks." I fell back weakly on my pillow, utterly drained from the short interview, my head pounding again.

"Think nothing of it," he said generously, "and, uh, take care of yourself, huh? You don't look as good as you used to, green eyes." He grinned and was gone.

The rest of Thursday was spent mostly sleeping, except for dinner, which came to my room on another tray. President Tomlinson stopped in afterward, and I thanked her for not opening her door to the hospital employees

385

and handing me over to them.

"When a person flies half naked through your front door in the middle of the night seeking refuge," she said seriously, "one doesn't just open the door to the persons chasing them. By the way, Lieutenant Bradley stopped by to let you know that the charges against Pudgie Brown will be dropped, although it will be a few days before it's official. You were sleeping, so I told him I'd tell you. And I had a long talk with Pudgie and told her the good news; I hope you don't mind."

"Oh, no. I'm glad. Thank you."

"She's very grateful to you, naturally. She is going to come up and see you in the morning, and will take you back to New York, if you feel like going back by then. But you should suit yourself. You're welcome to stay here for as long as you need to."

The big anti-nuclear march was on Saturday, and I wasn't going to miss it. "I'm sure I'll be ready to go back by then," I said. "But I hope you know how grateful I am to you for putting me up and saving my life and all that."

She smiled. "It was a nice change in my routine; summers can be a little slow around here. But seriously, I've been happy to have you — and feeling quite gratified, too, that it was an alumna who uncovered the truth about these 'Vassar Murders,' as the press persists in calling them. You did an excellent job, and the college is grateful."

I smiled my thanks, and she left for an evening of what she called plodding but necessary paper work; I fell asleep almost at once, and if I had dreams I didn't remember them the next morning. I did feel a lot better, though, and, since by then someone had brought over my purse and the extra clothes I'd left at Alumnae House, I rather shakily bathed and dressed. Then I got out my credit card and called O'Reagan in San Francisco to tell him all about what had happened.

"And the police aren't going to lock you in the slammer for breaking and entering, or even take away your license?"

"No, they were pretty nice, actually. But listen — do you think you can live without me for another week or so? Most of the time I've been here I've been working, and I'd like to spend a few days playing now. Not if you need me back there, though."

"You going to be up to working? I thought you said you had a concussion?"

"Only a mild one; it's pretty much gone now."

"Enjoy yourself then and I'll see you out here in a week — 'or so,' as you put it."

Right after that Pudgie knocked on the door and came in. She was smiling hugely and said, "Oh, Maggie, I am so grateful to you!" Then she sat down and burst into tears. "Sorry, sorry," she sniffed, dabbing at her eyes with a Kleenex and blowing her nose. "I'm just so happy and relieved, I'm a nervous wreck!"

We had a good laugh at that, and then she said, "Do you want me to take you back to New York today? Do you want to stay with us? I'd take very good care of you!"

"I'm ready to go now. I'll fill you in on all the gory details while we're driving down, all right? But I'll be fine at my cousin's apartment, if you'll just drop me there."

The drive into the city, and the re-cap for Pudgie's benefit, tired me more than I'd expected. When she dropped me off at Cousin George's I went immediately to the thin bed pallet and laid down, falling asleep at once. I woke up about midnight and had some left-over sushi. But I couldn't go back to sleep and found myself worrying about returning Richard's calls — or were they so far in the past now that it wasn't a question of returning but of initiating? I'd have to do that soon, in any case. It no longer felt so unpleasant, though, the thought of calling Richard, and I realized with some surprise and a lightening heart that somewhere within me, sometime during the past few days, the decision had finally been made not to see him again, at least not to live with him again. It even seemed, suddenly, quite amazing that I could have been considering going back to that unhappy relationship. I slept again, a deep and healing sleep without dreams, or none that I remembered when I woke.

THIRTY-TWO

Saturday dawned blue and beautiful, a perfect summer morning for the march. I was feeling, if not as good as new, at least tolerably strong and clear-headed, and was greatly looking forward to the day. I'd dressed and was just finishing breakfast when the phone rang. It was O'Reagan.

"I hate to have to tell you this," he said, "but it looks like I'm going to need you back here after all."

"When?" I asked, "and what?"

"Something big, but it's not certain yet — I don't even want to talk about it until it is. Irish superstition, maybe. How are you feeling?"

"Fine," I lied. "When will you know?"

"Tomorrow, but I thought I'd better warn you today."

"If I'm not here tomorrow, then I'll call you. Would Tuesday do, or Wednesday? I've got something planned I'd like to go ahead with, if possible."

"Yeah, that'll be okay. I'll let you know. Oh, by the way. I did find out something interesting about Franklin Steele, although of course it doesn't matter now."

"Ah, what?"

"He has some kind of bone cancer that's gonna check him out in about two years. So he doesn't have a motive to kill the old dame, but the son—"

"Would have about fifty million motives," I completed. "Lucky for him I got the goods on Horton. Although the kid did have an alibi, I suppose it could've been wangled."

Almost as soon as I put down the phone it rang again and Lieutenant Bradley's gravelly voice came booming across the line. "We got him. Or I should say, *we* specifically don't got him yet, but we will; I thought you'd like to know."

"My frontal lobes feel considerably safer," I agreed. "That's great news. Where is he?"

"Picked up trying to get into Switzerland from France. Another name, of course, but they were looking for him at all the border crossings and he didn't make it through. And the camera *was* under the desk; I've got the prints in front of me now. So there won't be any problem about evidence — and with your testimony, we can send him bye-bye forever. Not to mention, we found the nurse — his partner nurse, not the one you bopped."

"Found her where?"

"At a sister's in Trenton. Claims she was just taking an overdue vacation and denies everything, but that won't last, with the evidence we got."

"So it's all wrapped up, then. Thanks for letting me know. Now I can go out and really enjoy the day; I hope you can. Where are you, at work?"

"When aren't I at work? Anyplace else, I wouldn't know myself."

Then I set out to enjoy the first of the measly three days I probably had left in New York. Four days. Outside, all of New York's avenues were already filled with marchers heading toward Central Park. A huge sign carried by one group read TAKE THE TOYS FROM THE BOYS; a baby was being pushed in a stroller with the sign BABIES SAY NO TO THE WARMONGERS, YOU ARE NOT GOING TO STEAL OUR FUTURE!; a large cheerful group on Sixth Avenue paraded by with a big placard reading COMEDY WRITERS FOR PEACE. The mood was festive.

I took a subway down to Forty-second Street and met Muffy and my old film friend

Gerry and some others outside Grand Central. We started our march from there, going up Fifth Avenue, which had been closed to traffic to accommodate the marchers, as had First, Second, Third, Sixth, Seventh, and Eighth Avenues. It was expected to be far and away the largest gathering of people ever assembled in the city of New York, although *The New York Times* that morning had had nothing about the march on the front page, had merely referred the reader to page thirty-seven, and generally seemed to be playing it down.

Just behind us coming up Fifth Avenue were loud but ghostly sounds, the kind of sounds that might be left over after the end of the world. I turned and saw that they were coming from costumed members of New Hampshire's Bread and Puppet Theater blowing into huge conch shells. Others carried tall poles with giant ghost birds at the top — round white heads, long pointed beaks, and tattered wings. They floated eerily aloft, passing whitely against the background of Fifth Avenue's skyscrapers occasionally interspersed with dark old churches, and the effect, combined with the *wooo, wooo, woooo* of the conch shells, was just electrifying. There was a wagon with more costumed Bread and Puppet people and one of them walking alongside waved at me, a slim, blond-haired harlequin in red and orange, with pitch-black sunglasses that reminded me of the portrait from the de Chirico show. I waved back, in case he was waving at me, then kept going on up Fifth Avenue with my friends.

A group ahead of us began singing thinly:

"This land is your land
This land is my land
From California
To the New York island . . ."

Muffy and Gerry and I joined in happily, it was just like the old days,

"This land was made
For you and me . . ."

and I thought of Peter, Paul and Mary, and Pete Seeger, and all the marches of other years. The singing was interspersed with information about the march coming from a large megaphone just ahead of the singing group, saying things like: "Every *minute* thirty children die for want of food and inexpensive vaccines and every *minute* the world's military budgets absorb one point three million dollars," and "In

a nuclear war we wouldn't have enough bull-
dozers to scrape the bodies off the streets,"
and "One half of the people would die and
the living would envy the dead"; the conch
shells eerily hissed away behind us, *wooo,
wooo*.

> "I'd sing out danger
> I'd sing out a warning
> I'd sing out love between
>   my brothers and my sisters
> All over this la-a-and"

came from in front and from ourselves, and
the megaphone said that the radio estimated
there were already one million people in the
park and all the avenues were still filled with
marchers down to the U.N. building.

About halfway to the park, Muffy and I
decided we couldn't wait until we got there
to find a bathroom, so while the others waited
outside we slipped through the revolving door
of the Hotel Pierre, and made our way through
a large group of elegantly dressed people sip-
ping champagne who were gathered there for
some children's private-school function. Back
outside we were following the giant floating
white birds now, and another group, behind
us, was singing,

"Where have all the young men gone
Long time passing
When will they ever learn?
When will they ev-er
Learn . . ."

Just ahead of us four of New York's finest
were mounted on huge horses, traditionally
excellent mob flatteners should there be any
trouble. But the general mood continued to
be good-natured, a satisfying expression of
heartfelt concerns on a beautiful day. Finally,
we followed the columns ahead of us into the
park, passed a guy selling T-shirts and another
selling hot dogs, which I made a mental note
of, and found a place to sit next to a group
with a tall sign that read THE HUMAN RACE,
WE AREN'T PERFECT BUT GIVE US A
CHANCE. A rather cool summer afternoon in
New York, sunny and lazy, sitting in the dirt
with friends and listening to the stream of
information and song, Holly Near, Jackson
Browne, that come from huge speakers wired
to the central outdoor stage some distance
away:

". . . people who make and sell the stuff
— it would pay for fifty thousand health work-
ers to help the sick. What the hell kind of
society is this?" a New York-accented man's

voice asked angrily. "Tell them to take all their weapons and stick it up their ass!"

I was hungry after all the walking and, since no one else was, went by myself back to the hot dog stand I'd seen on the way in. Its proprietor was also pushing pickles: "Get your pickles here — you can *smell* 'em and you can *eat* 'em — seventy-five cents . . ."

Someone on the loudspeaker was introducing ex-Congresswoman Bella Abzug, whom I like a lot. I got two hot dogs, put mustard and relish on them, and prepared for a loud, rousing speech from Bella as I headed back to my friends. The blond harlequin with the dense black sunglasses whom I'd seen earlier came up and said, "Hello there, isn't this *great?*"

I agreed that it was and kept going. He followed next to me and said, "You don't recognize me, do you?"

I looked at him more closely but quite blankly. Then he took off the sunglasses and I saw that it was Carter Steele.

"Oh, it's *you*, Carter! — but what're you doing here? I thought you went back to the coast, had a job."

"I did, I do," he agreed. "But I couldn't miss all this" — he swept his arm toward the vast crowd and the stage — "also a friend in

Bread and Puppet invited me to come along with them. I'll be back at the dreary old job on Monday, though."

As neither of us said anything more for a bit the voice on the speakers blared loudly, "We were told there wasn't any danger in these bomb tests, we were *NOT* told not to drink the water, we *WERE* told there was no danger. I am a downwind person suffering from four kinds of cancer . . . in that community of eighty-one families there are only six without cancer. . . ."

"I'm very worried about my father," Carter said abruptly.

"Oh . . . yes," I pulled my mind back from what the speakers were saying, to Carter's father. "What a terrible thing."

"Yes."

"Maybe he'll pull through, though. Sometimes they think the cancer is fatal and it isn't—"

His hand jerked and the Coke he was holding splashed on me. He looked pale and grim and said through clenched teeth, "So you do know about him. I was afraid you would. Who have you discussed it with?"

"Discussed it with?"

"The fact that my father is dying."

His eyes flashed murderously, and I realized

I'd had no business saying anything to him about his father's illness. Alice *had* said Franklin Steele wasn't telling anyone about it, had told them in confidence . . . it was all the tragic people talking about cancer from the stage and I just hadn't been thinking. The loudspeaker continued: "Now they don't even announce the bomb tests . . . all the cancer and other radioactive-related illnesses and all claims to the V.A. denied . . ."

"I'm sorry," I said. "I had no business saying anything—"

"Heartbreaker!" an expensive-looking blond girl shrieked as she ran up and gave Carter a hug. "Old Carter Heartbreaker, why don't you ever call me, you beast?" She smiled up at him,, her arms still around his neck, and gave him a light kiss. Then one of the boys she was with called impatiently and she let go and rejoined her friends. "Call me sometime, Carter darling. I'll be in town . . ." She waved and was gone.

"Heartbreaker? Why did she call you that?"

"Just a nickname," he said, smiling a smile in which vanity was only thinly overlaid with a pretended modesty.

A series of alarms finally sounded in my nuclear-march-bedazzled head. Carter Heartbreaker. *C. H.* Initials marked next to the poem in Deborah Marten's book — *not* C. Horton but Carter Heartbreaker. "Just a rainy day or two, and a bitter word" . . . and Carter's father would have inherited all of Chloe's money if Pudgie had been convicted, if *I* hadn't got her off by providing the police with Horton. And Carter's father was dying. But Horton had *confessed*. Hadn't he? I tried to remember exactly what he'd said, something about "I get rid of that nosy old lady . . ." He *had* said that, or something very like it; even Bradley accepted him as the murderer now. But maybe Horton hadn't meant that he, himself, physically and literally had "got rid" of Mrs. Warren, as I had thought, had assumed—

"How's the murder case?" Carter asked.

"What? The case? Oh, fine. I mean" — I struggled to pull myself together, to think what I must do, what I should say — "things have gone very well. You probably saw in the newspapers that Pudgie's out on bail. I expect the charges to be dropped in a day or so."

"New evidence? Is that it? The papers said the police are looking now for some doctor from that convalescent hospital — 'to help with their inquiries.' Does that mean they suspect him now? I'm really interested, you know, in you, and what you're doing." He smiled down at me, a gorgeous, dazzling smile, and his dark eyes looked directly into mine. Searching.

I smiled back, trying to look flustered — well, that was easy — and turned-on, which was more difficult.

"I tell you what, Carter. I don't have time to really go into it all now, but did you say you'll still be in town tomorrow?"

"I could be, if it's a question of you and me spending some time together." God, he *was* sexy. No wonder poor Deborah Marten had been crazy about him.

"It'll have to be in the afternoon, but" — I did my best to simper — "since you're so interested, and since I *did* promise in Princeton that I'd tell you all about it if you were in New York . . ."

"Show me how a real detective works, and such a lovely one," he murmured.

I batted my eyelashes a couple of times and softly said, "Thank you. Let's see . . . why don't you meet me . . ." I looked around, thinking fast. "Here, tomorrow afternoon."

"Here?"

"Well, in the park, I mean. It's bound to be another beautiful day. We could have a little picnic of hot dogs and ice cream and I'll tell you all about de-tect-ing. And this case.

I know, let's meet in front of the zoo. Do you know where it is?"

"Sure. What time?"

I suggested two o'clock, and we went our separate ways. When I was sure he was out of sight I immediately sat down on the first bit of unoccupied ground I came to, feeling stunned.

Why had I been so sure it was Horton? And how was I going to prove, now, that it was this beautiful blond boy with the sexy eyes that had also, so briefly, flashed murder? When I'd let on that I knew about his father dying and which I'd glibly ignored, that murder look, until that girl had come along calling him by his nickname and made it all so clear that even *I* couldn't miss it. I'd have to figure out a trap somehow, but he wasn't stupid, he'd be on his guard, he'd be suspicious . . .

I went back and told my friends that I had to leave, not saying why, and started walking.

". . . Human needs instead of war and destruction," the loudspeaker blared. "If we are not heard today, we must continue what we are doing here again and again and again . . ." Was that Bella? Then singing started from voices grouped around the microphone and was picked up by increasing numbers of the

402

huge surrounding crowd as I reached Fifth
Avenue:

> "Some day-ay-ay-ay-ay
> O-oh deep in my heart
> I do believe
> we shall overcome
> Some day . . ."

So many people were singing, two million
anti-war people, that I could still hear them
as I crossed Park Avenue two blocks away and
turned south:

> "We'll walk hand in hand
> Some day-ay-ay-ay-ay
> O-oh deep in my heart
> I do believe . . ."

The words of the song jumped around in
my brain along with jagged fragments of
thought. Heartbreaker. Of course, it was so
obvious now that I'd been pounded over the
head with it; the kid was so enormously appealing, so beautiful; that girl Shirley had said
the boyfriend was gorgeous, and nobody in
their right mind would call Horton gorgeous.
Deborah'd met him in New Jersey. She
wouldn't have met Horton there; she would've

met *Carter* there. And of *course* the only person to benefit from Pudgie being convicted was Franklin Steele, and hadn't Alice provided me with the missing piece days ago for God's sake and O'Reagan again this morning? I'd even said that would give the kid fifty million motives and then blithely ignored it all, because I thought I already knew all about it, that's why . . .

In the elevator going up to Pudgie's apartment the beautiful song from the park finally faded away. Luckily, she and Hayden were both home; we went into the living room and I told them what had happened, and of the plan that I had begun to form while talking with Carter in the park, because I was going to need their help to carry it out. Then I called my old *cinema verité* film friend Pennebaker.

THIRTY-THREE

By noon Sunday everything that could be done before the meeting with Carter had been done. I tried to rest for an hour or so, but was too nervous; tried to read *Smart Women,* but couldn't concentrate; tried to meditate, but couldn't still my mind enough to even approach the required calm and emptiness. I put my shoulders on the shoulder stand, kicked off with my feet and flipped them up onto the wall, and stayed there for half an hour or so, which did calm me down a bit. Then I took some of Cousin George's Chi capsules, a blend of Chinese herbs that are supposed to enhance the power and clarity of one's thinking, and ran through my plans for the meeting with Carter. But I'd done that a thousand times and it was all seeming flatter and flatter, and less and less likely that he would admit to the murder and start talking to me about it. It was the only plan I had, however, so I tried to feel more faith in it as we went off, my plan and I, to meet him in front of the zoo.

I was early, but he was already there when I arrived, sitting on a bench and carefully scrutinizing the passersby. He was wearing sharply creased white linen trousers and a white shirt with thin green stripes, and looked wonderful: brown-skinned and blond, his dark eyes seductive and saying they were glad to see me. That was how he *looked*, but I could sense the strain and excitement in him. He had brought along a small backpack and a big paperback, *Bergman Film Scripts,* and he rose as I came up, greeting me with every appearance of delight and pleasure, taking my arm, looking down into my eyes and smiling. Did he also sense the strain in me? I wondered.

Carter insisted on paying for the hot dogs, but I bought the ice cream; then I suggested we walk a bit and find a place to eat away from the zoo smells. I steered us along a meandering trail that eventually led us to a big open field.

"How's this?" he asked, looking around. There were others picnicking or just lying in the sun. We chose a place at the far end, far from anyone else and about fifty yards from a pile of rocks and bushes at the entrance to the field. Music and singing could be heard from an outdoor concert nearby. Carter cocked his head to one side, listening, and then said, "Nice . . . What is it, do you know?"

"A Paul Winter concert. They announced it at the march yesterday — a sort of celebration for the day after. Have you ever been to one of his things?"

"No, I don't know him."

"I went to one in Bolinas once and it was *wonderful*. He has everybody bring an instrument, something good or just any old thing you can make sounds on — like a glass and a spoon. Then he divides everyone up into small groups and they just start making sounds together — group by group, I mean. Musical people, as well as totally *un*musical people like me. I left there feeling so high, I felt like I was walking along about three feet off the ground."

"Sounds great. I'll go to one sometime." He took a bite of his hot dog and then said, "So tell me about the case. You said you're expecting all the charges against poor Pudgie Brown will be dropped. Do you really think she didn't do it? I mean, I know she's your client and all that, but isn't the evidence against her awfully good? And I thought the police were totally convinced she did it."

I finished my first hot dog, wiped my mouth

with a paper napkin, and said, "It's a pretty long story — you don't have to leave anytime soon, do you?"

He shook his head, smiling, and prompted, "But the case?"

"All right; the case." I told him about my suspicion of Horton, and about finding the evidence of his fraud and getting him arrested. "So they say the charges against Pudgie will probably be dropped," I concluded.

He paled beneath his tan and looked anything but happy, although he was still smiling. "Oh, isn't that terrific," he said thinly. "But they *really* don't think anymore that Pudgie did it? I thought it was so open and shut. This Horton character — the fraud — that doesn't really make it likely he murdered *Chloe*; I don't see that they're necessarily so connected. But of course," he added thoughtfully, "something else could always happen that might show Pudgie *did* do it, after all. You say they caught this Horton guy in France? When they get him over here, I bet he doesn't confess to the murder."

"You may be right," I agreed, "and something else could always happen, as you say, to make it look again as if Pudgie is the murderer. But I don't think it will."

"You never know," he said, looking more cheerful.

"No. You never know. But I do know you won't get away with it, Carter, next time. Framing Pudgie again, I mean. That's what I really want to talk to you about, today."

He paused with the plastic spoon of ice cream halfway to his mouth and sat very still, watching me, the way an animal in the woods is still when it suddenly sees an enemy — or its prey. Then he put the ice cream back into the container and said, "What is that supposed to mean?"

"It means that Deborah Marten had a friend who knew that Deborah had a very good-looking boyfriend last summer with blond hair and a nickname." He didn't say anything, just waited. "The nickname of 'Heartbreaker.' Do you know many people with that nickname? I know only one."

There was a long silence while we sat there, looking at each other. Then he said, "All right. I *did* know her — but you can understand why I didn't want to say so, after she was murdered — especially since the murder seemed to be connected to the murder of — of a distant relative of mine. I only knew her for a few days, anyway, so naturally I didn't want to get involved. Anyone else would have done the same."

"Then there's also the fact that your father

is a good bet to die of cancer at about the time when, if Pudgie were convicted, he would inherit most of Chloe Warren's money — about fifty million dollars. You're his only child, really; Sally can't be counted either as a suspect or as an heir. So if you were to ask yourself which suspect would benefit from Pudgie being framed, how many could you think of, Carter? I can think of only one."

His beautiful dark eyes blazed with intense excitement now. "Why are you telling me all this, anyway?"

"Because I know very well that you're the murderer I've been looking for," I answered. "And while I may not have enough for the police, I think that what I have told you should be enough to discourage you from any more attempts to frame Pudgie. And I'd be willing to settle for that, at this point."

"I haven't heard enough yet," he said arrogantly. "I think I can still pull it off. I'm clever enough. I suppose it was that old chicken-neck hag Alice who told you about my father, wasn't it? I saw you talking to her at the reunion that night. And we were on the same plane the next day, out to San Francisco. So I listened at the door when my father was talking to them, at our house. That's why I followed you yesterday. I met you at the march

410

on purpose, did you know that?"

"No," I admitted, "I didn't."

"So you weren't suspicious until that stupid little cunt came up and called me 'Heartbreaker'?"

"That's right. If you'd stayed quietly in San Francisco and waited it out, if you hadn't followed me, then that girl wouldn't have seen you yesterday and called you by your nickname — and I might never have learned it."

"On the other hand you might have, though, some other way. But as you said, it's not enough to go to the police with. You really haven't got anything on me at all, except for a couple of coincidences."

I picked up my canvas carryall and pulled out the long black robe I'd found in the Triangle Club costume room in Princeton the night before.

"Where'd you get that?"

"You know where I got it, Carter. In the Triangle Club costume room, where I went last night to look for it. See, here's the tear at the bottom, just like the one Pudgie described to me; she'll be able to identify the robe from it, I'm sure. Identify it as the one worn by the murderer. How many other people connected with this case can you think of, that are also connected with Triangle Club?"

"Give me that!" He grabbed the robe and pulled it out of my hands.

"There were two rather large plastic buttons on the back," I went on. "Nice smooth surfaces for fingerprints — did you put on your gloves *before* you put on the gown? Did you leave them on until *after* you'd taken it off?"

He looked startled and uncertain for a moment, trying to think back. Then he checked the back of the gown and, when he saw that the buttons were gone, grabbed my purse and started looking through it.

"I don't have them with me, though by all means search my purse if you don't believe me. I don't know yet if the buttons have any fingerprints on them. But if they do, the police will be able to get some of your prints easily enough and see if they match, and Pudgie will be able to identify the gown as the one worn by the murderer."

His face was a sickly white beneath the beautiful tan now, his body as tense as a coiled snake's, and I had the feeling he was poised to run at any moment. Run, or attack me. Flight, or fight.

"But you're so young," I went on, "and you're obviously very talented; you have your whole life ahead of you. And you're so . . . beautiful, too," I added softly. "I hate to see

412

your whole life ruined for one mistake. And that man Horton *is* really a bad person, he was going to kill me — he probably killed some of those old people he was still collecting money for — so I don't really care if he gets blamed for the murders, as long as my client goes free. You won't get the money now in any case, but — why did you do it?"

"I needed the money," he said simply, relaxing just a fraction.

"*Needed* the money? At your age?"

"I'm old enough to know you don't get anywhere in this world without money," he said bitterly, "and lots of it, if you want to be free to do what you want. I've seen my father all these years, cutting out the cancers that always grow back, gross, disgusting things. Hating it, having to do it to get the money for his stupid women, the things he wanted . . ."

"And what do you want? What do you need fifty million dollars for?"

He looked at me thoughtfully and nodded his head. "And to think I didn't really take you seriously. That was where I made my big mistake, wasn't it? The cops fell for my plan without a whimper, but *you* . . ."

"I think your big mistake was in making the plan in the first place. Or at least in acting on it."

"I *have* to have money," he repeated. "And that mean, stingy old woman could have given it to me and never even missed it, you know that? I ran into her in New York one day and took her to lunch; I knew she'd like that, me, taking *her* to lunch. But when I told her about my script and asked her to help me — she just lectured me. Said I'd better realize I was going to have to earn my own way in the world, that I would get nothing from her beyond my education and I'd better realize it. Said to get my mind off *foolishness* like movies. Why should that fat Pudgie have it all? Chloe was totally unfair to my side of the family, and for no reason at all. I'm *glad* I killed her, glad I set up that prissy Pudgie, prancing around being the big heiress all these years while my sister and I had to be satisfied with scrawny little handouts and pretend we were grateful. *Grateful?* I hated her guts, and Pudgie's, too. That fat cow will never do anything the least bit interesting or useful or imaginative with the money, but I will. I figured it all out, during spring break, spring break when I couldn't go to Sea Island with everyone else because I didn't have enough *money*. So I took Chloe to lunch. Actually, I didn't just happen to run into her, any more than I did you. I knew she went into New York to shop, and

414

I found out when and then pretended to run into her. So when she sneered at me like that, about film, about what I wanted to do with my life — what I *will* do — listen! I have it in me to be a *great* film director, can you understand what that means? I mean *great*, like Eisenstein, like Bergman. But I can't do it without money, if I have to spend my best years licking ass—"

"The way everyone else has to—"

"Yes, but they don't have my extraordinary gifts, my *genius* for film, so it doesn't really matter, but—"

"So you decided even before you took Chloe out to lunch and she refused to help with your screenplay to kill her? You knew about your father by then, I suppose."

"Oh, yes, I knew about that at Christmas. He said he was telling me about it because he wanted me to know I couldn't expect anything from him in the way of money, graduate school, or anything like that. He was close to broke, and he was dying. He said he hoped knowing about it would make me give up what he called 'all that theater nonsense' and settle down to something I could make a living out of. I thought of the plan later, after he told me he wasn't telling people about the cancer; I knew that he had at least another year, probably two, so I thought I'd be safe as far as motive went. I just had to arrange it all for a day I knew he'd have a good alibi, but that was easy since he's almost always in surgery on Mondays and Tuesdays."

"You do have some feeling for your father, then, and wanted to be sure he wouldn't be suspected, was that it?"

"After the shitty way he's treated me all my life? Grow up! I just wanted to be sure nobody would think he'd committed the murder and framed Pudgie, so there'd be no problem about him inheriting."

"I see. How did you know Chloe and Pudgie would be going to see your sister that day?"

"Oh, Chloe wrote me Pudgie was taking her; she said Pudgie had some important meeting at the college that day, so I was pretty sure they wouldn't cancel it. She wrote about it when she sent my June allowance — what a joke. She sent it a couple of weeks early, said she knew I'd have extra expenses at the end of the term and might want it. So I set it all up for that day, called my father's office after I got up to Poughkeepsie to be sure he was in surgery as usual, and then just went ahead. It was easy."

"You got your friend to lie about your being in Princeton? That seems a little risky, not up to your usual standards. Or were you going to kill him eventually, too?"

"Oh no, he never knew anything. I put some sleeping pills into his drink, those green things, chloral hydrates. And changed the time on his watch after he passed out, then carried him up to bed. He has blackouts anyway when he drinks. I changed all the clocks in the house, too. So when I got back from Poughkeepsie the next day and woke him up, he thought it was two hours earlier than it was all day. We never watched television or listened to the radio, so I knew that would be okay. Then Monday night, after he'd been asleep for a while, I changed everything back."

"Well, that worked very well."

Carter was looking at me speculatively, and I felt I could almost read the thoughts going through his head. I believed he was thinking about whether he could get away with killing me then and there, or whether somewhere later would be better, and also trying to think how my death could be made to incriminate Pudgie again. I could feel his urgency, too — he had to do it all fast, before the police were too set on Horton as their murderer. I just sat there, watching him think and feeling cold, there in the warm summer sunshine; the way he looked at me made me feel very cold indeed.

417

Didn't Hayden and Pennebaker, shooting us with the telephoto lens from behind the distant pile of rocks and bushes, have enough on film and tape by now? Wasn't it time for them to step in and nab Carter? I glanced toward the rocks, but they were absent of activity of any kind.

While we'd been talking, the concert had ended and the people in attendance had started walking past us, a thin trickle at first, then more and more, unfortunately walking right between Carter and me and the hidden camera. Many made sounds on the real or improvised instruments they'd brought for the concert — a flutter of flute notes, a series of *bongs* on a shaman's drum, a *wh-aan wh-aang* on an ingenious homemade device of brass and pipes; small groups of people kept passing, playing and singing happily. They all looked incredibly high, and the spontaneous music they were making was wonderful — except that in addition to the people blocking Carter and me from the camera, their music was almost certainly making it impossible to pick out our voices from among the cacaphony of sounds now being faithfully recorded by the hidden wireless mike around my neck.

Carter stuffed the robe into his pack and took out a very small gun, pearl-handled and nickel-plated. He slipped it into his pants pocket, and the Jay Gatsby-style pleated linen fell in such a way that the gun didn't show at all. Then he slung the pack over his shoulder and stood up abruptly, his hand in the pocket with the gun.

"Let's go."

"Go?"

"Yes. Go. We're going someplace else to finish our little talk. Get up."

"Get up?" I didn't want to get up, and I certainly didn't want to go anywhere with him.

"Stop talking and get up *now*, or I'm going to shoot you."

"Don't be silly, Carter, there're too many people around; they'd see you."

"That's exactly why we're leaving now. I could very easily shoot you in the middle of this crowd, with all these weird noises, and by the time anyone noticed I'd be long gone. So you'd better get up and come along."

"Where do you want to go? What's wrong with talking here?"

"I have a nice empty place downtown where we can talk a lot better. Or maybe I'm hot for your body, aren't you hot for mine? You certainly acted like it, earlier. Now, get up — I'm not going to ask you again, I'm going to shoot."

He looked like he meant what he said, and furthermore, he was looking increasingly nervous, as if he might soon decide to kill me anyway, just because it would be simpler and less dangerous for him. I looked hopefully toward the rock where Hayden and Penney were, but saw only the exulting singing, whistling, howling faces of the departing concert crowd.

I got up.

"Good. Now walk slightly ahead of me, no, that's too much, slow down . . . that's right. Just keep going straight ahead until I tell you different. Try anything and I shoot you here and now — you familiar with Ram Dass, live in the now, die in the now?"

Walking off with Carter and a gun at my back was not an appealing proposition, but it was more appealing than dying in the now, as he put it, so I did what he told me to, walking as slowly as possible, trying frantically to think of a way of getting out of this one alive. Nothing at all occurred to me except that whatever I did, it had better be while we were still on the streets, while there were other people around, before he got me to the nice empty place he had in mind.

"A bit faster, Maggie, *don't* drag along as if we were going to a funeral or something!"

He laughed gaily.

I kept walking as slowly as I could, trying to think. We mingled among the people leaving the concert and no one took the slightest notice of us. Unfortunately, the range of the wireless mike was limited, and by the time we reached the edge of the park, even if we could have been heard above the music and singing all around us, I knew we were out of range. At Central Park West, Carter told me to cross the street staying slightly ahead of him and then to turn left. After we'd gone a block he pointed to a subway entrance, and we went into it, still more or less surrounded by people from the concert making weird and beautiful music, and shuffled down the stairs into the gloom and dirt of the garishly lit station.

By now Hayden and Penney should have realized something was wrong, by now they should have been able to see and hear that Carter and I weren't there anymore, but if they hadn't seen us leave, hadn't seen which way we'd gone, it probably wasn't going to do me much good. And wishing one or the other or both of them would come thundering down the subway steps on a white horse wasn't going to do me any good, either; I needed to think of something to do, myself, and fast.

ain't no cavalry
no more
no no more cav
al-reeee

I made up my own little song to the tune of the bluesy music coming from the group ahead of me and sang it softly as I tried to think of something useful but instead came up with thoughts like the fact that, after all, no one had tied me up and forced me at gunpoint to become a private detective and wasn't this just the kind of end a private detective was likely to come to, especially a careless private detective? Why hadn't I brought a gun along? Why hadn't I this, why hadn't I that . . .

At the entrance stile Carter tossed in a couple of tokens and the metal bar creaked twice as he pushed me through ahead of him. We were on the downtown side, and I started toward one of the benches against the wall, feeling weak in the knees and dizzy and hoping I could think better — or rather, begin to think, period — sitting down, but Carter gave me another nudge and jerked his head back toward the track.

"No, we'll stand over there and wait for the train, I think."

I walked ahead of him down to the left and

we waited by the edge of the track without saying anything. Then I heard the faint rumble of a subway coming from the uptown direction. I'd been away from New York and subways too long to judge how many seconds or minutes away it was, but it seemed like my best and perhaps only chance, so I waited until I judged it to be about half a minute away and then looked over Carter's shoulder and grinned, then back at him and said, "Don't look now, but the cops have come for you, Carter."

"Really, Maggie, I would have expected better than that from you; I'm disappointed."

I reached up and pulled the wireless mike out from under my blouse and waved it in his face. "This is a microphone, Carter, as you should know from your film experience, right? Not only is everything you said down on tape, it's all on video, too. They were in the park behind that big rock and now they've followed us here. Wouldn't it be pretty stupid of you to commit another murder, on camera and right in front of the cops?"

He looked uncertain for a moment, and as he glanced back toward the entrance behind us the train came thundering in. I jerked myself sideways and shoved, and he went over the edge, almost taking me with him, but I could hear a loud screech of brakes covering a horrible raw scream that was cut short and then there was just the sound of brakes and then they stopped, too. I was lying on the edge of the platform and people stepped around me as the subway doors opened; some of them just kept going, but one or two stopped and then others and soon there was a crowd. I felt sick and dizzy, and I couldn't seem to get the sound of that scream out of my head.

A few hours later, but seeming much longer, like days, or weeks, I signed my statement at the police station on Fifty-first Street. Lieutenant Bradley had been called down from Poughkeepsie, and Hayden and Pennebaker had been found wandering around the park looking for me and brought to the station. After all three of them, especially Bradley, arrived, the communication with the police got better; in fact, the police eventually were willing to put Carter's death down as accidental. Finally free to go, I stood for a moment on the steps in front of the station with Penney and Hayden and Lieutenant Bradley.

"Thanks for all your help in there," I said to Bradley.

"Thanks for all yours, green eyes. Boy, somebody tells you to bring in hard evidence, you really take 'em at their word, don't you? And not just once, either — twice!" He grinned. "But the way I missed the boat myself, the train, the trolly, the plane, and the spaceship . . . shit. I was *sure* she'd done it." Hayden glared at him, and he added quickly, "Glad I was wrong, of course."

"Well, at least you weren't alone, if that's any comfort. I was every bit as sure it was Horton, even before his so-called confession." I sighed, thinking it was the narrow, judgmental part of me that had caused the error or anyway encouraged it, then added, "Oh, well, to err is human, as somebody said."

To forgive, divine, he agreed, and went off in his police car. Hayden went home to tell Pudgie what had happened, and Penney and I stopped off at the Algonquin lounge, settled down into two of its wonderfully overstuffed chairs, and spent a couple of hours catching up on old times and new times. Then I passed on the idea of dinner, still rather wobbly and weak from Horton's knock on my head — and not feeling much like eating, anyway, with that horrible chopped-off scream still echoing from time to time somewhere down deep in my own interior. Would I ever be free of the sound? Penney said not to worry about it, that I couldn't have done anything else, that given the kind of person Carter was, I'd probably done the guy a favor and in any case I'd certainly done the rest of the human race a favor. But these reassurances came from that place of reason, and didn't affect my feelings at all, feelings of sickness, of wrongness, of stepping out of line in the scheme of things. We talked a bit longer, then Penney headed uptown and I took a cab to Cousin George's. I asked the driver to wait, went upstairs, and put some clean clothes in my canvas case.

Then the taxi took me on to Peter's apartment, where I put Albinoni on the stereo again and took a long, hot bath and washed my hair. I found some cheese and fruit in the refrigerator, made a cup of tea, and took a tray to bed. The room was filled with moonlight coming in through the huge square window, and I didn't bother to turn on the lamp. I was so tired . . . so tired . . . I fell asleep halfway through the tea, before I'd even touched the cheese.

I half woke much later as Peter got into bed and sleepily asked him how his conference had gone.

"Ssssh," he said, "go back to sleep, it's late. Conference was fine." He came naked into my open arms and I closed them around him, murmuring a welcome. Then, in spite of his good intentions not to wake me, we made love, quietly at first but then with a growing passion fueled by our being apart for several days.

Afterwards, Peter said, "Need to talk . . . tomorrow . . ." His mouth opened in a big yawn, and then another, and his eyes were closed. "Been thinking . . . what happens next . . ."

"I'll be right here," I said, but he was already asleep.

I was wide awake by then, though, and I lay there for a long time, my back snuggled into the curve of his body, thinking about tomorrow and the days after that. Thinking about my new freedom, about the cabin in the wilds of Connecticut, about the new job coming up in San Francisco.

Unable to sleep, my mind drifted on to thoughts of the past two weeks, of Vassar College and of my old friends there, of wealth and privilege, of murder. Thoughts of the afternoon, and of that horrible, short scream. Could I have done that differently? I hadn't wanted to kill Carter, only to get away from him, to keep him from killing *me*. . . . But perhaps the way it had happened was for the best, as Penney had said? Not from Carter's viewpoint, it wasn't . . . nineteen years old and beautiful and smart . . . and no soul at all. That's what I wished these schools could teach, the path of the heart . . .

Ah, well. It was done. And tomorrow was another day, another night. A sunny summer country day, a warm, black-skied starry night, a day and a night with Peter.

THORNDIKE PRESS HOPES you have enjoyed this Large Print book. All our Large Print titles are designed for the easiest reading, and all our books are made to last. Other Thorndike Press Large Print books are available at your library, through selected bookstores, or directly from the publisher. For more information about current and upcoming titles, please call us, toll free, at 1-800-223-6121, or mail your name and address to:

THORNDIKE PRESS
P. O. BOX 159
THORNDIKE, MAINE 04986

There is no obligation, of course.